Melissa Hill li
daughter Carri   ot writing or
reading, Melissa loves travelling, movies, The Beatles,
New York and interior design.

Find out more about her novels at www.melissahill.info
or @melissahillbks

Melissa Hill

The Love of a Lifetime

**SIMON &
SCHUSTER**

London · New York · Sydney · Toronto · New Delhi

A CBS COMPANY

First published in Great Britain by Simon & Schuster UK Ltd, 2016
This paperback published 2016
A CBS COMPANY

1 3 5 7 9 10 8 6 4 2

Simon & Schuster UK Ltd
1st Floor
222 Gray's Inn Road
London WC1X 8HB

www.simonandschuster.co.uk

Simon & Schuster Australia, Sydney
Simon & Schuster India, New Delhi

A CIP catalogue record for this book
is available from the British Library

Paperback ISBN: 978-1-4711-2765-6
eBook ISBN: 978-1-4711-2768-7

Printed and bound by CPI Group (UK) Ltd, Croydon, CR0 4YY

Simon & Schuster UK Ltd are committed to sourcing paper
that is made from wood grown in sustainable forests and support the Forest
Stewardship Council, the leading international forest certification organisation.
Our books displaying the FSC logo are printed on FSC certified paper.

To Sara-Jade
Thanks for all the amazing things you do

Chapter 1

It was an idea that never failed to entrance Beth Harper, the notion that a simple object – well, two actually – could be so utterly transformative. Just ask Dorothy Gale.

Positioning a pair of sequined red heels onto the black-and-white-striped-clad 'legs' she'd fashioned from a couple of cardboard tubes, Beth stood back and evaluated her work.

The famed ruby-red slippers were of course unmistakable, but perhaps the polystyrene farmhouse looked a little off? No, Beth figured most shoppers would get the theme. The Yellow Brick Road (hand-painted at home in her apartment the night before) was a giveaway.

Anyway, it wasn't as though she could call on Hollywood resources for her displays – nope, all Beth had at her disposal were basic craft supplies, her own imagination and, of course, some of the world's most beautiful shoes.

Thankfully she also had her boss's blessing, especially

when the management of Carlisle's – the popular Lexington Avenue department store in which she worked – realised that Beth's movie-themed shoe displays not only delighted shoppers, but attracted tourists to the shoe room in droves, during the holidays especially. Her in-store displays weren't quite as popular a tourist attraction as Saks' Christmas windows, but they were getting there.

For Beth, the opportunity to utilise her greatest passion – the movies – in her day-to-day work was a dream come true, and she loved delighting Carlisle's customers and staff all year long by using beautiful shoes to help recreate some of Hollywood's greatest movie moments.

Satisfied that her latest masterpiece was complete, she made a final check that everything was in place in the shoe department, before the store opened its doors to the public that morning. December was a time when people from all over flocked to the city for Christmas shopping, Broadway shows, outdoor ice-skating and the many other festive activities that made New York great.

Irish by birth, Beth had lived in Manhattan for the better part of ten years, and over that time had learned to appreciate the ramped-up energy of the city during the busy holiday season. Even though the accompanying chill wind played havoc with her hair ... That thought made Beth double-check that her medium-length blond ponytail was still in one piece after all her creative endeavours. It wouldn't do for her own appearance to let her down when the whole shop was decked in finery.

Christmas cheer exploded throughout Carlisle's, almost as though Santa's elves had come to do the décor. Delicate tree branches dusted with snow lined the ceiling, and fairy-lit pine cone garlands danced around the beams. Elegantly decorated fir trees twinkled on every floor, and beneath them were selections of the best Christmas fare the world's most famous luxury brands had to offer. The holiday merchandising team had even hung random bunches of mistletoe in different spots around the store, encouraging customers to join in the fun.

But while she loved this time of year in the city, just then Beth couldn't help but think about warmer climes. She and Danny, her boyfriend of seven years, had planned to leave for a long weekend with friends in South Florida today, but due to a pressing work issue on his part, they'd had to make a last-minute cancellation. Which was why Beth found herself on the sales floor in the first week of December, busying herself with a festive *Wizard of Oz* theme, and covering a shift for one of the part-timers in the department.

The distraction of setting up the new display was working wonders in helping keep her spirits up, but deep down she was a little disappointed. She had really been looking forward to a relaxing break away before the Christmas retail rush kicked off in earnest, but more importantly, she'd wanted some time alone with Danny. They lived together – had done so for the past five years – but there was something extra romantic about a break away with the one you loved, far from humdrum day-to-day habits and responsibilities.

Still, she thought, straightening a crystal and satin Kate Spade pump (which worked brilliantly as one of Glinda's Silver Shoes) on the central display, it was no great hardship to be here surrounded by such prettiness.

While her love affair with the movies had been inspired by her grandmother Bridie – who had introduced Beth to all the Hollywood classics at a young age – she guessed her appreciation of shoes had also begun with the first glimpse of her grandmother's vintage Mary Janes when she was a child.

She and her mother had found the wedding shoes amongst Nana's things after she died, and 12-year-old Beth, who had never known Bridie to wear anything other than comfortable lace-up brogues, had been entranced by this completely unexpected glimpse into her grandmother's past.

White satin, adorned with white fluffy ostrich feathers and tiny jewelled roses on the vamp, and in the low-heeled Mary Jane style that was the fashion of the time, they were impossibly glamorous and Beth had fallen in love almost immediately. And she listened captivated as her mother told her what little she knew about her own parents' wedding day, other than that Bridie and James had married just before the Second World War, and James had died in battle a year later while Bridie was pregnant with Beth's mother.

There were no photographs of the event, so no clue as to what her grandmother's wedding dress had been like. Beth's mum recalled Bridie talking about having to pawn her wedding ring to keep them afloat after James died, leaving the shoes as the only memento of that special day.

From there on in Beth had spent countless hours trying to imagine the wedding and how her grandmother had managed to hold on to those shoes when other, more valuable possessions had been lost. They must have been particularly precious to Bridie.

She realised then that her grandmother's great passion for 1920s Hollywood glamour wasn't just restricted to the silver screen, and that the romantic classics so beloved by her – and readily shared with Beth – had been an escape of sorts, a vicarious glimpse into the kind of romantic life Bridie had imagined for herself before her marriage was so cruelly cut short.

Beth remembered wonderful nights at home in Galway at her grandmother's house, tucked up under a blanket on the sofa in the darkness, she and Bridie watching rapt while Humphrey Bogart proclaimed his love for Lauren Bacall, and swooning as Spencer Tracy and Katharine Hepburn played out their great passion onscreen.

Her grandmother had been a huge influence on Beth, but had died when she was twelve, and she guessed evoking the movies was her way of holding on to those memories of her beloved nana so many years on, and especially now when she was so far away from home.

Thankfully, Beth's mum had let her hold on to Bridie's shoes, and to this day they remained in her New York wardrobe; in the original worn box, wrapped in the old delicate tissue paper. They were about her size, and Beth promised herself that as a tribute to Bridie, when (or if) she ever walked down the aisle to marry the love of her life, she would be wearing her grandmother's beloved Mary Janes.

Now, standing in front of the display shelves, she gently ran her fingers along the various shoe designs, caressing the soft silky material. As was her habit, she tried to imagine where each pair would end up, the kind of women that would wear them and the adventures they might have.

The sparkling silver and gold sandals were easy to place: these were ideally suited to glamorous, sophisticated events, a night at the opera or a gala ball at the Met. While the easily identifiable red-soled slingbacks were sexy and fun, perfect for a cocktail party or a girls' night out, the glorious satin crystal-encrusted creations were so exquisite that they were surely destined for a romantic encounter worthy of one of Bridie's beloved silver-screen classics.

Beth looked at her own feet and smiled as she imagined herself as a movie heroine wearing the shoes; her blond curls pulled up in a sophisticated chignon à la Grace Kelly, her petite figure dressed in a gorgeous flowing gown (Oscar de la Renta, maybe?) and in Danny's arms, dancing to Sinatra in some beautifully picturesque location ... under the Eiffel Tower or at the base of the Spanish Steps in Rome, beneath a sky awash with stars.

Her face broke into a grin as she allowed her imagination free rein, and heard the accompanying film soundtrack swell in a spectacular crescendo in her mind as she pictured

Danny wearing a tux, his dark hair slicked back Clark Gable-style, and his aquamarine eyes shining as he leaned forward and softly placed his lips on hers ...

Her idyllic Hollywood daydream was interrupted when a couple meandered into the department.

Ah – her first customers of the day.

Glancing around, the woman immediately made a bee-line for Beth's *Wizard of Oz* display and, stopping in front of it, she smiled and gleefully clapped her hands. The man pulled her close and planted a kiss on her cheek.

Buoyed by this obvious show of appreciation, Beth smiled and, smoothing down her red knee-length woollen dress, moved to greet the couple. 'Hello there – is there anything I can help you with?' she asked cheerfully, her green eyes sparkling with warmth.

The young woman turned her attention to Beth and beamed. 'I just love the holiday displays in here – this one is so wonderful, and *Oz* is one of my favourite movies!'

'Thank you. I love that movie too.'

The customer reached out and picked up one of the silver heels. 'But much as I love them, I don't think sparkling ruby slippers will quite work for what I need,' she giggled. Her face flushed happily, and she looked ready to burst with excitement.

Beth recognised that look. 'Ah, so you're planning a wedding then?' she ventured coyly, before the younger woman could say anything more.

She burst out laughing, and glanced at her companion.

'Well, yes, I suppose I am – *we* are. Though I didn't realise it until a couple of hours ago … we've just got engaged!' She offered her left hand, which, sure enough, was home to a gorgeous princess-cut diamond.

'How wonderful. Congratulations.' Beth looked back and forth between them. 'Nice job on the ring,' she added, offering the guy a wink. 'It's beautiful.'

He ran a hand through his dark hair and a blush crept up his neck, finding a home on his cheeks. 'Thanks.'

His fiancée grinned. 'I still can't believe it! We just arrived in the city yesterday for some holiday shopping. We were taking a stroll in Central Park this morning, and when we reached the Bow Bridge, it started to snow, and then out of the blue, Josh …' she giggled, indicating her companion, 'got down on one knee, and it was like … time just froze. It was *surreal*. I mean, we have been together for ages now – three whole years – and of course we've talked about it … but I mean, wow. So unexpected. And right there, with the snow falling all around us, it was so romantic it almost felt like something out of a—'

'Movie,' she and Beth finished in unison and they both laughed. The bride-to-be (clearly a kindred spirit) who introduced herself as Katie, was overjoyed and Beth was only too happy to be taken up in the excitement. She came across many would-be brides in this line of work, and she loved meeting couples at this newly engaged point, when everything was still fresh and romantic, before all the wedding preparations became overwhelming.

She also knew that such a time was strictly for browsing, with a heavy dose of wish-fulfilment thrown in.

Well, she could understand that.

'I'm so happy for you both. What a lovely time to get engaged. Have you set a date?'

'We're thinking this time next year. A Christmas wedding maybe?'

'Perfect. Well once you start planning, and find your dress, I'd be delighted to help you with shoes and accessories, if you want. I see you like those Kate Spades.'

'They're so beautiful. And thank you; that would be great. I know it's too early to be looking now. It's strange, though, because as soon as he asked me, I could almost envision the whole day in my head ... what Josh would look like as I walked down the aisle ... and I have this vision of me too, of what I will look like on the day, the dress I'll wear, and the shoes on my feet. *Especially* the shoes. Is that weird?' She glanced from her fiancé back to Beth.

Beth threw a quick look of reassurance to the guy, who had a perplexed look on his face. Understandable; everyone knew men didn't share the shoe – or indeed the 'Big Day' – gene.

'Oh, I'd say that's pretty normal,' she said. 'I think most women, myself included, have a pretty good idea of what they want their day to be like.'

Katie was shaking her head sagely. 'Exactly. And did yours turn out the way you envisioned it? Your wedding day, I mean,' she added when Beth looked blank.

'Oh ...' She opened and closed her mouth in quick succession, understanding at once that her words had been taken out of context. 'Well, I'm not married, actually,' she mumbled pleasantly.

Katie looked uncomfortable. 'I'm sorry, it just sounded like you knew so much about what I was talking about ... I was sure you'd gone through it too.'

Beth shrugged, keeping a smile on her face. This wasn't the first time she had gone down the 'gosh, you're not married?' route. At thirty-four years old and possibly a good ten years on the girl in front of her, she guessed she should have expected it. 'No, I'm not married. I mean, not yet, and I'm not sure if we ever will,' she added, laughing a little. 'My boyfriend and I have been together seven years and—'

'Seven years and *no ring*?' Katie gasped, cutting her off. Then spotting Beth's reaction, she immediately began to backpedal. 'I mean, sorry. It's not like ... it's just ... I thought three was long to wait ...' She trailed off and shook her head. 'But of course, every couple is different, right? Some people have things figured out, without all that stuff. It sounds like you do, anyway. I mean, some people never get married at *all*.'

At this point the guy nudged her, as if trying to signal to his beloved to take her foot out of her mouth. Beth remained calm and unaffected. After all, Katie wasn't insinuating anything; she just had a different perspective. Anyway, Beth was sort of used to it. This wasn't the first

time someone had reacted with surprise when they realised just how long Beth and Danny had been together, yet
seemed to have no intention of tying the knot.

'Anyway, I'm sorry. I'm blabbering now,' Katie blushed.

'It's no problem. Like you say, everyone's different. My
boyfriend and I always joke that if we got married, all the
romance in our relationship would just wither and die,'
Beth chuckled, trying to keep the mood light, before back-
tracking herself when she spotted the expression on her
audience's faces. 'I mean, not that the romance is going to
be dead for you two when *you* get married.' She gulped.
'It's just a silly in-joke of ours. In any case, best of luck to
you both and congratulations again. I'm Beth and here's my
card. Feel free to give me a call when you're back in town
and ready to choose your wedding shoes.' She extracted a
card from her pocket and handed it to the girl. 'And Merry
Christmas.'

'Thanks, and same to you ...' The young couple hurriedly took their leave, the bride-to-be regaining her sunny
disposition, and her fiancé looking mildly relieved.

Beth smiled after them as they walked away and put the
conversation out of her mind. It made no sense to think
too deeply about it. That sort of exchange had happened
before, and just like she did at other times when faced with
the question of why exactly she and Danny weren't married, she decided to sidestep the issue in favour of cheerier
thoughts.

'Let me guess, yet another bride-to-be salivating over

11

the satin Manolos?' Beth jumped in surprise as Jodi Cartwright, her longtime co-worker in the shoe rooms, sidled up to her.

Beth laughed. 'The Kate Spades, actually. They just got engaged. Down on one knee on the Bow Bridge in the snow. The park is such a perfect backdrop for a marriage proposal at this time of year, isn't it? So romantic.'

Jodi snorted. Ever cynical, the forty-something divorcee didn't share Beth's optimism about love and romance, and least of all about marriage.

'Yeah, it's romantic until one day you catch him with his mistress in the same place making his own romantic moment. And you know what's even more full of hearts and roses and unicorns that poop rainbows?' she added archly. 'Serving him with divorce papers at his mistress's house after he said he was away at a Vegas cop convention. *That's* my romantic moment.'

Beth blanched. She loved Jodi, but guessed she should have remembered who she was talking to. Her friend certainly wasn't one to be first in line with ticket in hand for the latest Nicholas Sparks movie. She should have remembered that Central Park was indeed the place Jodi had caught her now ex-husband Frank with this mistress. A million miles from romantic. She guessed Katie's foot-in-mouth syndrome was catching.

'Sorry, Jodi. I didn't mean ...'

Her friend patted her shoulder. 'It's OK, honey. Easy for you to romanticise marriage; you haven't been there. And

I say that not as a criticism but a *commendation*. Don't go there, Beth. Single life wins out every time.'

Beth wasn't completely sold on that, even though she and Danny regularly downplayed any considerations of marriage where their relationship was concerned. But she wasn't about to start another dialogue about the pros and cons.

'Anyway,' Jodi continued, 'what are you doing here this morning? I thought you and lover boy were heading south this weekend?'

Beth picked up some boxes and turned back towards the stockroom. 'Danny had something come up last minute. He encouraged me to go ahead anyway, maybe meet up with some of the others, but it would be no fun without him. I might as well stay here and do something productive.'

Ever suspicious, Jodi narrowed her eyes. 'And what came up that he felt you should still go?'

Beth smiled good-naturedly. As far as Jodi was concerned, there wasn't a decent man in all of Manhattan – hell, in all of the world. But Beth knew different.

'It's just a work thing. His firm has a new client starting a big PR campaign in January, and the entire office has been put into lockdown over something last minute. And that's fine by me. Especially since the company has been looking shaky as of late.' She frowned. 'He's had a lot of hours cut recently, so it's good that things are looking better. I don't want him getting laid off, so he needs to put in the time if they ask him. Simple as that. We can always do the Sunshine State some other time.'

'Hmm.' Jodi regarded her sceptically.

Beth swatted at her friend with a playful hand. 'Oh, stop it. Danny's a good guy, you know that.'

Jodi snorted again. 'Well, I'm glad that while you may be a hopeless romantic and always only a heartbeat away from re-enacting the best of Meg Ryan, at least you aren't caught up in that obsession most women over thirty in this town have about marriage. At least you're sane in that aspect. Because if you weren't we just couldn't be friends,' she added wickedly. 'I'm going to go put those boxes away, OK? Man the floor and I'll be back in no time.'

Jodi disappeared into the stockroom and Beth smiled after her older, cynical friend. It was true that she might be a hopeless romantic, but also that she didn't obsess about marriage – at least, not until faced with the question in the form of a happily engaged couple with a look of pity on their faces, she thought wryly. She and Danny worked well together, and Beth knew without a doubt in her mind that he was the one for her. They were in love, and dedicated and committed to each other for the long haul. She didn't need a white dress, a piece of paper (or fairy-tale slippers) to tell her that.

But still, she couldn't deny that things had changed since the early days. OK, so she didn't get as many butterflies in her stomach at the sight of him as she used to, but their relationship wasn't what you would call stale, not by a long shot. It was just *different*.

Though maybe that was simply what happened when time passed and familiarity grew. In romantic movies, nobody ever got to see what happened to the hero and heroine after the credits rolled. Possibly for good reason, as *after* happily ever after didn't necessarily make for an interesting story.

Still, Beth couldn't deny that she wished her and Danny's once-passionate kisses occurred a bit more often, and that these days unexpected romantic moments weren't so few and far between.

But, she told herself, she still had the memories: the romance that was part of her and Danny's story over the years. And that was it, Beth thought: it was their story that made them special together, that made them dedicated to each other. That was the foundation of their love. She and Danny Bishop had been writing their own particular romantic movie all throughout their relationship.

She remembered a moment, very early in the relationship, long before they had moved in together, before they'd even said, 'I love you' (though Beth had known it at the time). It was one of her favourite memories.

It was summertime, and they had just been out for dinner in Little Italy, she was still in her little black dress and Danny had thrown his jacket over her shoulders. They had found themselves at the foot of 58th Street, in a spot just overlooking the East River and the Queensboro Bridge, which was lit up with what seemed like a million little sparkling fairy lights.

And it was there that they'd sat and talked about everything and anything, until eventually the sun had started to peek out over the horizon. Beth remembered just how badly she wanted to tell dawn to wait a while longer, that she wasn't finished with the night yet – that she needed a few more hours of darkness as she learned about this wonderful man who was sitting next to her.

It had been magical. And though Beth didn't realise it until later, it had also been a scene – quite literally – from out of a movie. Woody Allen and Diane Keaton had filmed a famous piece from *Manhattan* in that exact spot, sitting on the very same bench. But she had never seen the movie until one night months later at her old apartment, when Danny was flipping through TV channels, and the iconic clip appeared onscreen.

As she watched, she felt as if stars had been trickling down upon her from heaven. It was a sign, a sign from the romantic movie gods – or perhaps even her beloved grand-mother – that she and Danny were meant to be together.

Instantly hooked, she had insisted on watching *Manhattan* from the very beginning, and while the more unconventional production wasn't usually her style, the film immediately took on a very special meaning.

Smiling at the memory, Beth realised that despite Jodi's misgivings, sometimes romance could indeed be like something from the movies – and in her and Danny's case it was even better.

Chapter 2

'Come on, Beth, you're really refusing to come out for a drink with me? You're a shame to your countrymen,' Jodi added wickedly, as after work the pair stepped onto Lexington Avenue and into the prickling cold that was the city in December.

Fairy-lit trees lining the path along the avenue twinkled in the darkness, and street lamps were adorned with Christmas lights shaped like angels, stars and candy canes. Beth, who never tired of the city at this time of year, gave a satisfied sigh at the romance of it all.

'I can't imagine the North Pole being colder,' her friend scowled, as a wave of steam from a nearby subway vent enveloped them.

Beth's hand went to her neck in an effort to keep it warm in the absence of a scarf. 'It really is chilly, isn't it?' She shivered as goosebumps appeared on the back of her neck, realising she had been out of the warmth of Carlisle's for less than thirty seconds, and was already freezing cold.

'Chilly? Honey, winter in New York is what made that guy coin the phrase "hell freezes over".'

'Ah, stop with the cynical New Yorker thing, you love this time of year too. Though I'm really regretting not bringing a warmer jacket and scarf. Still, it's nothing some hot chocolate and a toasty fire won't fix,' Beth smiled through chattering teeth, and Jodi rolled her eyes.

'The eternal optimist as always. Remind me again why we are actually friends. So act like one and be my wingman tonight? Otherwise I might just have to resort to asking the new guy, and cougar I ain't.'

Beth laughed. 'You mean Ryan from the men's department?' An attractive guy in his early thirties had started in Carlisle's the week before, and his movie-star good looks were sending much of the female staff weak at the knees.

Beth had to admit that he was pretty cute too, but agreed that he was perhaps a little on the young side for her friend. 'OK, OK, if you're that desperate, lead on. Never let it be said that I'm not a good friend – or a proper Irishwoman,' she joked, succumbing to Jodi's pleading (as well as the prospect of indoor warmth).

They ended up staying out much later than Beth had meant to, but that often happened when she agreed to one of Jodi's happy-hour schemes.

Eventually bidding her friend goodbye, she hailed a cab

to take her downtown, having done her duty. Jodi had attracted quite a few decent-looking men at the bar and, more impressively, had even landed an invitation to dinner the following week.

The cab pulled up in front of Beth's apartment building on Gold Street in Lower Manhattan. She pulled a twenty out of her wallet and handed it to the driver. Asking for some change and then providing him with a tip, she stepped from the car and fished her keys out of her purse.

She also grabbed her phone and tapped out a quick text message to Jodi, letting her know as promised that she had made it home without problems. At the same time, Beth realised that she had no new incoming texts nor had she missed any calls.

Strange, she thought. She had phoned Danny earlier and ended up leaving a voicemail for him, letting him know of her plans. But there was nothing back. Not a call, a text or a peep of any sort. He was usually very good about communicating.

Things must be seriously busy at work, she thought as she closed the distance between the kerb and the door of her building. Billy, the concierge, spotted her approach and rushed to the entryway of the lobby to greet her.

'Welcome home, Beth,' he said, opening the door. 'A late one for you tonight? They're keeping you busy at Carlisle's,' he continued in the lovely Scottish brogue he had yet to shake off despite over a decade living in Brooklyn. Like her, he'd left his native roots behind for the bright lights of New York City.

She smiled guiltily. 'No, I've been off for hours. I was actually out playing wingman for Jodi.'

Billy shook his head; he knew Jodi well and was known to flirt mercilessly with her whenever she visited. Her friend usually reciprocated, easily wooed by the handsome six-footer who was around the same age, and from what Beth could tell, also single.

'Ah, I see. Breaks my heart, you know. Breaks my heart. How can the likes of me compete with a Wall Street banker?' he said morosely, though he had a smile on his face.

In Beth's opinion, this lovely, kind-hearted Scotsman had plenty on a Wall Street banker in the scheme of things. Fat bank accounts weren't the only thing in life, and at least Billy had his soul intact.

'Have you seen Danny come in tonight?' she asked him. 'I know he was working late.'

Billy closed the door behind her and nodded an affirmation. 'That I have. But he went up and was back out again fifteen minutes later. Didn't get to talk to him, though. I was on the phone with Mrs Lovejoy in 15H and you know how she prattles on. But don't tell her that I said so.'

Beth smiled. Indeed, it was common knowledge in the building that Doris Lovejoy was a talker. You definitely didn't want to run into her in the lobby if you were in a rush. But even with chatty Doris in mind, Beth was disappointed that her boyfriend wasn't home. Another late night, obviously.

Brushing off her concern, she watched as Billy punched the button for the lift.

'I'm sure it's just something with work,' she said. 'We already had to cancel our long weekend away because his firm has a new client. It's OK, though. I suppose we have to pay for this stack of bricks somehow.'

Their apartment building was far from a 'stack of bricks', being recent in its construction, and centred in the heart of the Financial District. Danny had instantly fallen in love with its modern design and rare waterside location when they first viewed it a few years back. While the rent was way too expensive for Beth's taste (and indeed her occupation) Danny had been earning a lot more at the time, and had talked her round by offering to pay the bulk of the monthly costs.

'Glad to hear that things are picking up for him. God knows, things are still tough out there at the moment,' Billy commented. 'Though he did indeed look a bit stressed today when he was leaving.'

Beth knew that Danny's marketing job came with considerable pressure – especially during the busy holiday season – and he wasn't the kind of guy who handled stress well. He bottled up all his frustrations and worries, despite her encouraging him to include her and talk it out, as partners should. But she knew that wasn't his natural inclination. Much like his father, Danny Bishop was the type who would shut down his feelings and keep everything in, whereas Beth tended to wear her heart on her sleeve.

Melissa Hill

'I'm sure it will be fine,' she stated, more as an affirmation to herself than anything else, before throwing Billy a departing smile as the lift doors opened. She stepped in and hit the button for the twenty-eighth floor.

Solitary inside, Beth leaned against the back wall and closed her eyes briefly. Exhaustion fell across her in waves and suddenly the only thing she wanted was to cuddle her and Danny's little spaniel, Brinkley, named after the cute dog in *You've Got Mail*, and fall into bed.

The buzz she had from a couple of Baileys coffees earlier was gone, and in its place a headache played at her temples. Rubbing a finger on the side of her head, she visualised the bottle of aspirin in her bathroom, and couldn't wait to meet the sheets of her bed.

The lift pinged as it reached her floor and Beth opened her eyes and stepped out. Turning left towards her apartment, she rounded a corner and was met with Courtney, her teenage next-door neighbour, locking Beth and Danny's front door.

Seeing Beth, Courtney jumped as if she had been caught in the act of doing something wrong. Her right hand flew to her chest, and she placed it over her heart. 'Oh, Beth, you scared me. Sorry, I was just checking on Brinkley. I took him out at five o'clock and I just checked on him again, figuring he needed a potty break.' Courtney knew their work schedule and often helped out with the little dog's care.

Beth looked at her watch. It was close to nine p.m.

'Thanks for that. I hope we didn't keep you up too late?'

Courtney tightened the band that secured her dark brown ponytail. 'No prob. Anyway, Danny's not home yet either. I figured you guys would be, like, out together.'

'Still at work, poor thing.' Though the realisation of the lateness of the hour made Beth even more aware of how hard Danny was working just now.

'Right. Do you need me to come by tomorrow? I wasn't sure of your schedule since, like, your Florida thing got cancelled. That sucks, by the way. I read about this badass party Katy Perry was supposed to be hosting in Miami this weekend. Too bad you're gonna miss out.'

Beth had to smile. Courtney liked to believe she and Danny led a glam life (possibly based on the travel photos that decorated the walls of their apartment) and she didn't have the heart to burst the girl's bubble and tell her that there wasn't a chance in hell of them scoring an invitation to a celeb party.

'I'm sure we'll get there sometime. Thanks again, Courtney.'

'No biggie.' With a final snap of her gum, the teenager disappeared down the hallway.

As soon as Beth unlocked the door of her apartment she was greeted with the noisy patter of little paws as Brinkley streaked through the living room. The small spaniel lunged forward, bouncing the last few feet to close the distance between him and Beth. Grinning a happy doggy grin, his tongue lolled to one side of his mouth and he placed his front paws as far up as they could stretch on Beth's legs, throwing his ears back and licking the air around her face as she leaned down to greet him.

'Well, hello to you, too,' she cooed, kissing the dog's copper-coloured head and scratching behind his long, floppy ears. 'Did you get to see Danny when he came home?' The dog made some satisfied puppy noises; what they thought of as Brinkley's ability to answer questions in his own doggy language. 'Well, that's good. At least one of us did.'

Beth's flat-heeled boots clacked against the hardwood floor as she went through to the living room, flicking on lights. And even though it was dark outside and the apartment building was lit, she threw open the privacy drapes that covered the floor-to-ceiling windows lining the western-facing side. As she did, she took in what was undoubtedly the biggest selling point of this apartment (and the reason for at least fifty per cent of the rental cost); the breathtaking view that welcomed her from the twenty-eighth floor.

Lower Manhattan was awash in a sea of lights, and in the midst of all of it was the soaring spectacle of hope and optimism that was the Freedom Tower. Beth never tired of this almost celluloid view – the cityscape of Manhattan lying quite literally at her feet – and she lingered at the window for a moment, taking it all in.

Brinkley waited patiently beside her until she snapped out of her reverie and headed towards the kitchen, planning to make a cup of camomile tea and take some aspirin before settling into bed for the night. As she placed a mug of water in the microwave, she noticed a piece of paper on the worktop with Danny's familiar handwriting on it.

'Hi, sorry I didn't call. Hectic day, and just came home to grab some clothes. Going to pull an all-nighter at the office, so don't wait up. Need to power through on this creative brief for the new campaign. Call you in the morning. D. xoxoxo'

Beth sighed. Sometimes when the company's new client campaigns were hot and heavy, Danny did stay overnight at the office, loading up on energy drinks and caffeine before sneaking in a couple of hours' sleep on the couch in the waiting room. No doubt he would end up taking a quick shower in the morning in the gym attached to the company building on 34th Street.

The microwave beeped and she carefully extracted the mug with her hot water. Slipping in a camomile teabag, she waited for it to steep, when a picture on the wall on the other side of the breakfast bar caught her attention. Beth gave the teabag a few more dunks before shuffling out of the kitchen, and heading directly to the picture. The photo, held in an antique-looking gilded frame that was in direct contrast to the contemporary feel of their apartment's décor, had been taken in Venice, Italy, six years ago.

In it, Beth and Danny had their arms wrapped around each other as they sat in a gondola off the Riva degli Schiavoni. Bright greenish-blue lagoon waters not altogether dissimilar to the colour of Danny's eyes sparkled around them, and the island of San Giorgio Maggiore – which Monet famously portrayed at dusk – was behind them.

Beth remembered exactly how she'd been feeling right at that moment. She recalled the way the sun had lit up the café-lined street in front as the gondolier snapped their picture. She could still see in her mind the magnificent edifices of St Mark's Basilica and the Doge's Palace, and taste the freshness of the raspberries in the Bellinis from Harry's Bar on the Grand Canal.

She looked closely at the picture, as if trying to recommit every detail to memory. Danny's dark hair was a good deal longer than the shortened crop he sported now, his cheeks seemed fuller, and she noticed that his tanned and relaxed visage in the photo was a world apart from his current pale complexion. The outdoors really suited him, and Beth was struck by how the long hours at the office of late had clearly taken their toll not only on his demeanour but his appearance too. She was staring at the photo for so long that Brinkley finally placed one paw on her foot, his way of saying, 'Hey, I'm here too, get a move on.'

Her trance-like state broken, Beth took a tentative sip of her hot tea and looked down at the little pup, who regarded her expectantly. 'That, little man, was long before your time. But it was an incredible trip. A romantic, once-in-a-lifetime trip, in fact,' she said quietly, feeling a very strong and sudden longing to be back in that gondola right at that moment, with Danny's arms around her. She closed her eyes and could almost smell the sea air rushing off the Adriatic, and couldn't deny that her heart ached just a little. She loved Danny, and she knew that he loved her. But she wished for something else, too: the sweeping moments; huge show-stopping scenes. Those happened so rarely in their relationship these days, but it hadn't always been the case.

She scooped Brinkley up under one arm and headed to the bedroom. Within moments she was ready for bed, face scrubbed, aspirin taken, pyjama pants and comfy old T-shirt on. Brinkley made a home next to her beneath Danny's pillow, soaking up the temporary luxury of not having to compete with them both for space.

'Don't get too used to that, buddy,' Beth warned as she flipped on the TV, hoping she could find something that would lull her to sleep.

Roman Holiday, one of her favourite movies, was on Turner Classic Movies. Beth sighed contentedly, fixing her gaze on Audrey Hepburn and Gregory Peck at the Spanish Steps. She remembered this being one of the first movies Bridie had introduced her to, and felt a brief pang that her grandmother was no longer here to partake in the enjoyment. That was one of the most wonderful things about the movies, Beth thought, sitting quietly in the darkness, the experience was even better shared.

But then again she did have Brinkley.

'Rome was part of that trip, too. Your daddy and I ate gelato right where they are standing.' She pointed at the screen as the dog listened, tilting his head as if working to decipher her words. Beth smiled at Brinkley's response, and a feeling of fresh melancholy washed over her as she recalled the details of that incredible trip.

Venice, Italy – Six Years Earlier

Beth emerged from Venice's Santa Lucia train station into the bright sunlight of a September day. Stepping onto the Ponte della Costituzione, she was immediately struck by sensory overload.

The city's famous Grand Canal greeted her along with the bustle of activity that populated the famous tourist hub. On the other side of the canal, she spied the Palazzo Foscari-Contarini and Suore di Maria Bambina, and had a hard time prying her eyes away from the aqua-blue water that glittered like a sea of topaz gems.

Danny put his arm around her waist and pulled her close. 'Amazing, isn't it?'

Beth turned to him and nodded. This was her first time in Italy and while Danny had been here years ago as a child, she had been excited for weeks at the prospect of sharing this romantic experience with him. They'd been going out a few months and she'd been taken aback (but thrilled) when one day he'd spontaneously suggested the trip. From there they were heading to Ireland for a couple of days so that Beth could introduce him to her parents in

Galway. Things were moving fast but she'd known for a while that he was The One and she couldn't wait for her parents to meet the handsome New Yorker who'd stolen her heart.

Venice – indeed, Italy – had always seemed impossibly romantic to her, and she couldn't quite believe that the beauty of the place itself far outshone its celluloid depiction.

'It's just ... incredible ...' she gasped.

Squeezing her once more, he dropped his arm from around her waist and caught her hand. 'Come on. Let's get a taxi.'

Following his gaze, Beth noticed loading ramps in front of the train station, with great hulking water buses filled with people. She tried to make sense of the chaos at the dock as she followed Danny across the piazza and neared the water.

'How do we buy tickets for the water bus? And how do we know where to go? Does it pull up in front of the hotel? Or is it like the subway?'

Danny shook his head. 'No, we aren't taking the vaporetto. We'll take a water taxi, it's easier.'

Only then did Beth notice that there was a taxi stand on the water and a queue of people in line behind it. Aside from the fact that these taxis were glossy, wood-panelled speedboats and not yellow cabs, it was much like a taxi stand back home in Manhattan.

How glamorous ...

Suddenly, Beth pictured herself wearing a headscarf,

large black oversized sunglasses on her face, laughing into the wind like Carole Lombard or Audrey Hepburn in some fantastic Golden Age Hollywood movie. In her mind, she saw Danny at her side, devilishly handsome in an Italian-cut suit and dark sunglasses, channelling Cary Grant or Clark Gable, handing her a glass of prosecco as he helped her into the boat. She felt like swooning right at that moment, just like in the movies. Danny would catch her as she fell (elegantly, of course) into his arms, and he would stroke her temple and pepper her face with kisses. Until she awoke, thereupon he would spirit her away to their hotel room where they would make passionate love while a gondolier with an operatic baritone voice serenaded them, his song echoing up from the Canal below.

Then Beth's romantic vision came to a distinct halt as she heard the words, 'How much?' and the answer, 'Ninety euro.' Well and truly launched back into reality, she looked from Danny to the idly smiling water-taxi driver in front of her.

'Ninety euro? But Venice doesn't look that big,' she gasped, riffling through her bag for her map. 'Just how far do you need to take us?' she questioned the driver, after providing the name of their hotel. Truthfully, she could make no sense whatsoever of the Venetian canal layout and wasn't about to attempt to until she had a chance to explore and familiarise herself.

The driver, a dark swarthy man whose ancestors were likely pirates who had once commanded the waters of the

Adriatic, took the proffered map from Beth and gave it a cursory glance. Within seconds, he pointed to a spot, his finger on the identifier Ca' Satriano near the Venice Theatre. Quickly thinking back to the description of the location of the hotel advertised on their website, Beth knew he was being truthful.

'And where are we now?' she asked. The Italian pointed again, indicating the large bulky mass at the top of the map labelled as the Santa Lucia train station. When Beth realised the distance between point A and point B, she gulped hard. No way could that add up to ninety euro . . .

Turning to Danny, she said, 'No, Danny. Let's take the water bus, or walk. That's way too much for such a short trip.' She knew he wouldn't have as good a grasp of the currency value as she did.

Danny smiled. While he appreciated Beth's fiscal mindfulness, right now it was uncalled for. 'Babe, really, it's OK. I've been on the vaporetto, and I can tell you it's not overly efficient. This will get us there faster, and besides, those shoes you have on are not made for Venice's cobbled streets. Nor is dragging your suitcase. Spend a day in this city and you'll soon see.'

Beth bit her lip and tried to ignore the driver's eye roll. Indeed, her strappy, four-inch Tory Burch pumps were not made for walking, and she had to admit she had enjoyed the first-class cabin on the train from Florence to Venice.

'Besides we're here to celebrate my promotion. We can afford it. And you don't even take the bus in New York.'

She sighed and acquiesced. 'Oh, all right, when you put it like that.' She smiled at Danny and took his hand again as the water-taxi driver jumped to attention. The man busied himself with grabbing their luggage and lugging the cases to a boat standing at the ready in the canal.

A moment later, Danny helped Beth navigate the steps into the water taxi.

Noticing the luxurious wooden panelling and white leather seats, she allowed her mind to return to her previous fantasy, and her heart skipped with delight when they settled into the back of the boat and the driver produced two glasses of prosecco for their enjoyment.

Beth sipped the bubbles and felt herself relax. The boat's engine roared to life and motored into the Canal. A light breeze tickled her face and she breathed in the smells and sounds of this amazing water city. A moment later the driver took a turn down Fondamenta Garzotti and she pointed excitedly at the gondolas with which they shared the waterway.

'Oh, Danny, look, look. Gondolas! Oh my goodness, I just can't believe I am here, that we are here. Can we do that? Can we take a gondola ride?' She felt ready to burst with excitement and turned to face him, her eyes as wide as saucers at the unashamed glamour of it all. Italy was even better than she'd imagined – exactly like it looked in the movies, though even more wonderful in reality.

Danny laughed, throwing his head back in obvious enjoyment. She knew he was perplexed sometimes by her imagination, unbridled optimism and tendency to elevate everyday events to something worthy of Hollywood. He was always teasing her about those notions and joking that a constant soundtrack of movie music was playing in her head.

He pulled her close and placed a kiss on her cheek. 'Beth, we can do whatever you want. I planned all this just for us.'

Then Beth's leading man turned his attention to her lips, and thoughts of gondolas, prosecco and Venice left her brain.

At least for the moment.

A few hours later, Danny pulled Beth close and nuzzled her neck. Having checked into their hotel, a beautifully picturesque boutique building right on the water, they now were dedicated to exploring this beautiful city.

They had sat in a small café next to Rialto Bridge for almost two hours, chatting, people watching, and drinking a bottle of delicious Italian wine and, both happily flushed, were now immersed in the city's historical sights.

'I think Venice suits you, you know,' he murmured into Beth's hair as they meandered down Calle della Donzella.

'What makes you say that?' she asked as she leaned into him and wrapped an arm around his waist.

'It's beautiful, brilliant, gorgeous, inspiring – just like you. Exactly like you,' he repeated with conviction, and Beth felt her heart soar. 'I could secrete you away into some loft over the canal, listen to the sounds of the water sloshing against the building and lie in your arms for the rest of my life. Perfectly content. Perfectly happy.'

She felt tears prick the corners of her eyes. Not out of sadness, but because of the pure, unadulterated joy that she felt at that moment – indeed, every moment she spent with Danny. She truly believed they were on the same page. They were soul mates and he was her ultimate Hollywood hero. There was no other way to describe it.

'I love you, Danny,' she said simply.

'And I love you, Beth. Always you.' He pulled her into a secluded doorway off the small alleyway they were on and kissed her again. When they pulled away from their embrace, Beth felt as if her head was spinning. This was it. This truly was the real thing. Bridie would have adored Danny, she knew that. He was exactly the kind of leading man her grandmother would have chosen for her.

'Getting hungry?' he asked, once they had resumed walking.

'Amongst other things,' she grinned mischievously.

'Woman, you are insatiable.' Danny laughed as she walked in front of him to allow pedestrians on the other side of the narrow path to go in the opposite direction.

Then she suddenly stopped to consult her map. 'Do you want to try one of the restaurants the hotel recommended? It looks like one is right around this corner. At least I think it is.' She looked at Danny for input, still slightly bewildered by the city's impossible-to-decipher waterways.

He smiled at her and gave a brief bow. 'Lead on,

navigator. By the way, did you make a note of that shop with the Venetian mask you liked? I know you didn't want to carry a bag around, but if you want it, we should pick it up on our way back.'

She nodded and pointed. 'We'll be able to find it again, I think. And it looks like the restaurant is just here.' But then as they rounded the corner of the *strada* on which their intended restaurant was supposed to be, Beth's attention was diverted from food as they were faced with a tiny bridge over a small subset of the canal.

And while there were dozens upon dozens of such bridges in all of Venice, this one was unique. It was nondescript in every way except one – its ornate iron railings were decorated with padlocks of various colours, shapes and sizes.

'Oh, Danny, look. What is this place?'

'I'm not sure but—' He stopped speaking and then watched a couple who approached the bridge from the other side, hand in hand, smiling happily. The couple stood with their heads bent together for a moment. They appeared to be writing on something the man held in his hands – a padlock, Beth realised. Then when the woman was finished with her inscription, they found an empty space on the bridge and fastened the lock in place. A moment later, looking into each other's eyes, the couple kissed and tossed the key into the canal water below.

Captivated, Beth walked onto the bridge. 'Look, Danny. Years and years of these padlocks. Here's one, you can barely read the names, but the date is 11 August 1978. And another one: 1950 ... it's scratched on there. So many names. Amanda and Kevin. Denise and Bill. Susan and Tony. Lindsay and Bryan. Sadie and Robert. So many love stories.' So many hopes, dreams and love stories all tied up in one place.

She felt herself become overwhelmed by the romance of it all. She had never imagined that there could be a place so special, tucked away in a tiny corner of such a romantic city. 'Where can we find one for ourselves, I wonder?' she asked, looking towards the now-departing young lovers. 'Oh, Danny, we have to do this – it's like something you'd see in a ...'

Her words trailed off as they were approached by a young vendor with a convenient variety of padlocks for sale. Danny engaged in a quick round of negotiations, handed over the money, and then returned with the lock to Beth, who was still absorbed in inspecting other people's promises.

'What a magical place,' she whispered, truly awed. 'So many people have stood where we stand. Have been in love, right here, in Venice. Have wished and hoped and dreamed with someone special. Right in this place.'

Beth breathed deeply, as if she could somehow absorb the romance and wonder she felt at that moment.

Danny offered her the lock. 'We can add to it if you like. I know how much you love this cheesy Hollywood stuff.' He grinned and gave her the inscription tool he'd procured from the vendor.

'It's not cheesy. It's *romantic*,' she protested, but she knew he was just teasing.

Beth carefully etched her name then handed the lock back to Danny, allowing him to do the same. 'And the date, too,' she instructed.

Taking her direction, he inscribed the date and year beneath their names. Then he turned the key and the padlock popped open. 'Let's do this together then,' he suggested. 'Where will we put it?'

'Here.' She moved a few padlocks around and found a space where their token would fit. It was almost like a secret place, an enchanted location where she and Danny would stay huddled safe together for ever.

Silently, both kneeling alongside the rail, their hands worked together and closed the padlock around the iron bar.

Beth's hands stayed on it for just a second longer, as if committing the memory to touch, and she suddenly felt a little dizzy at what they were doing. Since meeting him six months before, this man had truly swept her off her feet, and the idea that she and Danny would be leaving a part of themselves – of their hearts – together in Venice seemed especially significant, somehow; that their love would exist here, in spirit, for ever.

Finally she took her hand away and allowed the neighbouring padlocks to right themselves against this new addition. Danny pulled her to her feet and their eyes found each other's.

He winked and held the key up to eye level, grinning. 'Now. Make a wish.'

'You first,' she smiled.

He thought for a moment before speaking again. 'OK, so how would they do this in Hollywood?' He laughed at her outraged expression. 'Sorry, sorry, I'm just joking.' Then his voice grew more serious. 'I wish ...' he began, in a tone that she'd never heard him use before and, despite his earlier teasing, his words now sounded heartfelt. 'I wish for our lives ... our destinies ... to be forever entwined. I love you, Beth Harper, and this lock represents that promise of a lifetime.'

A lifetime ...

In that moment, Beth realised that what Danny had just said completely mirrored her own feelings. This was it. He was The One. She and Danny Bishop belonged together.

'Was that worthy enough of one of your romantic heroes, do you think?' he asked.

Beth smiled. 'Much better. And my own wish is exactly the same.'

Then Danny pulled her close, and she watched silently as he cast the padlock key into the canal. It hit the water with a tiny splash, and as the two of them observed from the bridge above, the key sunk to the murky depths where it found a home and would remain in this romantic city. Forever.

A lifetime symbol of Beth and Danny's love for one another.

Chapter 3

The following morning, Beth climbed up the steps that brought her above ground from the subway station on 59th and Lexington, catching herself as she almost slipped on the ice.

Seeing the entrance of Carlisle's ahead, she swerved around a couple of lost tourists busily consulting a map, and gratefully entered the heated luxury of one of Manhattan's favourite stores. She called out hello to a couple of her co-workers and made her way upstairs towards her own department, keeping an eye out for Jodi, who was also in today.

Reaching the third floor, she saw that her friend was already at work and currently with an early-bird customer. Jodi caught Beth's eye and threw a brief smile her way before returning her attention to the shopper.

Beth took a right into the hallway connecting the shoe department with the men's department, and walked briskly into the common area where employees could store their personal belongings in lockers while on shift.

She undid the lock by entering a combination comprised of her and Danny's birth dates. *Six, eighteen, eleven, twenty-five,* she repeated in her mind, then clicked the lock open. She placed her bag inside and quickly checked her makeup in a magnetic mirror that she kept on the inner door. Satisfied with her appearance, she closed the door and redid the lock.

Running through a mental list of what needed to be done in the department that day, Beth turned quickly back towards the sales floor, only to collide full force into something hard and upright.

She was stumbling on her heels, and feeling herself beginning to fall when suddenly a pair of steady arms encircled her waist, righting her. Then those arms were stabilising her, helping her catch her balance and stay on her feet.

'Whoa there ...' The voice was silky, self-assured and decidedly masculine. For some reason, involuntary goose-bumps tickled Beth's skin at the sound of it.

She looked up and came face to face with Ryan Buchanan, the new guy from the men's department. With a strong jaw, longish sandy-blond hair cut like Bradley Cooper's, and a laconic smile that could light up a room, there was a good reason he was turning heads at Carlisle's.

Beth had only come across him briefly since he'd started, and never in close circumstances like this.

'You OK?' he asked, concerned, and she suddenly became very aware of his strong arms around her waist. They were standing so close that she could smell his cologne, something musky and masculine, and she forced herself to find her voice and pull her gaze away from his mesmerisingly green eyes.

'Thanks, yes, I'm fine ... sorry,' she stuttered, embarrassed, moving away from his embrace. As she went to create some distance, he too must have realised their proximity and quickly dropped his arms to his side.

'Oh, I'm sorry. Didn't mean to ... I just didn't want you to fall,' he explained, a faint blush deepening in his cheeks in a way that Beth found impossibly endearing.

And then there was that smile again.

She looked away, straightened her pencil skirt and examined her appearance – if only to break away from his handsome gaze. Inexplicably, she felt heat rising around her collar and knew at that moment a full-on blush was creeping up her neck. She willed herself to get it together, feeling a little like Meg Ryan or Kate Hudson in the midst of a classic 'meet cute' movie sequence.

'I'm not sure we've met properly. I just started here – I'm Ryan. Ryan Buchanan.' One of those strong, able hands was extended Beth's way and she snapped to attention as she realised he was waiting for a response.

'Yes, I know ... hello.' She reached out to shake his hand and the moment she touched his fingers, a jolt of electricity shot through her body. Beth flinched and snatched her hand away. She quickly glanced up at his face, wondering if he felt it too and, looking into those eyes again, she realised that describing them as green was an understatement. That description didn't do them any justice. They were almost like twinkling emeralds staring back at her.

And then the eyebrows over those emeralds shot up. 'And your name?' he asked with a grin, once again returning Beth to reality.

'I'm-mm Beth,' she stuttered.

'Well, M-Beth, it's nice to meet you properly,' he repeated chuckling. 'You're in shoes, right?'

'Yes.' She nodded, still a bit flushed, and completely bewildered as to what was happening to her.

'Even if I didn't know I could have guessed. Those are hot shoes.' He looked down at her flower-embellished Dolce & Gabbana heels – a gorgeous piece of shoe art from last season that Beth had managed to buy through the benefit of her employee discount. 'I love those movie displays you do over there. That *Pretty Woman* one was especially great. Major kudos for making thigh-high PVC boots a must-have with the Park Avenue crowd,' he chuckled. 'Clearly a born saleswoman. I'll have to pick your brains sometime.'

He flashed *that* smile again and Beth flushed afresh at the dual compliment.

'Thanks, I hadn't thought of it that way but ...' she began, and just then heard footsteps approach from behind. Jodi's voice followed, and Beth realised that her 'meet cute' was about to be interrupted. For some reason she felt guilty, not because she had been caught unawares, but because she half-wished that it *hadn't* been interrupted.

'Hey, Beth— Oh, sorry,' Jodi said, and Beth glanced at her, hoping that she herself looked perfectly calm and unruffled. She realised that this wasn't the case when her friend raised an eyebrow and gave her a puzzled look. 'Um, Sandra Bernstein is here.' Jodi pointed in the direction of the sales floor and Beth was brought back to reality: Mrs Bernstein was one of her regular customers. 'I can help her out if you want . . .'

'No, no, I was just on my way.'

'Better get to it myself.' Ryan smiled laconically, giving Beth another appraising glance and she tried to avoid his eyes as well as Jodi's questioning gaze.

She straightened her shoulders and nodded at him. 'I'm sure I'll see you around.'

'Absolutely. See you soon, Beth.'

She reluctantly pulled herself away and walked with determination towards the sales floor, feeling completely discombobulated. What the hell had happened back there?

All of a sudden, Beth understood exactly why Ryan Buchanan's recent arrival at Carlisle's had caused such a stir, and was sending female hearts all aflutter.

Later that morning, the phone buzzed on the bedside table, and even without checking the display Danny knew that it would be Beth calling. He meant to get in touch with her first thing, but his mind had been elsewhere . . .

Picking up the phone, he swung his legs off the bed and retrieved his shirt from where he had dropped it earlier.

'Can't it wait?' Adele asked, regarding him with her dark chocolate eyes. She pushed her lustrous black hair back behind one ear as she leaned closer, waiting for his answer.

'Sorry, I need to get this.' She seemed to take it as a brushoff, and moved to the other side of the room, fastening her hair into a loose ponytail.

Danny retreated to the attached bathroom for some privacy. He somehow felt less guilty about this entire thing when he was not in direct view of Adele's questioning, probing eyes. It was so much harder to lie to Beth, when Adele was listening and knew exactly what he wasn't saying aloud.

Pushing his arms into his shirt and hastily buttoning it up, he accepted the call and quietly shut the bathroom door behind him.

'Hey,' he greeted into the handset, hoping his voice sounded normal – hoping he could pull this off – again.

'Hi! Hope you got some sleep last night and aren't working too hard today,' Beth said, and he could hear the usual happy smile in her voice.

Danny's heart sank. He hated deceiving her, hated hiding things but at the moment there was really no choice. He couldn't help it. This is not how he pictured things years ago, *hell*, even a few weeks ago. Why couldn't he just come clean?

'Do you think maybe you could escape for lunch for a

half-hour?' she continued. 'I really missed seeing you last night.'

Despite himself, he raised a smile. There was something so appealing about Beth's unashamed adoration of him. For her there was never any game-playing or pretence of any kind, and he'd always loved how she wore her heart on her sleeve.

Unlike him, he conceded, guilt and self-loathing building afresh. 'I know, and again I'm really sorry about Florida. I'll make it up to you, I promise.'

'Ah, don't worry about that. I was more disappointed not to have you home last night. Not that Brinkley minded, though; he took over your side of the bed.'

Danny also appreciated Beth's unerring ability to pretend that everything was OK, as if they hadn't been through stressful times recently. He knew that despite her outward cheeriness and relentless ability to look on the bright side, deep down she had worried about his job, and the fact that the company had cut his hours, threatening his career and their livelihood.

But Danny also couldn't help but acknowledge that it was perhaps all the stress he'd been experiencing at work that had led to the predicament he was in now. The work-related strain had resulted in some recent nit-picking and tension in their relationship, all of which, he guessed, had brought him right to Adele's door.

It was a vicious cycle, and one that Danny didn't know how to stop. He loved Beth and yet . . .

'So what do you think?' his girlfriend continued. 'Do you want to meet for lunch today?'

Danny swallowed hard. He knew he couldn't see her now. He needed to shower and change his clothes beforehand, if only to try to get the stench of guilt off him. At this point, it was almost like it was coming out of his pores.

'Honey, honestly I would love to, but I'm probably going to end up working through lunch. I just ran out a while ago to pick up some takeout, something quick,' he lied, thinking of Adele on the other side of the door. 'I'm sorry; I was just trying to get through this day so I could maybe get home early this evening.'

It was clear Beth was disappointed. 'Oh, OK, well, I just thought that maybe I would just ask anyway, I wasn't sure ...'

Danny felt a lump growing in his throat and truly wished at that moment that he could reach out and pull her close to him, cry into her hair, ask for forgiveness, a fresh start, *anything*.

He felt desperate, but he also knew that it was completely unfair of him to expect her simply to accept any of this – to believe that she would just forgive his lies and still want to be with him. Especially when he had hidden so much already. How did couples move on when there were so many secrets, so much information concealed, not to mention trust breached?

'I'll make it up to you, I promise,' he insisted, meaning

it. 'This weekend. We'll do something special this weekend, OK? Anything you want.'

There was silence on the other end of the line and Danny felt the tension growing as he waited for Beth to speak. What if she was on to him? What if she knew that right now he wasn't working, wasn't eating takeout at his desk? What if she had already called his office only to have his assistant, Kimberly, tell her that, no he hadn't actually arrived yet and had left early yesterday, saying he had an 'appointment'. What if, what if, what if . . . ?

Finally, Beth spoke and once again Danny could hear her smiling on the other end of the line. 'That sounds good. I think we could do with that, to be honest.'

He felt himself exhale. 'Great. I'll see you later, maybe try to get out of here a little earlier if I can, OK?

Soon after, he and Beth said their goodbyes and Danny ended the call and stared at the phone after hanging up, just taking a moment as he thought through their conversation one more time.

Then he put his hand on the doorknob and steeled himself to face Adele, turning momentarily to look at his reflection in the bathroom mirror. Sure, he looked the same, more or less, a bit pale maybe, but he wasn't sure if that was due to the fact that he felt rattled by Beth's call, or something else. He just knew that he didn't *feel* the same.

And he worried that there was a part of him that was lost, as if part of his soul was crumpled and damaged and dark. He felt as if a great black blob of nothingness was living in his body, ready to consume him as punishment for what he'd been doing.

Danny breathed deeply, hoping to cleanse himself, steel himself, then he opened the door.

Adele took in his appearance and he knew that she could feel the tension rolling off him.

'You OK?' she asked, her eyes watchful.

He nodded, finding it hard to meet her gaze.

'You know you would feel better if you just told her,' she said simply. 'The truth will set you free, so they say.'

Danny shook his head. 'No, it wouldn't. It would change everything. You don't understand.'

'Danny, really, I do understand. I've been down this road a few times before, you know,' she said, and for a moment he was a little taken aback. But of course a woman like her would have experienced something like this before, he realised, feeling stupid. He certainly wasn't the first. 'But it's your choice,' she continued. 'It's your relationship, not mine. And I'm just trying to help.'

'You're right – it's none of your business,' he replied curtly, then immediately relented when he saw her expression. 'Hey, I'm sorry, that was out of line. I'm just ... I'm sorry, but like I said, I need to do this in my own time.' He took a few steps in her direction, but she held up a well-manicured hand.

'It's OK. I get it, and I know it's difficult. Really, it's all right. Take your time. But don't take too long ...'

Danny nodded, completely understanding the subtle

warning. Suddenly he felt awkward. They'd been seeing each other for a few weeks now, but he didn't really *know* her as such.

'So ...' he said, absently, wondering how to take his leave.

'Right, so, see you next time? Same time, same place?' she said, catching his drift. 'Give me a call.'

'Sure.' Danny swallowed hard, considering his weaknesses, his deficiencies and then answered, 'I'll be here.'

He couldn't stop himself if he tried.

Much later at home, Beth lay curled up in bed with Brinkley next to her when she heard the front door of the apartment open. Looking up from reading an old dog-eared romance novel, she looked to the door of the bedroom expectantly and stole a glance at the clock.

Nine-thirty: not exactly an early finish, she thought, remembering Danny's claim on the phone earlier that he was going to try to make it home from work at a reasonable time.

She tried to shake off some of her disappointment and reminded herself that he was just trying to do well at work, especially in the run-up to Christmas, when the company would be handing out bonuses. She shouldn't really be annoyed if he worked hard; after all, it wasn't as if he was running around the city with his friends, hitting bars and partying it up. And she'd been enjoying an early night curled up with a book, in any case.

Quiet footsteps moved closer to the room, and Brinkley jumped to attention the moment the door opened. Danny stood with his hand on the door handle, a hesitant look on his face.

The moment he saw Beth he broke into a half-smile. 'Hey, I thought you might be asleep,' he said quietly as Brinkley jumped from the bed and crossed the distance between them. 'Early night?' He leaned down to place his briefcase on the floor and picked up the dog, scratching him around the ears, much to Brinkley's enjoyment.

Beth smiled and stretched her arms above her head. She kicked her legs from under the bed sheet and stood up. 'Yeah. It's so cold out, and I was just reading.' As she drew closer and opened her arms for a hug, instead of welcoming her embrace Danny quickly handed her Brinkley, almost as if he wanted to avoid physical contact.

A curious act that didn't go unnoticed by Beth.

'What? No hug?' she joked.

Avoiding her gaze, Danny kissed her on the cheek and moved around her on his way to the bathroom. 'In a minute, for your own sake,' he chuckled. 'Sorry, it's been a long day and I really need a shower. I, uh ... just hit the gym.'

Beth nuzzled Brinkley's neck and thought about his words, feeling slightly crestfallen that he'd gone somewhere else instead of being home early like he'd promised. 'I thought you were working late at the office? How did you find time to head down to the gym?'

Danny shrugged out of his shirt and threw it into the laundry hamper. 'I was so stressed from work, I needed to blow off some steam. A new place opened just a few blocks away. Actually, I almost slipped on the ice trying to rush home.'

Beth followed him into the bathroom as he undressed and started the water. A moment later, with steam billowing from the bathtub, he opened the shower curtain and slid in. While she had always been an admirer of Danny's toned physique she had to admit lately there was something different about him.

'Have you been working out harder recently? Or dieting even?' she asked.

He stuck his head out of the shower and considered her words. 'Me – diet? Nah. Just doing the usual. If anything, I'm eating more junk at the desk lately.' His head disappeared once again and Beth thought about it. He looked leaner, as if he had definitely been working out harder, or eating less. 'Why do you ask?' came the question from the shower.

She shrugged. 'You just look like you've lost some weight lately. Nothing major. I was just wondering if you were doing something different at the gym. Getting pumped up or something, trying to impress the ladies ...' she added, chuckling.

There was a brief pause from the other side of the curtain. 'No, nothing different. It's probably just stress, to be honest.'

Beth nodded and pushed the thought from her mind. It was true that while she had the tendency to put on a few pounds when she was worried about something – finding comfort in ice cream and chocolate – Danny usually went in the other direction.

Typical, she thought, men shed pounds when they're stressed or busy with work. Whereas she tended to pack them on, especially at this time of year. Only today at lunchtime, she'd popped over to Lindton Fifth Avenue, where they routinely handed out free Lindor truffles for the holiday season. That would have to stop, or she'd soon end up looking like one of those spherical chocolates herself.

She smiled and put Brinkley down on the ground, where he immediately went about sniffing Danny's discarded clothes.

'Get out of there, silly. I'll take care of those.' Beth bent down to pick up his trousers at the same time Danny stuck his head out of the shower again.

'Hey, leave those,' he said abruptly. Taken aback by his vehemence, Beth stood and quickly dropped his clothes back onto the floor. 'I mean, there is some stuff in my pockets still,' he explained in a softer voice. 'I'll take care of it. It's just … I don't want anything to get lost.'

'I can go through the pockets for you—'

'Don't worry,' he insisted. 'I'll do it. I'm finished here anyway.' At that moment, the water stopped and Danny grabbed a towel from the rack next to the bathtub. A second later, he emerged from the tub, still wet, and grabbing his clothes, swept quickly past Beth and out of the bathroom.

Perplexed by his curious behaviour, she followed him into the bedroom to find him emptying his pockets, shoving assorted pieces of paper and other flotsam into his briefcase. He then wadded his discarded trousers up and tossed them into the hamper where he had put his shirt minutes before. Then he turned to Beth and smiled sheepishly. 'Sorry, didn't mean to be tetchy, just some business cards and stuff that I couldn't lose. Meant to leave it all at the office.'

Beth regarded him sceptically. She was not a sensitive or suspicious person, but then Danny had never given her any reason to be. He was never secretive, nor was he one who didn't like others touching his things. He always left stuff lying around – would allow his phone to remain unattended on the kitchen counter and his laptop open on his desk. But then she realised uncomfortably he'd been doing less of this of late.

Danny slipped on a pair of pyjama pants, then he approached her holding his arms out. 'So what about that hug?' he asked with the smile that had always melted her heart. 'I've missed my favourite girl today,' he added quietly as he enveloped her in his arms.

Breathing in his freshly showered scent, Beth let the tension that had crept into her body ease away as she allowed herself to be held.

A moment later Danny broke the embrace and swung

her legs up, carrying her like a bride as she chuckled in his arms. Collapsing them both onto the bed, he kissed Beth before whispering into her ear. 'If I remember correctly, you said you were lonely last night. Here's to making up for lost time.'

Chapter 4

'Here you go, Miss Dempsey,' Beth said on Monday morning, handing the 16-year-old blonde a huge Carlisle's glossy bag containing at least a couple of thousand dollars' worth of footwear. 'It has been a pleasure to help you today, as always.'

Sitting on the plush red velvet sofa surrounded by discarded shoes and boots, the young socialite didn't make eye contact, but snapped her gum and twirled a lock of her hair as she stared at the screen of her phone.

'Right. Well, yeah, but like it would have been better if you had those Jimmy Choos I wanted in a size eight. I guess I'll have to go to Saks now. Inconvenient. Ugh.' Another snap of gum and Beth resisted the urge to sigh. Marley Dempsey was, to say the least, a challenging customer, but she was also one of the biggest spending ones.

'Well, as I said, I would be happy to order them in for you. It should take only a day or two—'

'Whatevs,' the younger woman said, rolling her eyes. 'Not going to help me; I catch a plane for London with Daddy later. And besides, there's probably better stuff on the other side of the pond. New York is so meh during the holidays. What a waste. I can't believe anyone hangs around this city right now. Old, cold and sooo many tourists.'

The blonde uncrossed her long legs and picked up the shopping bag. She bent down to get her purse and flipped her long (extension-filled) locks over her shoulder. When she stood back up again she looked around and took in someone who'd just walked into the shoe rooms.

'Whoa. Total hottie, twelve o'clock,' she muttered under her breath as she started to take her leave. Beth looked up and smiled.

Ryan Buchanan.

As Marley passed him on her way to the lift, she threw a come-hither glance over her shoulder that Ryan seemed oblivious to. Beth snorted back laughter and then felt uncomfortable as she recalled the strange reaction he'd provoked in her a few days before. Their paths had crossed a couple of times since then and, much to her relief, she had managed to keep her cool and behave halfway normal around him.

He smiled that heart-melting lopsided smile as he got nearer, and threw a thumb over his shoulder. 'Was that ... Marley Dempsey? The hotel heiress?'

'The one and only,' Beth smiled. 'And I think you might

have turned her head,' she added coyly. He chuckled but resisted turning round to watch Marley's taut derrière walk away, something which Beth couldn't help but appreciate. His restraint, not the younger girl's derrière.

'Not my type. Too much silicone for someone so young. Plus from what I hear she comes with a lot of baggage . . .' He grimaced and Beth laughed, recalling how Marley's scandalised father had been threatening to sue left, right and centre when topless photos of his daughter had been leaked on Twitter. It was later revealed that the attention-seeking youngster had herself been behind it all.

'Well, I'm sure you've already realised that it's a common theme around this store. Carlisle's tends to cater for Manhattanite kids who have way too much money and who are very, very, bored. Lucky for us, though.'

Ryan smiled and put his hands in his pockets. 'Right. I have gathered that, and I've only been here two weeks. But speaking of bored Manhattanites, I'm new to the city and I haven't really got my bearings here just yet. I was wondering if you'd be interested in showing me around, maybe grab a drink or even dinner sometime?'

Beth's heart beat faster and she felt as if she was a teenager again, being asked out by the cutest boy in class. She automatically felt the word 'yes' forming on her lips when she remembered something that she had been too easily forgetting lately whenever she came within close proximity to Ryan Buchanan.

That she had a long-term boyfriend, the love of her life.

She and Danny had had a great weekend – one that Beth was sorry to see end, if only for the fact that it had been nice to spend a bit of one-on-one alone time with him. But even in light of the fact that he had been attentive and loving to her since getting home late last week, she couldn't deny that something felt 'off' lately. She couldn't put a finger on it, or why she was even feeling that way. She just knew that something wasn't right.

Of course, there was that trouser pockets issue. She had briefly forgotten about it once Danny had turned on the charm and started kissing her – which had led to other things – but when she woke up the following morning, her mind immediately returned to the incident. She had racked her brain to figure out just why he had been so possessive about his things the night before. She had even thought about checking what he had put in his briefcase that time, but knew that she didn't want to be that person: the suspicious, snooping girlfriend, constantly looking through her boyfriend's belongings, searching for evidence of some kind of . . . wrongdoing.

So she had tried hard just to put it out of her mind and take Danny at his word – that it was just work stuff that he didn't want to misplace. After all, he had never been one to be sneaky or to lie to her. Beth probably could have done this easily if it had been the only *thing* that had happened, but then there had been that situation with his phone . . .

Danny had placed the phone on the breakfast counter on Saturday afternoon after he and Beth returned from a cosy lunch at Union Square, and had retreated to the tiny room they used as a study, to check his work email.

Beth had been in the kitchen when the phone had started vibrating on the granite countertop, indicating an incoming call. When she had called out to Danny and had reached for the device to bring it to him, he had come running almost at a full sprint, and practically snatched it out of her hand. And if that wasn't enough, he'd then retreated again to the other room with the phone, talking in low tones to whomever was on the other end, only to return minutes later and refer to it as 'a stupid work thing'.

Beth hated that her antennae were fully alert at the moment. And she equally loathed the feeling of insecurity and suspicion that had entered her psyche since. She wasn't sure if she could even imagine Danny – her Danny – doing something underhand. And frankly, after so many great years together, she couldn't face the idea that something might be wrong with them, with their relationship.

She had loved this man for so long, had built a life around him, not to mention placed so much of her heart in his hands, that she couldn't even begin to imagine an alternative scenario. That maybe he was getting bored, or his head had been turned. What if he was interested in or – worse – was falling for something else? Was it even possible that he might not love her any more? Yet that didn't make sense either, she argued with herself. After all, he had been so attentive and loving towards her all weekend.

But what if that was just all part of an act while he tried to figure out the best way to leave her?

Beth knew that such a thing sometimes happened. She had seen enough of those movies, and knew that it never turned out well for the heroine. At least, until the real hero swooped in to mend her broken heart.

But Danny had always been her hero, her leading man. No, a shift to deception couldn't *possibly* be the storyline of her romantic movie. She was meant to have a happy ending with Danny. Theirs was the love of a lifetime. It just wasn't possible that there'd be an unexpected, heartbreaking plot development.

Was it?

'Well? What do you say?' Beth heard Ryan ask then, bringing her right back to the present and offering her an entirely different dilemma. 'I've been living in LA, and New York is just such a different animal. You must remember what it was like for you when you first came here,' he continued. 'You're not from town either, right?'

Beth looked back up and met Ryan's emerald-green eyes, seeing right through the fellow city-newbie line. She smiled, trying to shake off how inexplicably drawn to this guy she felt and shook her head. 'I appreciate the invite but I can't.'

He didn't break her gaze. 'Another time then.' But by the way he looked at her, Beth realised it wasn't a question, it was a declarative statement. And she guessed he was the kind of guy that wasn't used to being turned down. Or prepared to take no for an answer.

This realisation gave her a tiny *frisson* of satisfaction but she quickly pushed it away.

'Sorry, but I really can't,' she insisted. 'You see, I have a boyfriend. Danny. We've been together for seven years, and call me old-fashioned, but I don't think going out or spending time with another guy, even as friends, would be appropriate.'

Ryan's expression didn't flinch. 'Seven years. Whoa ... that's a long time. You know what they say: the seven-year itch and all that,' he added jokingly. 'Think there's any truth in it?'

It was simply impossible not to be discombobulated by the way he was looking at her, let alone his words, and Beth's internal thermometer spiked afresh. She worked very hard to control the expression on her face, but felt quite hot and bothered, and was pretty sure Ryan immediately got the answer to his question without her having to verbalise it.

Trying to regain a semblance of composure, she raised her eyebrows. 'I'm not sure what you mean ... isn't that a movie?' she asked, unafraid to play dumb.

He laughed a little. 'I guess it is. But there's a lot of truth in the expression too. I just got out of a relationship myself, primarily because I moved here. My ex and I, well, she was a California girl through and through. No way would she move here, and I guess that's probably a good thing. She was great, but not long-term material, you know? I mean, I want to settle down at some point. You more or less know when the time is right, right? And Lauren, my ex, well, she was younger. Doing the club scene every night, which just isn't my style. It's fun, but it gets old eventually. Now I know I want to be with someone I can just curl up with on a couch, open a bottle of wine, watch a movie. Know where I could meet a girl like that in New York?'

His question was loaded with meaning, and Beth felt a little weak at the knees by all this attention. She was thinking of all the girls who would just *jump* at the chance of settling down with Ryan Buchanan ... And she couldn't help but wish that Danny would be this way, full of purpose regarding *their* future. What was *he* waiting for? Was she not marriage material? Where were they going as a couple?

She shook her head, ridding herself of such troublesome thoughts, and instead tried to focus on the fact that this was simply a flirtation, and likely, it was because Ryan was a little younger than she. This was just the sort of game younger guys played. He wasn't looking for a partner, he was looking for a challenge, she was sure of it. And Beth certainly wasn't going to throw her hat into the ring to play that game. She was in an adult relationship, one that was everything she'd ever dreamed of, and more.

'Well,' she replied nonchalantly, 'New York is a big city. Lots of great girls out there.' She smiled, trying to get across to him once and for all that she wasn't interested in doing this particular dance.

Still Ryan didn't look in the least bit discouraged as he considered her answer. And even as he handed her a piece of paper with his phone number on it, 'just in case you are ever bored', Beth told herself that she would simply throw it away later.

But when, later, the slip of paper materialised in her pocket as she clocked out of Carlisle's for the day, she put it in her purse. No big deal, it was just a number. She had contact details for many of her co-workers, after all.

And really, what was so wrong with having a new friend?

'Hey, Billy,' Danny called out as he beat the concierge to the front entry of the building. 'No worries, I got it,' he added, opening the door himself.

Billy stood back as Danny made his way into the lobby of the apartment building. 'How you doing today, Danny boy? Life treating you well? Haven't seen you around much lately; they must be working you hard over on Madison Avenue.'

Danny smiled uncomfortably as he passed the Scotsman, and punched the up button for the elevator. 'It is what it is. Work has been busy, yes, a lot to do.' He glanced at the elevator doors, willing them to open faster. Billy was a nice guy but Danny wasn't in the mood for making small talk, and the last thing he wanted was to get into a discussion about why he hadn't been around lately. While the concierge would of course be none the wiser about any of Danny's activities, he still knew he was a lousy liar, and speaking anything but the truth always made him feel guilty.

Billy nodded. 'Yeah, I understand that for sure. Beth's already home, you'll be glad to hear. She came in about an hour ago. Practically dancing on air. That girl is always happy but today you could tell that she had a real spring in her step. You two going out tonight then?' The concierge smiled knowingly and Danny couldn't help but wonder why. He swallowed hard when he realised that he hadn't yet spoken to Beth today.

'No plans. Not that I know of, anyway.' What he did know was that whatever was behind Beth's apparent good mood had nothing to do with him. To Danny's knowledge, the only thing that his girlfriend had done today was go to work. Hardly anything exciting about that. He knew that she was great at her job, threw everything into her movie-themed shoe displays, and made terrific commission from some of her very rich clients, especially at this time of year. But in his mind, unless someone had walked in and spent twenty grand on stuff, there was little about a day in Carlisle's to be overly giddy about.

Billy chuckled merrily. 'Ach, well, maybe you do and you don't know it. You know what women are like: always keeping us on our toes,' he joked in his Scottish lilt. 'Though I have yet to find one to do that for me,' he added, somewhat wistfully.

'See you later, Billy.'

As Danny got out of the elevator and approached the door to his apartment, he heard the sound of cheery music from inside: 'Sleigh Ride' by the Ronettes, one of Beth's favourite Christmas tunes. She loved this time of year and, much to Danny's amusement, always insisted on playing a Christmas album while they were decorating the tree.

But they hadn't done that yet this year.

Frowning confusedly, he fished his keys out of his pocket and, as he opened the door, the music got louder. He placed his briefcase down and was immediately met with a dancing and singing Beth in the kitchen.

Danny had to smile. She had obviously not heard him enter, nor did she realise that her performance now had an audience. With Brinkley at her feet, and pans strewn across the counter as she prepped the dinner, she spun around the kitchen, extracting a corkscrew from one cabinet and pirouetting to the small wine rack they kept on an opposite counter. She then did a twirl, using the wine bottle as her microphone and continued to sing about how lovely the weather was for a sleigh ride.

Just as she was about to reach the cabinet where they kept their wine glasses, she faltered and started to laugh, embarrassed. She had finally noticed him standing there.

'Bravo,' he smiled, applauding. However he might be feeling, it was impossible not to get caught up in Beth's infectious joy, and Danny's heart twisted a little as he realised just how much he loved this girl, despite everything.

And more to the point, how it would kill him to intentionally break her heart.

'Why that song? We're not decorating the tree tonight, are we?' Danny called out over the music.

She put the wine bottle and corkscrew down and did a small curtsy for show. Then she picked up the remote control to the iPhone dock and pointed it across the room, decreasing the volume of the music.

'Nope, just in a good mood. Felt like some Christmas cheer, that's all.'

But Danny continued to probe further, noticing that Beth had a semi manic look about her just then. The way someone might look if they just got off a roller coaster: face flushed, cheeks glowing, eyes happy. It was one thing to be in a good mood – indeed, Beth was in a good mood pretty much all the time – but something else was going on here.

And that bothered Danny because he couldn't put his finger on it.

'A good day at work, then?' he asked.

She shrugged noncommittally, and turned her attention back to the cabinet to reach for a wine glass. 'Yeah, it was fine, typical holiday shopping craziness. Marley Dempsey came in too, you know, the hotel heiress? That will be a nice commission cheque next month,' she smiled, and flipped her hair over her shoulder.

OK, so a good sale, that must be it – but . . .

At that moment, Beth turned back towards him for a

split second and that's when he noticed it. Yes, her face was flushed, no doubt from the exertion of dancing and singing, but there was something else. The faintest blush was creeping up around her neck, making its way to find a home on her face. He had *seen* that blush before. That much, he was sure of. Beth blushed like that when she was nervous, and excited, or ... guilty about something.

Danny's eyes narrowed. But what was she guilty about? Something was going on. He knew Beth's moods, knew *everything* about her. One thing was for sure, he could read her like an open book and he knew without a doubt that something had happened. Something, or someone, had caused Beth's jubilant mood. And he also knew it certainly wasn't him.

That thought troubled him. But then he wondered why he was being this way. After all, *he* had been keeping something from *her*. Something huge. Wasn't he being a hypocrite here? Or was sneaking around like this making him paranoid?

Goodness knew it wasn't the first time he'd seen her happy and dancing around the kitchen like the kids from *Footloose*. Though that had mostly been in the early days, Danny thought wistfully. There hadn't been too many opportunities for fun and whimsy over the last couple of years, since money had become tight and more grown-up issues had gotten in the way.

So, yes, it could be that Beth was just in a happy mood, he thought. But again, this was a particularly jubilant one, and the giddiness certainly suggested more. She hadn't looked this happy in quite some time, and Danny knew that the last time he'd seen Beth so flushed and giddy he had inspired it. He tried to think back. Probably that time they were in Charleston a couple of years back, when she convinced him to do that thing from *The Notebook*.

Beth had coaxed Danny into re-enacting the famous movie kiss. It had been kind of embarrassing at the time but she'd been so eager to try it, and so thrilled afterwards that it was impossible not to join in. There was a picture of it somewhere, Beth in Danny's arms, her legs wrapped around his waist as they joined their lips, the camera's self-timer coming into play, as they couldn't quite brave asking a stranger to take part in such an intimate moment. Of course, it wasn't raining and she had been nowhere as graceful as the girl in the movie, but it had been good fun ...

Or maybe it had been when they'd rented a sailboat and took it out on the river last summer?

No matter, deep down Danny knew one thing: the last time Beth had looked as if she was walking on air with happiness it had been because of something he had done.

He shook his head out of frustration when he realised that Beth had been speaking. He was completely distracted, his thoughts going a mile a minute. 'Sorry, what was that?' he asked.

She raised an eyebrow. 'You OK? I just asked if you wanted a glass of wine before dinner.'

'Yes. I mean no. I mean, yes, I'm OK. And no, I don't want a glass of wine before or with dinner actually,' he replied absently, as he tried to wrap his head around all this.

Suddenly, Danny felt a tightening sensation in his chest as if a boa constrictor was wrapping itself around his body, squeezing the life out of him. He had confessed as much to Adele earlier, that he didn't know how much longer he could go on living a lie. He knew that coming clean to Beth was exactly what Adele wanted, what she'd been telling him to do right from the start, but to her credit, she didn't push it. And he certainly wasn't going to come clean tonight, and bring Beth's happy world crashing down – not when she was in such a great mood. She didn't deserve that; didn't deserve any of this, not when all she'd ever done was love him so completely, and never wanted anything in return.

Right then Danny felt nauseous.

Beth took a sip of wine out of the glass that she had poured for herself. 'I was going to make spaghetti. I thought that since you're home earlier tonight, maybe we should do something nicer for dinner. A bottle of wine, some pasta, and move the table over to the window? Watch the Freedom Tower and all the lights. After all, we have a skyline view that people would pay good money for in a restaurant. Then afterwards, if we have time, we could put up the tree . . .' She smiled encouragingly, but Danny's mind was elsewhere. He'd barely heard a word she'd said.

'Right,' he murmured distractedly, his mind racing. 'Ah ... why don't you go ahead without me. I have some work to finish up; I'll probably be a while.'

He turned away from Beth, lost in his own guilt, and didn't see the crestfallen look that swept across her face.

'OK. Maybe I'll just have it in front of the TV then,' Beth replied, her good mood instantly deflated. 'And the Christmas tree can wait till another time ...'

Chapter 5

For the next few days Beth felt as if she was on high alert, looking, watching, keeping her eyes peeled around the store. She felt giddy like a schoolgirl – and a bit idiotic in the process – but while she loved Danny deeply (despite the rough patch they seemed to be going through lately), she had to admit she was enjoying this ... flirtation of sorts with Ryan.

She knew that she shouldn't feel this way – that she shouldn't even be entertaining the idea of liking the attention – but the attention *was* nice. And that's all it was, she told herself, she was just enjoying the unique glow that came with being made to feel special. It was harmless fun, that was all.

She supposed her current state of mind also came down to the fact that she was feeling a little ignored elsewhere. Danny's rebuff of her efforts a few nights before had really hurt. She had tried to do something nice, cook them dinner, spend some time just relaxing together after a rough few weeks. And his response? That it would be better for her to eat alone. That he had *work* to do. Again.

So that's what Beth had done. She had sat alone on the sofa and eaten by herself, watching the TV instead of the city lights. Though technically not alone. Rather, she had eaten the pasta while Brinkley drooled and begged for tit-bits alongside her.

Danny didn't emerge from the confines of his office for the rest of the evening, and she had gone to bed before him.

Then this morning, when she woke, she discovered he had already left for work. She couldn't deny that the thought of something being truly wrong with their part-nership scared her. But at the same time, what was she supposed to do? And just where exactly was their future headed if they continued on this course, with Danny being so remote and absent? Certainly nowhere near ...

Beth felt her brow furrow at the thought, and realised that her subconscious was leading her to say that word – a word that she and Danny so rarely uttered that it seemed like some form of taboo. *Marriage.* And why didn't they mention it very often, she wondered now – or, indeed, at *all*?

Beth knew why. And much of the onus fell on her. When all of their friends had, over the years, coupled off and sub-sequently gone down the aisle, Danny had said that he just wasn't interested in get married for the sake of it. Beth had just gone along with this at the time because in a way she agreed with him. It seemed there was a lot of engagement and wedding competitiveness amongst those same friends, so much so that the commitment they were supposed to be making seemed buried in the madness. Danny was right: the real romance was in the commitment, not the wedding, and she felt proud and happy that they were on exactly the same wavelength in that regard.

But much further down the line, years later, whenever the question came up amongst those now (mostly unhappily) married friends as to why Beth and Danny hadn't taken the plunge, the discussion seemed to cause discomfort and friction. So they began avoiding the conversation altogether.

While it hadn't bothered her before, Beth realised that it was starting to bother her a lot now. It was what people in love did, wasn't it?

She knew that she and Danny had taken a step in the right direction that time in Venice, when they'd privately and symbolically locked their love on the bridge, supposedly for a lifetime.

But surely after so many years, instead of ducking and diving the issue, the next step was to publicly commit to spending the rest of their lives together; and proclaim to the world that this was the person they each wanted to be with, forsaking all others.

As if on cue, Beth spied Ryan passing through the main promenade of the store, on his way to the men's section. She smiled as she noticed him scoping out the shoe department; clearly he was looking for her. So while it seemed that Ryan had taken the news that Beth was already attached into consideration, it evidently didn't stop him being so friendly.

'What are you doing wandering around by ladies' shoes?' she teased, as he crossed the floor to approach her. 'I'm beginning to think you might have a fetish.'

Ryan laughed and his emerald-green eyes danced. 'What? You think I like to parade after hours around my place in a pair of five-inch platforms?'

Beth looked him up and down. 'Somehow I don't see you in platforms. You're already tall. Platforms are just for shorties like me who need a leg up.' She did a little, lady-like jump. 'I see you more as a strappy sandal kind of guy.'

'You aren't that short, titch,' Ryan laughed. 'Anyway, I didn't come over to talk shoes, I'm sure you do enough of that on a daily basis, so I'll spare you the monotony.'

'What's up?' she asked.

He put his hands in his pockets and smiled at her, an adorable dimple forming on his right cheek. 'Well, since it's close to lunchtime, I just wanted to find out if you'd like to grab a bite somewhere.' He extracted his hands from his pockets and put them up innocently. 'Purely platonic, of course. I get that you have a guy at home and that's cool. Not trying to step on anyone's toes ... in platforms or otherwise,' he added chuckling, 'Just hungry, and thought you might be too.'

Beth smiled and felt immediately at ease. OK, this was fine. He'd said it himself, purely platonic. 'So, what do you say? Lunch? I need a fellow New York transplant like you to show a newbie like me where I should be eating,' he continued, with a lopsided smile that truly was irresistible.

Just lunch. Completely harmless.

'All right,' Beth acquiesced, with a resigned smile. 'You're on.'

Half an hour later, sitting at a high-top table in La Birreria, a rooftop brewpub in the Flatiron District above Mario Batali's Italian grocery store, Eataly, Ryan had Beth in stitches as he recounted how when he first arrived in the city, he had accidentally worn a Boston Red Sox baseball hat to a sports bar playing a Yankees game.

'How on earth did you make it out alive?' she laughed as she plucked a chip from her plate and popped it in her mouth. When Beth had first arrived in the States, being Irish, she hadn't a notion about baseball or the famed rivalry between the New York Yankees and Boston Red Sox teams, but Danny had very quickly filled in the blanks. Over time she'd begun to follow and appreciate the game as much as she used to enjoy Gaelic hurling and football back home in Galway.

Ryan splayed his hands, expressing complete innocence. 'I didn't do it on purpose. It is just a hat I have. I really thought I was going to get my ass kicked.'

'That would have been a mild punishment. Honestly, if you're going to live in this city, you're going to have to be schooled in what to wear, or more likely what *not* to.'

Though Beth noticed he was doing quite nicely with the former in his Tom Ford shirt and J Crew trousers. 'You're not in Kansas any more, Toto,' she added, grinning mischievously. 'Besides, where'd an LA guy get a Red Sox hat? And you don't seem like much of a baseball guy, if you don't mind me saying.'

Ryan chuckled and stole one of her chips. 'What, I look like a pretty boy to you just because I can put myself together for work? I have a life outside of that, you know. Besides, I'm originally from Boston; I lived there till I was about ten or so.'

Beth feigned shock. 'So you *did* know better! Hmm, now I get it. You *like* to live on the edge. I don't even think that I feel sorry for you now.' She laughed aloud and took a bite of the burger in front of her. 'Not that I can judge. I'm a Mets fan.' Danny was a lifelong fan of the team, and Beth had gone along to countless games with him and the Bishop family at the stadium in Flushing Meadows.

Ryan watched her with narrowed eyes and Beth suddenly felt self-conscious. 'What?' She picked up her napkin and wiped the corners of her mouth. 'Do I have something on my face?'

'No, no. You're fine. I guess I'm just impressed. Not only about the Mets thing. I haven't known too many women who would dig into a whole burger at lunchtime, or really anytime. Getting used to East Coast habits again is going to be an education. Not to mention the weather. Brrr.'

'So how long were you in LA?'

'Since I left Boston, so for the best part of twenty years now. My parents still live there, in a retirement community in Malibu. I'll go back to visit now and then, but I am done with that scene. What about you? With that accent, you're obviously not from New York ... Irish, yes?'

She smiled. 'And my family keeps telling me I've lost my accent. Yep, I'm from a small town just outside Galway in Ireland. Came to the US after college and ended up staying. Travelled quite a lot in between, too, but there is no other place I would rather live. And—' She stopped mid-sentence, realising what she was about to say.

'And what?'

But she knew Ryan wouldn't let her off the hook too easily so she continued, feeling a bit silly about what she was about to admit but deciding to go ahead anyway. 'Well, this city ... from a very early age, I always felt like I already ... knew it. And when I finally came here, I realised I did – know it, I mean.'

He looked intrigued. 'How so?'

'Because of the movies.' When he looked blank, she went on. 'Every street corner, every skyscraper, Fifth Avenue, Tiffany's, Central Park, the Empire State Building – they were all so familiar to me. So when I finally got here I didn't need to worry about settling in because it already felt like home.'

Beth thought back to the early days with Danny when she had persuaded him to take one of those open-top bus tours available all over Manhattan. After some initial protest, simply because it was such a touristy thing to do, he finally agreed, and even seemed to enjoy himself.

That was one thing that Beth had to admit. There were times when Danny might protest over something – calling it clichéd or silly – but then his mood always changed, lightened, when he saw the joy it inspired in her. Of course, some of the stuff on the tour *was* cheesy – like rubbing the Wall Street bull's bronze testicles, or taking photographs with the Naked Cowboy on Times Square, but life was too short to be so cynical or judgemental over something that would provide some laughter and create a memory.

The tour had been fun too, and it gave Beth the opportunity to relive some of her favourite New York movie moments. The bus had coursed through Manhattan, past Fifth Avenue and Tiffany's, where Holly Golightly had stood in her Givenchy gown eating a Danish and drinking coffee while feasting her eyes on a window-full of jewels, imagining her prince.

They passed the New York Public Library, where Big had so cruelly jilted Carrie on her wedding day in *Sex and the City,* then onwards to the Empire State Building, where in *Sleepless in Seattle* Tom Hanks and Meg Ryan had recaptured the romantic essence of *An Affair to Remember.* Beth and Danny had then gone by Cadman Plaza and Furman Street, near the Brooklyn Bridge, where Daryl Hannah had longed for the ocean, as an incognito mermaid in *Splash.*

The bus had also sailed through the East Village and

passed where the four-storey nightclub Danceteria had been located until 1986. Beth had practically jumped out of her seat when the tour director asked who had got 'into the groove' there and in what movie. Inevitably, she had proudly shouted out Madonna and *Desperately Seeking Susan,* before knowledgeably adding that while Danceteria was a memorable movie location, the mystery meeting point in the movie was actually Battery Park. The tour guide had bristled in annoyance at her stealing his line.

And while this iconic movie location wasn't on the tour, Danny had secured a reservation at the famous Serendipity 3 on East 60th Street, where he took Beth after the tour ended. There, they sat at the star table, the same spot in which Jonathan and Sara had sat eating frozen hot chocolate in the movie *Serendipity.*

Though her boyfriend had pretended to humour her and tell her that the tour was 'fine for tourists, but not something real New Yorkers do', she had scoffed at him because she knew that despite himself he had had an enjoyable day too. And he definitely hadn't had any qualms about scarfing down his dessert and then helping Beth finish hers.

She reflected back on the memory, searching for more details in order to make it last longer, but she felt something else sneaking into her brain, ruining her reverie. A realisation that they did that so long ago. It had been so spontaneous; she and Danny *had* been so spontaneous once upon a time. But it seemed so far in the past.

'You came to New York because of the movies?' Ryan's

words brought Beth back to the present. He was smiling but, much to her relief, he wasn't laughing at her; if anything he was intrigued by the idea. 'That's so cool ...'

Beth had tried to explain to people before how the city as the backdrop to so many of her favourite films had been an irresistible draw. Some got it; others didn't – and most New Yorkers, especially Jodi, thought she was nuts – but Ryan was clearly one of the former.

'I guess I know what you're saying. I passed by Katz's Deli the other day and couldn't resist popping in for fun.'

She laughed. 'One of many guys hoping for a re-enactment of *that* Meg Ryan scene, I'm guessing ...'

He winked. 'Nope. I just heard they do a good pastrami sandwich.'

'Yeah, right.' She shook her head. 'Oh, I know it's probably hard to understand, but when you love the movies as much as I do, then this city ... it's just ... heaven.'

Ryan was shaking his head. 'I suppose I should have guessed you were a movie aficionado. Is that where the shoe display thing comes from?'

She smiled. 'Of course. Aren't I always telling my customers that a pair of shoes can indeed change your life?'

'A decent philosophy, though I'm not sure it would work in my department. Can't see the guys looking for chinos buying into that, somehow.'

'True.' Beth finished the last piece of her burger. 'So now you know why living anywhere else would feel like being on the moon to me.'

Ryan nodded and took a sip of his soda. 'And your boy-friend? The Mets fan? He from here?'

She nodded.

'And what does he do?'

Beth straightened up a little at the mention of Danny. 'He's in marketing. For one of the Madison Avenue firms. It's been rough lately, they were going through some lay-offs, but since the economy started to rebound things have been picking up again. And that's good; it's good for his career. I mean, he's been busy lately, but that's to be expected. Same thing happens with me in Carlisle's around this time of year, as I'm sure you'll find out soon.'

Ryan eyes narrowed. 'Sounds like there is a "but" coming, though?'

Beth blinked, wondering how he'd picked up on that note of worry. It must have been in her voice. She shook her head, determinedly negating the assumption. 'There wasn't a "but".'

'Oh yes there was,' he argued matter-of-factly.

'There wasn't,' she insisted, setting her mouth in a straight line as if preparing for a challenge.

He put his hands up. 'All right, all right, there wasn't a "but". I was just following your lead, that's all, but if there is nothing to discuss, then I'm cool.'

She regarded him for a moment, feeling a little strange. What had she really wanted to say? And why was she con-sidering telling someone she hardly knew about something very private?

'OK,' she said, taking her napkin off her lap and placing it on her plate, a clear indication that she was finished. 'So, there was a "but".'

He looked up. 'I know; I'm kind of good at reading people.' When she didn't reply, he went on, 'Hey, I didn't mean to say anything that makes you uncomfortable. I apologise if I overstepped.'

Ryan wiped his fingers on his napkin and pushed his plate away. Then he reached across the table and gently placed a hand on Beth's arm. As soon as he touched her, she again felt a brief surge of electricity and surprised herself by the fact that this time she didn't automatically pull her arm away.

She shook her head. 'No, no, it's not your fault. There has been ... stuff happening, I guess you could say, and I am probably just being silly. It just feels weird, that's all. I mean ... I haven't spoken to anyone about it. So, it seems odd, saying certain things aloud when I've only been think-ing them.' Feeling shocked by her words, Beth couldn't explain what had got into her just then. Or why she was telling this man – one that she couldn't deny she felt an attraction to – what was going on in her relationship.

'You don't have to talk about any of it. It's none of my business,' he continued softly.

Beth found herself pressing on, realising there was some-thing actually quite cleansing about unloading it all like this. 'No, it's OK. I'm probably being overly dramatic. I suppose I've just been feeling a bit in second place and ...

oh God, that probably sounds really needy, and I am totally not a needy person. *Not at all.*' She laughed nervously. 'Danny has just been really tied up lately, like he has a million things on his mind. And I'm not always sure if I make the cut.' She felt a lump growing in her throat, and to her horror, realised her eyes were beginning to well up.

Oh, for goodness' sake, stop it! she remonstrated with herself. You will not do this ... not here and certainly not now.

'Beth ...'

'Oh God, I'm sorry. You wanted just to go and get a bite to eat, and here am I going all serious on you. I'm—'

But Ryan was unfazed. 'Beth, it's OK, honestly,' he said, his voice soft as he reached for her hand, urging her to look at him. 'I'm sorry that I started this, I didn't mean to make you upset.' She chuckled a little, trying to make light of everything. 'I suppose I should just say thank you for listening to me. Good therapy.'

Ryan laughed. 'And not as expensive as a shrink, huh?' She smiled weakly.

'Really, though, in all seriousness, I didn't mean to bring up things that make you sad, Beth. I don't want you to be sad. But I do feel honoured that you would consider talking to me.'

'Anyway ... I think we better get the check now? Time for us to be getting back.' She made a big show about looking around for their server.

A moment later they had their bill, which Ryan insisted upon paying even though she protested.

'If you're my shrink, shouldn't I be paying for lunch?'

'Consider it a business expense,' he teased, putting a few twenty-dollar bills down on the table.

'Well, thank you,' she said, standing up. 'I appreciate it. Next one's on me.'

'You got yourself a deal.' He stood up next to her and put his hand on her back, helping her navigate her way through the crowded restaurant.

The gesture did not go unnoticed and just as she thought the words, *stop overreacting, he's just being a gentleman*, Ryan leaned close to her ear, and said in a whisper that sounded like a promise, 'Just for the record, Beth, you are not the type of girl anyone should put in second place. If your guy is doing that, with all due respect, he's nuts.'

And Beth's stomach did a little backflip.

Chapter 6

It was the following week, and Jodi sat on the couch in Beth's living room, barefoot, feet curled up under her, munching on popcorn while Beth scrolled through Netflix, trying to decide what they should watch.

The two women were having a movie night in, something they did regularly.

'So *Sleepless, Definitely Maybe, When Harry Met Sally, Valentine's Day,* or *Music and Lyrics*?' Beth asked.

'Has Netflix profiled you, or what? Do you ever watch anything other than "Romantic Comedies 101"?' her friend asked archly. 'Why don't you try something different once in a while? There are probably a few classics that you have never considered. Like maybe *Scarface* or *Die Hard*. A little blood and violence never hurt anyone.' She laughed into her glass of wine.

Beth shook her head. 'Judge all you want. At least I have a *positive* attitude towards love and life.'

'Oh, yeah? And what attitude would that be? The more the merrier?' her friend shot back with no small measure of sarcasm.

Beth quickly turned back towards the TV as she felt a familiar blush creeping up her neck. 'What's that supposed to mean?'

Jodi sat her wine glass down on a coaster on the coffee table and unfolded her feet. She sat upright, leaning forward to where Beth sat on the floor. 'You know full well what I am talking about. The hot guy at work – Ryan. He's been spending *a lot* of time in the shoe department lately, and he doesn't look like the cross-dressing type to me. What's going on? What are you up to?'

Beth had known to expect this question. She had been trying to avoid Jodi's enquiring gaze for days – the mocking expression she'd worn every time Ryan had ventured over into their department, making Beth laugh, inviting her to lunch, bringing her coffee from Starbucks to stay alert during one long afternoon ...

Yes, it was true that she was seeing a lot of him lately. But they were *friends*. OK, so they'd had lunch together a few days since, and Beth couldn't deny it had all been enjoyable. In truth, the little bit of flirting that was taking place between them was akin to the way she handled relationships back in school. It was harmless.

'So? Did you hear me?' Jodi persisted.

Beth put the remote control down and turned to face her friend. 'Yes, I heard you. I was just thinking.'

Jodi's eyes narrowed. 'You haven't done anything you regret, have you, sweetie? I would never have taken you for a cheater.'

Beth blanched at hearing that word spoken aloud. She knew what Jodi thought about cheating and most definitely didn't want her friend to include her in such a category.

'No, of course not. I wouldn't do anything of the sort.' She glanced down at her hands and wrung them in her lap, trying to figure out what to say next. 'It's really nothing. I've just made a new friend. I didn't think there was a law against that.'

Jodi tsked. 'Beth, let me tell you one thing. *Friends* don't look at each other the way you and that guy Ryan do. *Friends* don't smile and tease, and try to make some kind of bodily contact with one another at every available opportunity.' Eyes wide, Beth opened her mouth to speak; denying that she did any such thing, but Jodi shushed her with her hand. 'Don't tell me that's not true. I know you, honey. And if people around you can feel the sparks flying when you and Ryan are near each other, there is no way you aren't aware of it too.'

Beth wanted to deny it, but also knew that her friend wasn't an idiot. Yes, there were sparks. Definite sparks.

'OK, so maybe there is a teeny bit of attraction there. And I can't deny that it's fun. But that's all it is – harmless fun. I already told him, Jodi, I told Ryan that I wasn't available. I was upfront with him about Danny from the start. He knows that I am in a serious relationship.'

Jodi shook her head and sighed deeply. 'Oh, Beth. Look, I believe you when you say that, and I know you are a genuine person. I also know that you love Danny. But something else is going on, too. You have to admit that. It might be something as simple as you liking the attention that Ryan is giving you. And while you believe that your intentions are pure and you can deal with this situation, maybe Ryan is less concerned about your relationship? But if this so-called harmless flirtation – or whatever it is – is allowed to persist, it's you and Danny who stand to lose. It'll be your relationship that suffers. Ryan is footloose and fancy-free – he has nothing to lose or to fear.'

Beth once again looked down at her hands and became very focused on her nails. She could feel Jodi's gaze upon her, waiting for her to respond but she felt completely at a loss for what to say.

We *are* just friends, that's it, Beth reassured herself. She felt her mind wandering through movies she knew – stories where men and women were friends, where no rules were broken, where things were able to stay platonic.

Gone with the Wind, she thought immediately. No, maybe not a good example. The chemistry between Rhett and Scarlett was there from the outset. And when they finally recognised it themselves ... explosive.

That more recent one, *Silver Linings Playbook*? They were friends, sort of. Beth tried to recall the relationship between Pat and Tiffany, played by Bradley Cooper and Jennifer Lawrence in the movie, and realised that the only thing that stood out was the way they came together at the end. Yes, they were friends, but they too had fallen in love.

OK, she thought quickly, *You've Got Mail*? That's a good one. They can't even stand each other. *Until the end,* she reminded herself, where Joe makes a distinct effort to woo Kathleen, to first win her friendship – and then her love. *Say Anything . . .* ? Nope. *Reality Bites*? Not so much. *The Wedding Planner*? Not a chance.

She bit her lip, frustrated that she couldn't find one onscreen example of a man and woman who were able to remain friends when mutual attraction was clearly evident.

'Earth to Beth . . .' Jodi snapped her fingers and brought her back to reality. 'Do you realise how well I know you?'

Beth was puzzled. 'What do you mean?'

'I know *exactly* what you are doing right now. You are calling upon your vast encyclopaedia of movie knowledge to find an example of a man and woman who clearly have the hots for each other, are able to stay friends and keep sex and love out of it by the time the credits roll. Aren't you?'

A little unsettled by just how well her friend did indeed know her, Beth rolled her eyes and picked up the remote control, as if signalling an end to the conversation. 'I am *not*. I was just thinking and—'

Jodi snatched the remote control away and stuck it on the side table next to the couch, far out of Beth's reach. 'You are. I *know* you are. Because I've known you for five years and I get how your mind operates and what makes you tick. Look at what you do at work. You set up these amazing Hollywood-style showcases for every new goddamn shoe design that arrives in the department. Furthermore, you feed all these irresistible movie fictions to the women who buy those Cinderella slippers from you – the places they'll go and the things they will do. But let me tell you one thing, Beth. Life is not a movie. Now, I know you appreciate happy endings and tear-jerkers and the way the music swells just as Jack and Rose kiss on the front of the *Titanic*. But you know what also happens in that story? The *Titanic* sinks. And that is going to be *your* story if you keep playing with fire. Because I can tell you happy endings do not occur when there are three people involved in a relationship story. Someone gets hurt. Always.'

Beth looked at her friend and knew that Jodi was speaking from her own experience. And it was a place where she definitely got hurt. She was that third person; had ended up being the odd one out in her marriage. Briefly Beth wondered if Jodi's ex-husband, Frank, ever tried to use the reasoning that he and 'the bimbo' were just friends. And she wondered how long it took for him to realise that he was not capable of living that lie.

She rubbed her temples and gave a small groan. 'Jodi, you know me. I'm not that kind of person. And I would never do anything disloyal to Danny.'

Was flirting, even harmlessly, with Ryan being disloyal, though? Beth didn't think so, not when she'd already made her feelings and intentions crystal clear to him from the outset. Or at least that's what she'd been telling herself.

Jodi was nodding in agreement. 'I know that you love him. But with that being said, I have to ask where *is* Danny? I know, I know, you said he had to work late tonight. But where *is* he? In your heart and your head?' she persisted. 'And what's going on there? Because if you even make a tiny bit of room in either of those places for anyone else, then something in your relationship isn't right.'

Beth swallowed hard. She guessed it was time to confide in Jodi about her concerns of late. If only to get her take on it.

And she found that once she started telling her everything – the way Danny had become possessive over her handling his phone, fishing out whatever had been in his trouser pocket, how he lately seemed so reluctant about spending quality time together – she couldn't stop. Thankfully her friend listened (for once) without interruption, and it was only when Beth finished that she offered her opinion.

'Well ...' she sighed heavily. 'I know I can be cynical when it comes to these things, but I'm not liking the way this sounds. I have to say I never felt Danny, of all people, was the unfaithful type. Even though it seems like I distrust all men, I actually don't. And I've always had a soft spot for your guy.'

Beth nodded, grimacing. 'I really didn't want to consider the notion either. But I'd be stupid if I didn't start to wonder if *something* is going on – and it doesn't feel good.'

Jodi looked at her curiously. 'Haven't you tried talking about it with him? Let him know how you've been feeling.'

Beth swallowed hard, hating the prospect of confessing any of her worries to Danny, especially when he was under so much pressure elsewhere. 'I can't say this to him,' she said quietly. 'I just *can't*.'

'Why not?' Jodi asked. 'Why can't you say anything if you truly think something is wrong? I didn't take you for a doormat, Beth.'

Beth shook her head in disagreement. 'No, I'm not a doormat. I just don't *want* to. Not when he's got so much on his plate lately. And not only that but I suppose I feel like ... like it's admitting defeat somehow. That something is less than perfect with us. And that's not how I want our relationship to be. It's not how we have been in the past. Danny and I never argue. I mean, not really. And things have always been so good and—'

'Oh, Beth,' Jodi interrupted. She threw back the remainder of wine that was in her glass as she continued to shake her head out of obvious bewilderment. 'Why do you think you can live your life like a heroine in some movie? How can you operate under the notion that you must have a perfect relationship? All those movies are fairy tales, sweetie. Danny is not your leading man, he's real-life flesh and blood.'

'I'm not operating that way, I'm just—'

'Oh yes, you are. Newsflash, honey – relationships aren't perfect. *No one's* relationship is perfect. And like I said, life

92

is not a movie. Look, I don't mean to be a killjoy here, but someone needs to say this to you. Relationships are messy and dramatic and sometimes sad and then, happy too ... but they are all of those things. And if they aren't? Then someone isn't holding up their end of the bargain. And with you and Danny, I am willing to bet it might be both of you at the moment. He very well might be under a lot of pressure and maybe he's hiding something too. *Something* might be going on with him. But if you aren't talking and have imposed a "let's not talk about the bad stuff" rule, then it's your fault, too.'

Beth stared at her friend and considered her words. Admittedly, they stung. But were they true? When it came to Danny and their relationship, was she unable to talk about – or confront – problems? Recognise them, even? And worse, was she then in fact partly to blame for whatever was going on with him?

'I suggest that you take a long hard look at yourself and the way you've been dealing with things, Beth. Really think about what I just said, because I don't want you to get hurt and I don't want Danny to get hurt, and even though I don't really know Ryan, I don't want him to get hurt either. And remember what I said, in a party of three, there is always an odd man out.'

Having said her piece, Jodi sat back in her seat. The two women were both silent for a moment, until eventually she spoke again. 'Speaking of which, I saw Frank and the floozie while I was picking up a pizza at Sal's last night. I stopped at the corner bodega for a pack of twenty right after that.'

While Jodi knew how Beth felt about her smoking, she also understood what her friend was dealing with if she had spied her ex with his new love in public. Even though the marriage had been over for almost two years, it didn't take Sherlock Holmes to realise that Jodi still had a soft spot in her heart for Frank. Beth reached out to take her friend's hand, as she continued to recount her tale.

'It's like, I think I might have forgiven him. If it had just been sex. If only it had been something as simple as that. But it wasn't. It was love, and that is what I think hurts the most. Men, for the most part, you know they think with the head down south.' Jodi grimaced and rolled her eyes. 'And I'm not excusing a cheater. Not in a million years. But I think that if Frank would just have admitted, "Jodi, honey, it was just a roll in the sack. It was a mistake," and then promise me it would never happen again – after I had kicked his ass, of course – I might have been able to move on.'

Squeezing Jodi's hand, Beth whispered, 'I'm so sorry, Jodi. You are so wonderful and Frank's an idiot for not realising it. I know what you're saying and yes, you might call me silly, but I truly do believe that everything along the way happens for a reason. Maybe Frank isn't the love of your life, and was never supposed to be the one you end up with.'

Jodi chortled. 'Quit it, Pollyanna.'

Beth had to smile, realising she did indeed sound a bit Pollyannaish. But she truly believed what she was saying; it was how the world made the most sense for her: the idea that all the various plot strands in life eventually put you exactly where you were supposed to be. While Jodi, given her recent experience, was perhaps right to be cynical, at least for the moment, Beth wasn't going to give up on that idea for anyone. And she knew all the way to her core that things would work out for Jodi. There was a Hollywood ending in store for her friend. She would bet on it.

'Anyway, speaking of happy endings – or lack thereof – you promise me you will think about this? About what I said about Danny? And how life isn't like the movies?'

Beth gave a little nod – a reluctant affirmation of agreement, at least for the moment.

'OK. Good.' Jodi grabbed the bottle of wine and filled both her glass and Beth's. She picked the glass up, took a drink and then pointed the remote control at the TV. 'And now for our next lesson of the evening. Why men and women who are attracted to each other *cannot* be friends. If you want a movie example about your love life, Beth Harper, watch this. *When Harry Met Sally*. Hopefully, this one will drive the message home.'

Chapter 7

The following morning seemed to crawl by for Beth. Jodi was off today and the sales floor was quiet. The weather was cloudless, sunny and relatively mild, resulting in many of their potential customers taking advantage of the welcome break in the winter chill to spend time at the ice rinks, outdoor Christmas markets and other festive activities rather than at the department stores. Undoubtedly, the rush would pick up again once the weather turned, but for now it was peaceful.

She was planning on taking a walk herself at lunchtime and wondered if Danny would get the opportunity to sample the beautiful day. He certainly needed a little Vitamin D, she thought, realizing how rundown he was looking lately. All that time cooped up inside the office wasn't good for anyone, though she understood how desperate he was to hold on to his job.

Her thoughts were interrupted by two people walking

into the department at the same time. One was dressed in the low-key, slackerish garb of a bike messenger with a delivery, and the other was Marley Dempsey, teenage hotel heiress, evidently back from her recent jaunt to Europe.

''Tis either a feast or a famine' was a favourite expression of Beth's grandmother, and that was certainly true of today.

Beth waved a hello and indicated to Marley that she wouldn't be long – it seemed that the bike messenger would need a signature.

The young man, who looked to be in his early twenties, had a messenger bag slung over his chest and was carrying a cup of coffee. As he approached, he started to search through the bag.

'Hi, there, can I help you?' Beth enquired with a smile.

The guy popped his gum and returned her smile, albeit with less enthusiasm. 'Yeah, I have a delivery for Beth Harper?'

She perked up. 'Well, that's me,' she said, her smile growing, wondering what had been sent to her. She had never received a delivery at work via bike messenger specifically for her.

'Awesome,' the guy said as if this was the end of some long and drawn-out quest. He extracted a clipboard from his bag and handed it to her, along with a pen. 'If you could just sign here,' he indicated, pointing to an area on the clipboard. 'This isn't like, a traditional delivery, I guess you would say.'

Curious, Beth signed her name and looked back up at the young man. 'What do you mean?' she asked, handing the pad and pen back to him and expecting the usual envelope or package.

'It means, here you go.' With that he handed her the generic coffee cup he'd been carrying in his hand. 'I'm assuming this is how you take your coffee. I was told triple shot grande white mocha. With whip?'

Perplexed, Beth automatically reached out for the coffee cup. A bike messenger for a coffee delivery? 'I don't understand . . .'

The guy shrugged. 'I don't know either, but it's not the weirdest thing I have seen, that's for sure. One time, I had a woman send her husband another woman's underwear to his office. I'm guessing she'd found them in her bedroom or something. That was awkward.'

Beth shook her head, the messenger's story of marital infidelity completely going over her head as she considered the mysterious cup she now held in her hand. This was much more interesting to her. And yes, it was indeed her coffee of choice, but why on earth would anyone send her a drink via bike messenger? And at work, too?

'Well, do you have the sender's name?' Beth asked.

The messenger shook his head, and looked uncomfortable as he checked his clipboard. 'No, the sender asked to keep that private. Sorry.'

Her eyes widened. 'I don't understand, why would someone send me a coffee anonymously?' What a weird, but kind thing to do. And she couldn't deny it was intriguing. Sort of like something from a . . .

'Actually there's something else too.' Now the guy looked discomfited, as if whatever he was about to do was definitely *not* part of his job description. 'I am supposed to say, "Best enjoyed with a box of Cracker Jack."'

'Come again?'

The messenger rolled his eyes and repeated, '"Best enjoyed with a box of Cracker Jack."' He said it faster this time, as if he was eager to get all of this out of the way as quickly as possible.

Beth looked from the bike messenger to the cup of coffee in her hand. 'I'm sorry, I really don't understand. I'm supposed to drink this with Cracker Jacks? Isn't there anything else—'

But the bike messenger cut her off. 'I have no idea, ma'am. That's all I've got written down here. Sorry.' And with that, he took his leave.

Beth considered the message, all the while staring at the cup, which felt warm and fresh in her hand. *Best enjoyed with a box of Cracker Jack?* What on earth was that all about? She didn't even particularly like Cracker Jack. Especially not with coffee.

'Um, hello?' Beth's confused train of thought was interrupted by Marley Dempsey, who had until now been waiting, albeit impatiently, on the shoe sofa. 'I don't have all day here.'

'Oh, I'm so sorry, Marley! I'll be right with you.' Beth

tried to figure out what to do with the cup of hot coffee, and decided for the moment to put it behind the cash wrap, out of view of the shopping public. She would deal with it later. It certainly wasn't the time or the place to drink it. She looked at her watch: just after ten thirty, a good hour before she was even due to take a coffee break.

Feeling intrigued and more than a little excited, though unsure exactly why, Beth knew that before she could ponder it further she had to deal with a demanding social-ite, who apparently needed more new shoes.

Half an hour later, Beth waited as Marley tried on her fifteenth pair of boots – seemingly unimpressed as the teen-ager had the Prada on her feet for less than two seconds before she was scowling and shaking her head. 'No, these put like thirty years on my feet. It's like I'm your age or something,' she complained, scowling.

Well, thanks. Beth pressed her lips together as she did the sums. Apparently Marley thought she was pushing fifty. 'If it helps, I personally like the Jimmy Choos best on you,' she offered as she watched the girl kick off the fifteen-hundred-dollar boots with little grace or delicacy.

'Whatevs,' Marley said. 'I guess I will take the Choos and those Louboutins. I want the brown, black, and taupe.' The girl paused for a moment and furrowed her brow, apparently thinking hard. 'And throw in those purple shoes too.'

Beth smiled at the girl's ability to be so flippant over shoes that averaged a couple of thousand dollars a pop, and began gathering up the boxes that Marley had scattered all over the floor of the department within the past half-hour. Lucky for Beth, the girl's lavish purchase would mean another decent bonus next month.

'So, it doesn't look like you were in Europe for very long then?' she chatted to Marley as she went. 'Didn't you just go to London with your father?' Beth tried recalling what the girl had said last time she was in the store. She hadn't listened very closely to the details at the time, but she knew that Marley would have no problem talking – especially about her favourite subject – herself.

The younger girl nodded as she popped a fresh piece of gum in her mouth. 'Yeah, I was only there for a couple of days. It was grey and rainy and I was totally bored. My dad said that I should hop on over to Monaco for a while – my mom was there. But like, she's a total downer, just had a ton of plastic surgery and is recovering, so like, what's the point of being with her?'

Possibly to keep her company? Beth thought, a little uncharitably. She'd love the opportunity to spend a little time with her own parents. It had been almost two years since she'd managed a trip home to Galway, and as it was expensive for her mum and dad to come and see her, opportunities for time together were few and far between.

'She's on this big detox too – completely ugh.' Marley complained. 'So I just decided, better to come back to New York, especially with both my folks safely an ocean away.'

And Beth had no doubt that the lack of supervision was the last thing this girl needed. Based on history alone, it was clear that whatever trouble Marley got herself into here would ultimately make it onto Page Six, and wouldn't take long to reach her parents on the other side of the Atlantic.

'Well,' Beth began, feeling at a loss for what to say to this overindulged, but she guessed ultimately very lonely teenager, 'I hope you behave yourself.' Marley rolled her eyes and Beth instantly regretted what she had said. She did indeed sound matronly.

Beth picked up the boxes that Marley was about to take home and headed over to the cash wrap, her thoughts immediately returning to the coffee cup and the strange message. She set down the boxes and carefully moved the now cold cup of coffee aside, so as not to spill it. Then she set about scanning the SKU code on each box and added each one to a large Carlisle's bag – and then two – so as to not make it too heavy for Marley as she left the store. Though no doubt there'd be a driver waiting two steps or so away from the entrance so she wouldn't have to struggle on the pavement.

Just as she finished this task, Marley approached and very ungracefully plopped her large Miu Miu handbag on the counter with so much oomph that the bag toppled over, spewing its entire contents directly onto Beth's work area and knocking over the cup of coffee. Whitish-brown liquid spilled everywhere.

Thinking and reacting quickly, Beth pulled the Carlisle

bags containing the boots back just in time, as cold coffee cascaded down the workspace.

'Oh my God, I'm like, so sorry!' Marley said earnestly as she quickly went to collect the contents of her handbag.

Beth held up her hand, thankful that none of the actual merchandise was damaged. 'It's OK, sweetheart, it's no problem. Let me just run and get something to mop this up with.' She hurried to the back room and returned a moment later with a roll of paper towels to clean up the spilled coffee. She handed some to Marley, who went about drying off her belongings and placing everything again in her bag.

'I'm really sorry about that,' the girl apologised again, now sounding much more like her young age.

Beth shook her head as she finished mopping up the mess; she wasn't mad at all. 'Really, it's no problem. It's my fault, that coffee cup shouldn't have been there in the first place.'

She pulled a rubbish bin from below the cash wrap and started throwing the soiled paper towels in it, feeling grateful that the mess was contained. Then she reached towards Marley, who also had wet paper towels to dispose of, and took them from her. The socialite reached down, grasped the now-empty coffee cup and was handing it to Beth when she stopped and frowned.

'Hey, that's weird, there's writing inside this cup. Did you know that?'

Beth felt a little tingle travel up from the base of her spine. *Writing in the cup?*

'Really? I had no idea. What does it say?' she enquired, moving to the other side of the cash wrap where Marley was inspecting the inside of the cup.

The younger girl squinted and turned the container around in her hands as she read. 'I think it says, "Meet me there. We could have this engraved, couldn't we?"' She frowned again and looked at Beth. 'Huh? What does that mean? You must have gotten a bad cup,' she added quickly, dismissing the cup and handing it to Beth for disposal. 'Take it back to wherever you got it and give 'em hell. That's what I'd do.'

But given the circumstances of its delivery, Beth was pretty sure it wasn't a 'bad cup'. She peered into the container herself, at once making out the handwriting. The message must have been written with a Sharpie before the cup was filled because it wasn't at all smeared by the hot liquid. It had definitely been written deliberately and Beth felt sure it had something to do with the bike delivery guy's accompanying verbal message.

A shiver ran down her spine. 'I don't know. This is really strange. I wonder—'

'Wonder what?' Marley asked.

Beth read the message out loud. '"We could have this engraved ..."' Engrave what? The coffee cup? Something niggled in her mind; she looked to Marley. 'Does that sound familiar to you, somehow? I'm pretty sure I've heard it somewhere before.'

Marley shrugged. 'Nope. Never heard anything like

104

that in my life. Could be a new Starbucks marketing thing maybe?'

Well, yes, that was a possibility. But the coffee cup was unbranded, and how to explain the other accompanying message from the delivery guy?

'You know that bike messenger who showed up at the same time you did? He delivered this coffee to me.'

Marley's jaw dropped. 'He delivered a *coffee*? You *know* there is a Starbucks, like a block away? I'm all for splashing cash, but having a bike messenger deliver your coffee is just *totally* diva.' She regarded Beth with some scepticism about her apparent indulgent behaviour and Beth couldn't help but smile. This coming from a teenager who was just about to put almost six thousand dollars' worth of boots on her father's credit card.

Beth shook her head. 'No, I didn't have it delivered. Someone sent it to me.'

'Who?' Marley asked, intrigued.

'The guy said the sender asked to remain anonymous.'

The younger girl's eyes grew wide. 'OMG. Seriously? Imagine if that coffee had been, like, *poisoned*. What if I just saved your life?'

Beth couldn't help but smile as Marley stood up straighter with the idea that she was her generation's Florence Nightingale. Talk about a drama queen.

'Well, of course I would thank you, if that was the case, but I am not sure if I was a target for poisoning, Marley. The coffee wasn't the only thing delivered. There was

105

a message too. The delivery guy was told to say, "Best enjoyed with a box of Cracker Jack",' Beth repeated for her now very rapt audience. 'It must tie in with this message in the cup.'

Marley shook her head in bewilderment. 'OK, but like, what does it all *mean*? I'm serious, this is way weird.'

She was right about that much.

Beth bit her lip, deep in thought. 'Coffee, Cracker Jack and engraving ...' She shook her head, her mind spinning. 'Of course it shouldn't make sense but for some reason ... I also think it does. There's just something familiar about ...' She racked her brain for a very long moment as Marley continued to stare at her as if she was crazy. Then she shook her head. 'You're right, it is weird. It doesn't make sense at all. And even if it did, why would someone send me this stuff?'

Marley stared at the coffee cup in Beth's hands with a blank look on her face and then sighed heavily. 'Oh, IDK.' Beth quickly tried to summon up her minimum text-speak knowledge and realised that this meant 'I don't know'. 'Maybe they want you to do something,' the younger woman suggested then. 'Whoever sent it. Like maybe it's a clue of some sort.' She shrugged then, already becoming bored by it all. 'You should probably just Google it. That's what I do if I don't understand something, you know?'

'You're probably right – I'll check it out later.' Though, Beth knew that spending the rest of the day trying to keep her thoughts off the mysterious delivery and *on* her customers would be hellish.

But sometime later, as she was wrapping up a purchase, the shopper's silver charm bracelet shining beneath the overhead lights caught her eye, and she stopped short.

'Everything OK?' the woman enquired, looking up at Beth's sudden sharp intake of breath.

'Of course, yes – thank you.' She smiled absently but her heart was pounding. Something had just popped into her head related to that strange message with the coffee cup. She couldn't be certain, and she was *desperate* to get home to check.

But if her suspicions were correct – and Beth was pretty sure they were – it merely made this morning's delivery all the more mysterious . . .

Chapter 8

Danny was feeling claustrophobic. Adele was studying him, waiting for an answer and he just didn't want to talk. Why couldn't she understand that? Why did she have to press him so much? It was as if she didn't truly get the situation he was in. She was looking at it all completely one sided.

'Well?' she enquired. 'Haven't you said anything yet? And if not, *why* not? You know this isn't going to end well, Danny. The longer you draw it out, the harder it's going to be on her, on everyone.'

She was pushing. He hated when she did this. And lately it seemed as if she pushed all the time. He buttoned his shirt up quickly and averted his eyes from her gaze.

Even though Adele knew so much about him, and had seen him both at his best and his worst recently, Danny still felt as if they didn't really know each other. And what scared him more was that right now she looked so determined. Almost as if she was tempted to pick up the phone and tell Beth herself.

He knew that she wouldn't – that she *couldn't* – do that but sometimes when Adele looked this way, well, he wasn't so sure. As if, rules and boundaries be damned, she would take matters into her own hands and maybe do what she felt was right on a woman-to-woman level, or something.

Danny swallowed hard. He couldn't begin to imagine how that would work out.

'This isn't just something you casually announce over a cup of coffee, OK? It's a bit bigger than that,' Danny said quietly, wishing they could get off the subject. 'I thought you understood.'

Adele nodded, her look softening. She pulled her long hair back and threw it over her shoulder. It was interesting, he noted, how she was Beth's polar opposite. Where Beth was fair, soft and petite, Adele was angular, dark and chiselled.

It must be her Mediterranean background, Danny thought. Adele Rovere. Although like him a New Yorker born and bred, she'd told him she had Italian ancestors.

'I understand that, I really do. I'm just not sure if you are handling this well. You are making it worse and more complicated with every day that passes. And if you think that Beth doesn't realise something is up by now … well, I wouldn't be so sure. Call it women's intuition, but we sense this sort of thing. We *know*.'

Danny wanted to argue with that, wanted to deny it,

but he knew that it was probably true. If anything, Beth's behaviour of late suggested that she did sense something.

But then again, if he was different or acting off, then she was too. That recent dancing around the kitchen thing like she was starring in a Nora Ephron movie attested to that. And he knew that that wasn't necessarily caused by him. He had done nothing to invite that kind of behaviour, and he had to admit that bothered him. That she could be so happy when he was feeling like this. They had always been so in tune with one another, he thought sadly. How had things ended up like this?

'Yeah, well, if she senses something, then let's just say I am realizing a few things too,' he replied darkly, feeling glum.

Adele's eyebrows raised on her smooth forehead. 'What does that mean?' she asked, her chocolate eyes narrowing.

'Well, despite what you think, Beth seems in particularly good spirits at the moment. And it's not because of anything I did. So much for women's intuition. What do you suppose that means?'

Adele shrugged her shoulders. 'I have no idea – how could I? I don't know Beth, after all. All I know about her and what she's like is based on what little you have told me. Yes, she's happy-go-lucky but a delicate soul, and you don't want to turn her life upside down and all that,' she intoned, and he looked at her, annoyed.

Was she trying to suggest that Beth was weak? Because that certainly wasn't the case. Yes, she might prefer always to look on the sunnier side of life, but there was nothing wrong with that. It was actually one of the things that had made Danny fall in love with her.

Adele was shaking her head again. 'Anyway, I'm not the one you should be talking to about all this, Danny. I've told you before, I think you should come right out and just tell her. No tiptoeing around it, trying not to hurt her. At this point, that's impossible anyway.'

He waved a dismissive hand, feeling irritated by her today. 'Like I said, just let me do it in my own time, OK? You don't know her like I do . . .'

Adele reached out and tried to put a comforting hand on his arm, but he moved away. 'Come on, you know I'm just trying to help. I care about you. I know that none of this is easy on you. Because it happened so quickly, and it's so close to the holidays now . . . I get it. But I think that despite what's gone on you're still reluctant to admit it *is* happening, Danny. All this . . .' she waved towards the bed and around the room. 'You have to make a decision. And soon.'

Danny placed his head in his hands, frustrated. 'And at the end of the day what would that solve? If I tell her now, do you think she'd ever be able to forgive me?' He stood up and straightened his shirt collar, readying himself to leave. He couldn't handle this conversation any more at this point. He thought again about what she had said, and wondered if he truly was just sheltering Beth from the truth like you would a fragile doll.

111

Sensing that the conversation was definitely closed, Adele followed as Danny made his way to the door.

'Well, you might think you know what you're doing,' she warned in parting, her words echoing in Danny's mind as he took his leave, 'but keep this up for much longer, and you might just be making Beth's decision easier when she does find out.'

After work, Beth returned home to Gold Street to discover that once again she'd reached the apartment before Danny, but today she was too distracted to worry or be concerned about it.

After disposing of her work clothes in lieu of a pair of yoga pants and a T-shirt, she shovelled down a cook-from-frozen lasagne for dinner, then headed into the living room, Brinkley skittering at her feet.

Sitting down on the sofa, she turned on the TV.

Smiling, she patted the space next to her and the little dog jumped up, taking a seat on top of a nearby cushion. Powering up her laptop, she waited for the machine to go through its startup and then eagerly opened up her browser and prepared to enter a search query. Immediately, she saw what she was looking for: a YouTube clip from a movie scene; one that she recognised all too well. Clicking on the clip, Beth's eyes widened happily as she realised that she was right.

'We could have this engraved, couldn't we?' said a male voice. The instantly recognisable Paul Varjak played by

George Peppard, was speaking to a salesman at Tiffany's. Beth watched raptly as the salesman took the ring that Paul had just offered and examined it.

'This, I take it, was not purchased at Tiffany's?' the salesman was asking.

To which Paul replied, 'No, actually it was purchased concurrent with ... uh ... well, actually ... came inside of ... well, a box of Cracker Jack.'

Beth smiled delightedly. THAT was why today's set-up all seemed so familiar, the coffee cup, Cracker Jack and more importantly the curious line, 'We could have this engraved.' It was from a movie.

And not just any movie ...

'I knew it.' Beth tossed her computer onto the sofa and jubilantly threw her arms in the air in celebration of her discovery. Brinkley jumped up from the cushion and barked suspiciously, apparently miffed by the disruption. 'Coffee – like the coffee that Audrey Hepburn drinks as she stands outside the windows of Tiffany's in the opening scene of the movie. And Cracker Jack – Paul got the ring out of the Cracker Jack box so he would have something to engrave at Tiffany's,' she cried, exalted by her discovery. The clues all pointed to the movie *Breakfast at Tiffany's*. 'You know what this means, Brinks?'

The little dog tilted his head at the question, as if he was waiting for her to tell him.

She thought again about the hidden message inside the coffee cup, and what it represented. Clearly the sender *did*

Melissa Hill

want her to do something, and the *Breakfast at Tiffany's*-related inscription on the cup was not just a message, but an invitation. *Meet me there.* Beth was unaccountably thrilled and delighted, not only at the prospect of such an adventure, but where it might take her.

'Seems somebody wants me to go to Tiffany's.'

Chapter 9

The next day at lunchtime, as she approached the famous Tiffany's store on Fifth Avenue, Beth's excitement reached a peak. That morning she'd barely been able to concentrate on work at all.

Thankfully a new stock delivery had kept her busy for much of the time, but it also meant she hadn't had the chance to talk about any of yesterday's events with Jodi, whom she guessed would be just as excited and intrigued by it all as she was.

Or maybe not. With Jodi you never knew.

Beth took in the store's front façade, which always looked especially beautiful during the holiday season. This year the merchandisers had made it look as though the store itself was wrapped up with a huge glittering red bow, which ran the entire length and width of the corner building. While it was one of the most exclusive jewellery stores in all of Manhattan, it was also a world-famous

landmark – thanks to Audrey Hepburn and the epony-
mous movie – and regularly amassed extensive crowds
both inside the store and outside. Throngs of New York
Christmas shoppers and tourists crowded around the front
just then, many of them looking to pose for photographs
in front of the window that the beautiful Ms Hepburn had
made famous in 1961.

Meet me there.

OK, so she'd figured out that Tiffany's was the place she
should go. But *where* exactly? There was nothing about
any specific meeting spot (or indeed time) in the clues she'd
been given.

Beth spied the huge picture display windows and wondered if this area was where she was supposed to be. Maybe
there would be something obvious in the content or theme
that connected everything?

She quickly but politely made her way through the
crowds, having been waylaid by a small group of giddy
teenage girls – who all had their hair in up-dos and
were sporting big Jackie O-type sunglasses and fake fur
coats – to take a photo in front of the window where Holly
Golightly stood in the movie.

Beth's eyes took in everything. The stunning vintage
Christmas-themed showcase full of glistening adornments
that were worthy of royalty, elaborate designs using precious
stones, the jewels alone easily costing thousands of dollars,
if not hundreds of thousands. But all in all it was simply a
festive display. The store's holiday windows were merely

tempting those on the outside with their wares – there was nothing in the display or amongst the arrangement that connected to her clue.

And, disappointingly, there was no one (at least not anyone she recognized) looking for her by the windows, or indeed anywhere around the store's exterior. Who was she supposed to meet? And where?

Beth decided to refocus her efforts. There had to be someone waiting for her inside. There just *had* to be. Why else go to such elaborate lengths to get her to meet whoever it was if the person wasn't going to turn up?

As she pushed through the revolving doors that led to Tiffany's glittering inner sanctum, she wondered just what she was hoping would happen, or who she'd be meeting there.

Her mouth grew dry and she swallowed nervously. Was it Ryan? The thought had crossed her mind more than once since yesterday's curious delivery. If so what was he up to? Had their recent conversation about Danny given him reason to think that Beth's head might be for turning?

Or could it be Jodi, her friend trying to distract her from what she'd already warned was a potentially troublesome dalliance? No, that seemed a little over the top and not remotely like Jodi, who always preferred to cut to the chase and say straight out what was on her mind.

In any case, it certainly couldn't be Danny (who'd arrived home from work at some godforsaken hour yet again last night). To say nothing of the fact that he was up to his eyes at the office, he'd barely had the time to speak to Beth these last few weeks, let alone go to the trouble to concoct such an elaborate gesture.

No, it had to be Ryan. Beth thought back to recent conversations that the two of them had had over lunch. About New York movies, baseball, relationships and so much more. It was totally like him to do something like this. But Tiffany's? That seemed a little excessive for a guy she didn't know *that* well, didn't it? Unless he really was that swoonsome romantic type like the hero in *Sweet Home Alabama*, who'd closed off this very store to propose to his girlfriend.

Of course Beth knew this wasn't going to be a proposal or anything like it. In fact she still had no clue what it was all about, but she couldn't deny that this kind of spontaneity, almost playfulness, was exactly what her life had been missing lately – something exciting, something adventurous and *fun*.

Still, she had to be careful. By going along with all this – thrilling though it was – wasn't she in danger of ending up somewhere she wasn't yet sure she wanted to be?

Well, she was here now anyway, Beth argued with herself, so despite her misgivings about what was going on or who was behind all this, she might as well find out what happened next.

Walking into the store, she eagerly returned the smiling doorman's greeting and then looked around. Trying to make sense of the mass of people here – as well as determine just what exactly she was looking for – was definitely going to be tricky.

Beth tentatively made a loop around the jewellery floor on ground level – taking a moment to appreciate the stunningly beautiful robin's egg-blue and white Christmas trees dotted around the room, all adorned with those famed little blue boxes.

Realizing then just how big the Tiffany's flagship actually was, she tried to figure out how in the world she was supposed to know if she was in the right area – let alone the right floor.

Wondering where her intended meeting companion might be, she actively sought out the gazes of people who happened to catch her eye – store clerks, other shoppers, innocent-looking tourists – until she realised that she was probably looking like some kind of weirdo desperately staring down everyone in sight. So she decided to abandon that plan completely.

Beth paused for a moment next to a display case filled with sparkling diamond necklaces, earrings, and the odd engagement ring. Her mind wandered a little as she took in the beautiful sparklers – symbols of love and commitment – and immediately a wave of melancholy washed over her. Peering down at her unadorned left hand she thought about Danny and wondered if she would ever have a ring like that on her hand.

Seven years together. But nothing tangible to show for

it. No greater commitment had been made. And why was that? Beth wondered.

She continued staring at the case of diamond rings, trying to imagine what one would look like on her finger; picturing what it would be like if Danny proposed, what he would say. And then, without any control of her thoughts, her mind switched gears. What if it was someone else – say, Ryan – doing the proposing?

She felt flushed at the thought and immediately abandoned that line of thinking. Again, she was getting way ahead of herself. She barely knew Ryan. And she felt guilty too. Danny was the one, the only one she wanted a ring from.

Wasn't he?

Just as Beth was about to move away from the display counter and concentrate afresh on finding the person she was supposed to be meeting, a Tiffany's saleswoman behind the counter said, 'What's it gonna be, Angelina?'

Beth looked up confused, and trying to determine if the woman was in fact addressing her. But there was no one else around. She was at least a ten foot radius from anyone else on the sales floor. Plus, the woman, who looked to be in her mid-fifties, was looking directly at Beth. Clearly she was talking to her.

But why was she addressing her as *Angelina*?

'I'm – I'm sorry?' Beth muttered, looking at her in that confused and embarrassed way one gets when in an uncomfortable social situation.

'What's it gonna be, Angelina?' the woman repeated, this time with a wry smile on her face.

Beth's brow crinkled and she shook her head. 'I'm sorry, my name isn't Angelina. I think you must be looking for someone else.'

But the woman didn't look at all deterred. In fact, her smile broadened. And her next question made Beth's heart leap in her chest.

'I assume you like Cracker Jack?'

This certainly got Beth's attention, and she moved back towards the counter, placing her hands eagerly down on the glass. 'Of course I do,' she exclaimed, and then blushed at her obvious enthusiasm. 'I mean, I haven't had Cracker Jack in years. But ... so you know about it, yes? The coffee cup and this meeting I'm supposed to be having here?' she pressed, eager for answers.

The woman nodded and flashed a knowing smile at her, but remained maddeningly silent. Beth's heart hammered and her mind raced, wondering what she should do next. Was this the person she was supposed to meet? But then, based on the salesperson's expectant expression, she realised that the woman seemed to be waiting for *her* to say something.

Was there some kind of code word or ...? But then something struck her, and the message written inside the coffee cup automatically popped into her mind.

Maybe we could have this engraved ... Could the line from the movie *Breakfast at Tiffany's* be like a code, or a password of some sort? Was she supposed to repeat it out loud?

'We could have this engraved, couldn't we?' Beth uttered slowly, feeling utterly surreal to be doing such a thing. The woman would think she was crazy. But no, the assistant's grin grew wider, and Beth knew that she had struck gold.

The woman held up a finger as if to indicate for Beth to wait a moment, and then turned round, heading to somewhere out back.

Tapping her foot nervously, Beth felt relieved when eventually the salesperson re-emerged and approached her once again. The woman held a robin's egg-blue box in her hand, wrapped with a white ribbon. The iconic Tiffany's little blue box. Beth felt her heart almost stop.

What on earth . . . ?

Was this for her? She was almost afraid to think about what would be in the box, for fear of ruining the moment. And she wondered if this was the intention all along: to indeed send her here for a *Sweet Home Alabama* moment.

Danny?

Her heart soaring, Beth glanced briefly around, wondering if her boyfriend, the love of her life, who was admittedly acting very secretive lately, might somehow materialise. But no, there was no sign of Danny or indeed anyone else who might want to take responsibility for this curious situation.

The salesperson placed the little blue box on top of the glass display counter in front of Beth. Then she took a step back, silently indicating that it was up to her to open the box.

With trembling hands, and her mind in an absolute tizzy, Beth reached out and pulled the box closer to her. She looked up and smiled nervously, looking for any indication of what was in the box, any clue at all as to what on earth was going on. Briefly she shot another glance around, but still no Patrick Dempsey-type suitor (Danny or otherwise) materialised, and she couldn't help but wonder now if she'd been set up by a candid camera-style show – or at the very least, was being punked by Jodi or someone else.

This isn't a proposal, she told herself, feeling more disappointed than she cared to admit. *Just open the box.*

As if understanding her nervousness and trepidation, the Tiffany's saleswoman stepped forward and placed a calming hand on her wrist. 'It's OK, Beth, just open it.'

At first slightly worried that the woman could read her thoughts, Beth fumbled with the ribbon. But then another thought entered her brain. The woman knew her name. So why had she addressed her as 'Angelina' earlier?

What's it gonna be, Angelina?

Trying and failing to make sense of the situation, Beth decided to carry on, hoping that some answer to this mystery would be contained in the box. She pulled the ribbon quickly and without further thought, took the lid off and placed it to the side.

Reaching inside, she extracted, not a piece of jewellery, as she'd expected, but a piece of paper.

A note.

We could have this engraved, couldn't we?

The line from the movie echoing once again in her mind, Beth read the words on the paper. '*Someday if I had the money, I'd take you ... we'd sail away ... around the world and back again. I promise you.*'

Beth's eyes opened wide with surprise.

Sail around the world? ... I promise you?

What did it mean? It sounded like a proposal of sorts, she supposed, but given the absence of a husband-to-be (or indeed a ring), that just wasn't possible. Then rereading the words, she noticed the presence of quotation marks, indicating that it must be a quote of some kind, just like the one hidden in the coffee cup. Then the realisation struck her and she smiled.

This wasn't a proposal or a romantic gesture. It was another clue.

She looked up at the salesperson, who was studying her face, almost as if wondering whether Beth was working this all out in her head.

Beth looked down and read the words out loud. '"Someday if I had the money, I'd take you ... we'd sail away ... around the world and back again. I promise you." It's another clue. Isn't it?' she asked, but the salesperson stayed silent. However, her wry smile remained.

Beth searched the recesses of her memory, trying to fit the pieces together, trying to work it all out – make sense of what was going on here. Of course the saleswoman had to be part of this; there was no other way to explain it and she was definitely in on it. In fact, she'd been instructed by someone – the instigator – on what to do, hadn't she? Which suggested that the words she had first spoken to Beth had something to do with this puzzle, too.

'What was it that you originally said to me?' she asked her, urgently. 'When I first arrived earlier? Will you say it again?'

The woman simply smiled and nodded, only too happy to oblige. 'What's it gonna be, Angelina?'

Beth listened, working hard to make a connection and find a deeper meaning.

'What's it gonna be, Angelina?' she repeated. 'It's part of a clue, isn't it? I know it.' She looked again at the salesperson, but the woman's face gave nothing away. And then she smiled delightedly. 'Is this . . . some kind of scavenger hunt?' she asked. It had to be, though, admittedly a very elaborate one. 'Or,' she clarified, eyes shining with anticipation, 'a . . . treasure hunt?'

The woman's next words confirmed everything that Beth needed to know. She grinned broadly. 'Good luck and happy hunting.'

Chapter 10

Danny felt as if his skin was a sheet of ice. He couldn't wait to get indoors somewhere, away from the bitter cold that was freezing the hell out of New York this December. Although everyone seemed to think the weather had been mild lately, to Danny it felt like being in the Antarctic.

But then, he wasn't feeling great these days anyway. With all the strain he was under, he was exhausted and weak. He had a load on his mind, and still there was so much to set straight: with Beth, Adele, as well as various things work-related and otherwise, that were in danger of running away with him. He had messed up, and he really had no idea how to go about putting things to rights. At this point, was that even possible?

It seemed, though, as if fate was trying to intervene today, in some manner anyway. He found himself now in Beth's neck of the woods. He'd just finished a client appointment a couple of blocks away, so he decided that no matter what might happen tomorrow or the next day, the very least he could do was try to reconnect a little with Beth. They'd barely seen one another over the last while and he really wanted to make it up to her.

Turning the corner and facing the main entryway to Carlisle's, he pulled open the door and was met with a blast of warm, centrally heated air. Sighing with relief, he felt himself becoming eager – excited, almost – to see Beth, as if it was their first date instead of their one-thousandth. He tried to recall the last time that he had surprised her at work like this – indeed, surprised her at all – and realised that he couldn't. A fresh wave of guilt washed over him and to try to fight it, Danny focused on a good memory of him and Beth together.

He recalled one of the dates they had gone on early on – when they had sat on that park bench all night in the summertime, with the Queensboro Bridge as their audience, laughing with each other, learning about hobbies, interests, passions – beginning their relationship.

Danny had very quickly realised that he and Beth were almost re-enacting a scene out of Woody Allen's *Manhattan*, one of his favourite movies and one that somehow movie-mad Beth hadn't seen at that point in her life. Her fascination after learning of their connection to that iconic spot, and the significance she'd attached to it, had made Danny fall even deeper in love with her. It was rare to find a person with such passion and wonder for everyday life, who found such happiness in ordinary things and was able to imbue them with the extraordinary. Who had such a good heart and who truly believed in fate and possibility.

But that was years ago, almost a lifetime ago. And things were very different now, that was for sure. Danny longed to recapture some of that old joy and excitement but he wasn't sure if it was even possible now.

Since meeting Adele, had that ship truly sailed?

Trying to push aside his troubling thoughts, he found his way upstairs to the ladies' shoe department, keeping his eyes peeled for Beth. He knew that she was working today and it was still a little before her usual lunchtime break, so she had to be around here somewhere. It would be a welcome relief to spend some time together, catch up on what was going on with her.

Danny looked around and saw that the department was decidedly empty of salespeople, including Beth. Standing in between a display of shiny heels and a table of aggressive-looking studded pumps, which looked more like weapons than accessories, Danny stuffed his hands in his pockets and craned his neck, looking for someone who might be able to direct him Beth's way. She could be out back checking stock or something. And, knowing Beth, marvelling at every piece. He never quite got her – or indeed any woman's fascination – with what were essentially just trussed-up pieces of leather, but as a guy, why would he? Though he did appreciate the sentimental attachment Beth always had to her grandmother's wedding shoes. Nostalgia he understood, dangerous-looking studded stilettos, not so much.

Just as he decided to go find a sales associate in a neighbouring department to help him, someone walked from the inventory room onto the main sales floor. Not Beth, though, but Jodi.

'Hey, Jodi,' Danny called out, happy to see a familiar face. 'How are you? Long time, no see,' he said cheerily. True, Jodi was loud and a bit abrasive, but she was also a good friend to Beth – and pretty funny when she was in the right mood.

'Danny. What are you doing here?' she asked with a slight frown, and his smile faded ever so slightly at her less-than-enthusiastic greeting.

'I came in to see Beth. Thought I would take her to lunch today. She is working today, right?' he enquired, his mind running through a million other scenarios, including the idea that maybe she had got a new job in another department and he hadn't been listening when she told him.

'Yes, she's working today.' Jodi looked around and her gaze focused past him on a position to the upper right of her vision, before returning her eyes to meet Danny's. He thought she looked nervous and a little jumpy, and completely devoid of her usual devil-may-care attitude. 'But ... I think she already went to lunch. Had to go out a little bit earlier today, she said; you just missed her. I'd imagine she won't be back for an hour or so.'

Jodi seemed to make a great show of tidying a shelf in front of her, despite the display looking barely touched, and somehow Danny felt as if he was being dismissed.

'Oh, I see. Well, do you know where she went? Maybe I could go and meet her.'

'I really have no idea. She just said something about an errand. I'm sorry, Danny, I wish I could stay and chat but I have tons to do.' Jodi looked around as if she had a long queue of waiting customers vying for her attention and, realizing it was an empty sales floor, motioned with her hand to the stockroom. 'When she gets back, I'll be sure to tell her you were looking for her, OK?'

'Well, I wouldn't want to keep you if you are busy,' Danny said. Jodi *was* trying to get rid of him. Why was she so jittery?

One thing was for sure: she was hiding something. Whether or not it had anything to do with Beth was the question. But if so, what could she be hiding and, more to the point, why?

'So, well ... I'll see you around, OK?' She scurried off then, as if afraid to be in the same room as him.

Danny was completely confused. Jodi was treating him like a total stranger, as if they hadn't known one another for years. What had he done to make her behave this way?

He couldn't think of anything. Unless, his absences of late had indeed been noticed by Beth, who had in turn vented to Jodi? And now, through some bond of sisterhood and solidarity, she was taking Beth's side.

He started heading down the hallway towards the men's department, mentally cursing the fact that his plans for a heart-to-heart had been ruined, when, just then, Danny heard it. Beth's laugh, like sleigh bells tinkling. He moved quickly towards the source of the sound a little way further down in the men's section, and saw his girlfriend, giggling like a schoolgirl, near a display of Tommy Hilfiger sweaters.

And she wasn't alone. She was chatting with some guy.

For some reason Danny stopped in his tracks, and, realising that he was seconds away from being spotted by Beth, he quickly jumped behind a rack of suits. Unsure as to why he'd felt the need to hide, he studied the scene a little away from him, Beth laughing with ease at whatever this guy was saying.

He was a stranger to Danny, but judging by how close together they were standing, and the easy tone of their voices, it seemed the very opposite where Beth was concerned. This was someone his girlfriend seemed to know very well indeed.

'Ha, as if! *Elf* is *not* the most romantic Christmas movie of all time,' she was laughing. 'I mean, I suppose it's a love story of sorts, but it doesn't hold a candle to *Love Actually*.' Beth laughed again and Danny listened intently to the tone of her voice. Was she *cooing* at this guy? He felt his hackles rise, and alpha male instincts coming out. OK, so he hadn't been the easiest to live with lately, but Beth was *his* girlfriend.

It sounded as though they were talking about movies, Beth's favourite subject.

'Look, I have my reputation to think about here. If a big

macho guy like me admits out loud to liking *Love Actually*, they are going to take my manhood card away, OK?'

Now he was smiling, showing those cheek dimple things that all women seemed to love. And, what's more, he was *flirting*. Danny recognized a play when he saw one.

His eyes narrowed. Even worse, Beth seemed to be eating this crap up.

'Anyway,' said Beth, 'I should be getting back. Jodi's been covering for me while I was out and there may be a rush on. Thanks for the sandwich.'

So much for 'just missing her', Danny noted, thinking back to Jodi's insistence that Beth would be gone for an hour. Sounded like her so-called errand was an opportunity to share a sandwich (what else?) with this guy. No wonder Jodi had been so edgy when he'd arrived asking for Beth; she must have known she was out with this guy and was covering for her in more ways than one.

Man, was he getting his payback right now or what . . .

Danny couldn't help but realise that maybe this served him right, and he was experiencing a dose of Beth's beloved serendipity. While he'd thought of this as a harmless opportunity to take Beth to lunch, karma was, in reality, a bitch that played dirty, throwing all of this in his face.

Trying to get his thoughts, never mind his feelings, in order, he watched as the guy smiled again at Beth. It was obvious he had a thing for her and, by the sound of it, very possible that she had a thing for him too. It was written all over their faces. They were acting like high school kids, for crying out loud. And it was driving Danny nuts.

'So, how about a drink later? We both get off at the same time. Think the universe is trying to tell us something?'

'Thanks, Ryan, but no.' This time Beth looked genuinely hesitant, making Danny feel a little better.

'Don't you go out with Jodi for happy hour sometimes?' he pressed, smiling. 'No big deal. It's just what friends do.'

Friends. OK, so they were friends; Danny felt somewhat reassured. Not that Beth was that type of girl – she definitely wasn't a cheater. Or was she?

He knew for a fact that she was flirting. It was written all over her face. And this likely explained her giddy behaviour at home of late ... Danny continued to examine their body language and he felt his temperature rise afresh.

He took stock of Ryan's appearance once again. OK, so he was attractive enough, he supposed, with that whole dimpled smile thing that women seemed to love. Danny's mind raced as he tried to make sense of what was going on, and how this impacted his plans, and he belatedly noticed that Ryan and Beth had already said their goodbyes to each other, and she was now on her way back to the shoe department. He wasn't sure whether or not to follow her as Jodi would surely tell her that he was looking for her, and she'd have to wonder why he was still around some fifteen minutes later.

But he also came to the conclusion that Ryan wasn't just Beth's lunch companion, but apparently worked in the department Danny was now camping out in. And was, in fact, now making his way over towards him.

He stood up, and was staring blankly at a suit jacket when Ryan spoke. 'Good afternoon, sir, is there something that I can help you with?'

Danny stood up straighter, coming face to face with the man who'd just been flirting shamelessly with his girlfriend, the woman with whom he'd been sharing his life for the past seven years. Now, the flirty, smooth-talking persona was gone, and the guy was back on a different kind of sales job.

'What?' Danny replied, trying to collect his wits.

'Would you like to try on that jacket? Are you a size forty-four?' Ryan persisted helpfully.

Danny started shaking his head. 'No, no, sorry, I don't want to try it on, I was just looking. I was actually, um, shopping for a Christmas gift for my ... wife,' he muttered, shoving his hands into his pocket – conscious that he wasn't wearing a wedding ring and didn't want Ryan to get suspicious.

It was only when Ryan's eyes widened a little that Danny understood how odd a man's Tommy Hilfiger suit would be as a Christmas gift for your wife. 'I, um, wanted to buy her some shoes. Some, um, nice shoes. But I think I'm a bit lost.'

Ryan smiled. 'Right, well, I know someone who can help you. I have a friend in the ladies' shoe department who would be delighted to assist, I'm sure. I can walk you over there and introduce you?'

But the last thing on earth that Danny wanted was to come face to face with Beth now. He couldn't. Not until he processed all of this and what it might mean. 'No, no, it's OK, thanks. Actually, I just realised I've forgotten something ... my phone ... I mean, my wallet. My phone and my wallet. So, I have to go.' Danny pushed past Ryan, who watched him quizzically. 'Thank you for your help. I just have to go,' he mumbled again, guessing that the guy must be thinking he was dealing with someone who was clearly off his rocker.

'Of course. Well, if I can be of any assistance in the future, be sure to let me know.' Ryan withdrew a business card from his jacket pocket and handed it to Danny, who had to resist the urge to crumple it and throw it on the ground.

Instead, he took the card politely and tried to regain some of his composure. 'Sure. Thank you,' he glanced at the card as if he didn't already know Ryan's name, 'Ryan. I appreciate your help.'

Danny turned on his heel, walking away quickly and didn't look back, though he guessed that Ryan was watching him. Feeling almost as if he was a prison convict trying to escape, he burst out of the double front doors and onto Lexington, immediately breaking into a cold sweat. He paused to catch his breath, completely in shock and feeling confused by all he'd just witnessed.

Yes, it had to be true. Karma had wanted him to see all that. Karma had been intent on clueing Danny in on what was coming next – and why. He tried to process it and worked to recall each part of Beth and Ryan's conversation. Yes, they had been flirting. Yes, it was very clear that they were attracted to each other. So maybe Beth was going to leave him anyway.

This is what you get for keeping secrets, he thought, feeling even more confused than ever. He couldn't believe that he had been naïve enough to think that he could simply tell Beth the truth and hope that their relationship could recover. How could he be so dumb?

Danny looked down at the business card in his hand. Ryan Buchanan.

Unease crept up his spine and he felt a sharp pain in his stomach. His hands felt cold yet clammy, as if Fortune had just cast her eye on him and found him lacking – weak – unworthy. He waited for the episode to fade, and then felt a sense of resignation replace his panic.

As he walked away, with Carlisle's in his wake, Danny thought about all that was happening. He was beginning to understand just how much he and Beth had lost sight of one another lately.

And it seemed that while he had been keeping his secrets, Beth had also been keeping her own.

Chapter 11

Beth barely had time to stow her handbag in her locker and clock in on the store computer before Jodi was all over her, explaining that Danny had called in to take her to lunch, and guessing that she was out with Ryan, Jodi had covered for her.

'But I wasn't out for lunch with Ryan; I told you I had an errand to do. I asked him to pick me up something from the deli when he going on his sandwich run.'

'Oh. Well, I didn't know that, did I? Especially as you two seem thick as thieves lately. I just didn't expect to see Danny, so I was caught unawares. You guys only missed each other by like ten minutes.'

Really? Beth wondered why Danny had popped in to see her unannounced. She had no idea that, according to Jodi, he had an appointment in this part of town this morning. Would it have killed him to tell her about his plans earlier if he wanted to get together for lunch?

While she was feeling a little irritated, as well as jittery about all that had just happened at Tiffany's, a little voice reminded her that maybe she shouldn't be so hard on her boyfriend. He was being spontaneous, and wasn't she always complaining that the spontaneity had disappeared from her relationship?

He was trying, she thought, softening inside and feeling her heart bloom ever so slightly. But there was no denying that lately she felt conflicted, torn, *confused* over her feelings and love for Danny, the evergreen emotions that seemed always to be there – even though she needed to be reminded of certain things lately – and the fact that there were, steadily increasing feelings for Ryan.

Feeling afraid and panicked at the thought, she quashed the admittance.

'Beth, what's going on?' Jodi asked, looking at her shrewdly. 'And where were you at lunchtime?'

Beth took a deep breath and, in between customers, tried to explain what had happened recently, from yesterday's curious delivery to the even more curious events at Tiffany's earlier.

As expected, Jodi met Beth's tale with equal parts scepticism and sarcasm, as well as just a touch of paranoia. 'So you are telling me that you are receiving weird, cryptic messages from some stranger, and now willingly intend on chasing down "clues"? Honestly, Beth, this is how most slasher movies begin. You automatically think this is a Nora Ephron-style romance, but in reality some psycho serial killer has other plans,' her friend tsked.

'It's not some serial killer; what kind of deranged killer would arrange a meeting at Tiffany's? For goodness' sake, Jodi, why do you have to think so negatively all the time? It's just fun. There doesn't always have to be some dark ulterior motive to everything.'

'Fun?' Jodi said as she raised her eyebrows. 'Honey, anonymous messages like that are not fun, they're spooky. And if there are romantic undertones, that's even more ominous to me. Who do you think might be behind all this? If it's Danny, that's one thing. He's the only person that should be sending you romantic messages.' She stared at Beth, who knew exactly what she was getting at.

Truth be told, save for that brief moment when the blue box first appeared, it hadn't really crossed her mind that Danny might be behind the treasure hunt or adventure or whatever this was. It just wasn't his sort of thing. Maybe he might have thought about doing something like this at one point four or five years ago, but sweeping romantic 'nonsense', as Jodi had called it, didn't seem to be on her boyfriend's radar these days.

She wanted to make sure Jodi's attention was quickly deflected from Ryan, though – she didn't need another lecture. So she simply shrugged and gave a little smile. 'It must be Danny,' she lied. 'That's likely why he came to see me today, to see if I'd made it to Tiffany's, and found the next clue, as planned.'

Jodi studied her friend's face for a second and then opened her mouth as if she was about to speak. But then she must have changed her mind, as she returned her attention to her work. 'OK, so it looks like, regardless of what I say, you are going to continue on with this crazy scavenger hunt—'

'*Treasure* hunt,' Beth corrected.

'Whatever. Anyway, so you are going to follow these ... clues. I'm guessing you told me all this for a reason. Namely because you want help.' She put her hands on her hips and took a deep breath. 'So, go on then, tell me more about the latest clue, the one you got at Tiffany's. Maybe I can help you solve it. At the very least if I have some idea of where you are going I can point the police in the right direction to recover your mutilated corpse.'

Beth laughed. 'You are unbelievable. You know, positive thinking can really make a different in a person's love life, did you know that? I recently read that somewhere. Maybe that's why you have issues with the opposite sex. You're such a Negative Nancy.'

Jodi snorted. 'Please, I'll have you know I'm not having any issues with the opposite sex, or my sex life, for that matter. Beside the fact that they are useful for essentially only two things – reproduction and killing spiders – men are pointless.'

Beth rolled her eyes. 'Not all men, Jodi. And since *when* did you have a sex life?'

'You met him, actually,' she said matter-of-factly.

Beth's eyes widened, surprised by this abrupt turn in conversation. She searched the recesses of her mind. 'Met *who*? And *when* did I meet him?'

'I believe he was bachelor number two. That last time we went to happy hour at 123?'

'No way.' Beth thought hard but couldn't conjure up Jodi's mystery man from the weekend she and Danny had called off their Florida trip. 'I'm sorry, I can't remember. Was he the bond trader?' she guessed, knowing that at least one of the guys that Jodi had met that night was a Wall Streeter.

Her friend shook her head. 'No, wrong guy, but he does work on Wall Street – for a hedge fund. He's a tax attorney.'

Beth raised her eyebrows. 'A tax attorney? I bet your sex life is wild. Off the scale.'

'Hey, don't judge. His name is Trevor and he's fun. And while tax law might sound like the epitome of boring, this guy certainly knows how to live. We've been having some good times lately. I mean, it's probably nothing serious. But, you know, he, um – he's nice and charming, and he seems to enjoy my sense of humour, which makes a nice change. It's all been nice.'

Suddenly, Beth realised that while Jodi was acting nonchalant, she was actually playing coy. She had just used the word 'nice' three times in quick succession. She was completely downplaying this crush. She *liked* this guy, certainly – and as such, Beth decided to quash the teasing. After all, if there was one thing she did know it was that her friend deserved a bit of happiness in the romance department. If this Trevor was making Jodi's heart sing, even just a little, then he was OK in Beth's book.

'I can't believe you didn't tell me,' she admonished, and her friend blushed.

'I wasn't going to, 'cos it's still early days. And I'm not the only one who's been keeping things under her hat, am I? Still, at least *my* admirer has a name,' Jodi said, expertly turning the subject back onto Beth. 'Let's take a look at that clue and see if we can figure out yours.'

When Beth returned home from work later that evening, Danny could tell she was distracted. Yes, she had greeted him pleasantly enough on arrival, apologised about missing him at lunchtime earlier, and had even kissed him, but her mind was elsewhere, he could tell.

And when he casually suggested maybe sitting down and watching a movie together, Beth feigned tiredness, and said that she needed to get to bed – she had an early start the following day and she felt a headache coming on.

'The last thing I need is to wake up with a migraine,' she said. 'I'm going to take some Excedrin and hit the sheets.'

Maybe she really did have a headache, he thought, maybe she really was tired. But it was strange for Beth to turn down the opportunity to watch a movie.

It was only after she retreated from the living room and shut the bedroom door behind her, that he realised that she hadn't said one word about the so-called 'errand' she had been on.

*

Beth breathed a sigh of relief as she shut her bedroom door behind her. Truthfully, she *had* been tired, though not as tired as she claimed to Danny – and she certainly didn't have a headache coming on. If anything, she knew that she would be lucky to sleep that night. She had so many thoughts rushing through her brain that her entire being was operating on overdrive.

Angelina . . . Sail away . . . around the world . . . I promise you.

What did it mean? And how could she find out? More to the point, what was it all about?

A treasure hunt – she knew that much – but what was the end goal? If it was Ryan who'd instigated this, it really was taking flirting to the next level after all their playful (but harmless) banter over the last couple of weeks.

Notwithstanding what or who was behind it, there was no denying Beth liked it. She enjoyed the mystery it presented. And was dying to figure out what would happen next or what she was supposed to find.

If Ryan had concocted this treasure hunt, then he certainly wasn't acting like the friend he'd so innocently proclaimed himself to be. And what's more, if Beth decided to continue on this little adventure, she was condoning it – almost giving the green light to take things further, so to speak.

She swallowed hard. Of course, there was always the option to completely abandon this entire crazy thing. She could ignore the new clue; after all, there wasn't anything saying that she had to play this game. She could voluntarily opt out.

And that's all it was, a game. So if she just ignored this – maybe went back to Tiffany's tomorrow and told the salesperson to pass on the message that she wasn't going to pursue the clue – then she would have a clear conscience. There would be no secrets, nothing to worry about, and definitely nothing to lie about as far as Danny was concerned.

But . . .

Beth knew that it was dangerous and that clearly she wasn't thinking correctly, but she didn't want to do that. This was intriguing, challenging . . . it was daring, almost. She wanted to keep going with the hunt. She hadn't had this much fun in ages.

She loved the adventure and the mystery – and OK, yes – the movie-like drama of it all. She had a mystery to solve, and she was pretty sure she'd be able to understand the clues. She'd cracked the first one, after all. She almost owed it to herself to continue on. It was a test of knowledge of sorts.

And at the end of the day, what was wrong with having a little fun?

Beth smiled to herself as she made up her mind. She would continue on the treasure hunt for as long as she could. No harm, no foul.

Having made her decision, she settled back against her pillows, turned the light off, pulled her computer closer and started a new search.

Angelina. Sail away. Around the world. I promise you.
Tens of thousands of different results came back.

Beth was sure that the clue didn't have anything to do with Angelina Jolie, *The Amazing Race* TV show, or purity rings for teenagers.

'Weird what Google thinks you might be looking for,' she said under her breath. But then she realised the folly of her words. She was being too obtuse, too vague. And Google didn't have a human brain or the ability to know the context of the search.

'I need to be more specific,' she muttered, and racked her brains, wondering how she was supposed to narrow it down. Then in a flash, it came to her and Beth typed one more word into the search bar.

Movie.

Since *Breakfast at Tiffany's* had provided the context for the first clue, she guessed that this treasure hunt, if it had been created and devised by someone who knew her well, might centre around one of her favourite passions. The romance of the silver screen.

And based upon what Google was showing her now, Beth guessed that she just might be right in her assumption. Scanning over the latest results, she considered the chances.

The first movie listed was indeed a classic – she even owned it on DVD. It was a bit trickier to decipher than the *Breakfast at Tiffany's* clue, though, because that movie had her intended destination right in the title of the film.

But at least she had a movie in mind. Now she just had to

figure out what she was supposed to do with that information, or how the clue was connected to a local destination in the here and now.

She furrowed her brow, thinking hard. This movie, she thought, might be the one she was looking for. Well, it only had a few scenes set in New York , if she recalled correctly. So where was she supposed to go next? She needed to get her thinking cap on, that's for sure. Once again she summoned up her grandmother's spirit. Bridie would know immediately. Her grandmother's movie knowledge had been almost encyclopaedic. Google had nothing on her.

But right now, Beth's brain felt muddled, and it was true that she was tired. Maybe she should give in to the sandman – after all, she had made a bit of a stride in understanding this next clue. The rest could wait.

She set the computer aside, realizing her eyelids were growing heavy and that maybe – just maybe – sleeping on this puzzle might give her the clarity that she needed in the morning to solve it.

Chapter 12

'Remember *Romancing the Stone*?' Beth asked Jodi at work the following morning.

Her friend nodded. 'Of course. Kathleen Turner before she gained pounds and years. And Michael Douglas before the surgery. Haven't seen that movie in a while, though.'

'Well, I think at the very least I've figured out that the treasure hunt clues are movie-themed,' Beth told her excitedly. 'I just can't figure out what to do with this information. Am I supposed to go somewhere, like I did with the Tiffany's one?'

Jodi thought for a moment. 'Hmm, if it's supposed to send you somewhere, I don't remember much of that movie being in New York. Are you sure you aren't supposed to jump a plane to a jungle in Colombia or something?'

Beth frowned. 'I can't imagine that being the case. Seems way over the top. I feel that since the *Breakfast at Tiffany's* clue was New York-focused, then this one might be too.'

Jodi nodded and looked as if she was trying to order her thoughts. 'OK, so the parts that were in New York – wasn't Kathleen Turner an author or something in that flick?' Beth nodded. 'So, maybe one of the big publishing houses on Park Avenue? Or maybe you are supposed to go to a bookstore? I don't know ... I also think there is a connection to a treasure map in the movie but, as I recall, that takes Ms Turner somewhere else entirely.'

Beth shook her head. 'I don't know, I thought of the treasure map as the obvious choice, too. But that just doesn't really feel right. So, think of the clues; they must do more than just point me towards the movie. The woman at Tiffany's said to me, "What's it gonna be, Angelina?" And then in the clue, the quote talked about "sailing away".'

Jodi paused for a moment as she considered Beth's words and then suddenly the shoe dropped. Quite literally, as she let go of the Valentino slingback she'd been holding. 'Of course. The boat.'

Beth shook her head, confused. 'What? What boat?'

'The boat in the movie,' Jodi explained. 'Remember? At the end. Michael Douglas is on that boat right in the middle of the street – it's being towed or something – and he sweeps Kathleen Turner off her feet, and they kiss and the "boat" sails off – right in the middle of Manhattan. That *has* to be it.'

Beth felt her heart race with excitement at finally making a New York connection to the movie. But there was one not so insignificant problem with that. 'Where am I supposed to find a boat in the middle of Manhattan? That's not exactly a regular occurrence,' she said, realizing that the idea of a boat being towed down Fifth Avenue or any other street on the island was indeed a movie moment, but not at all likely to happen in real life.

But Jodi didn't look at all deterred by this. In fact, she was smiling.

'Why do you look so happy?'

Jodi laughed knowingly. 'Oh, just because for once in our friendship it is *you* who is thinking too literal and negative, and *me* who actually sees the big picture. Me who is keeping a positive mind. Me who's solved your little clue.'

Beth grimaced impatiently, wishing that Jodi would just get on with it. 'Tell me then. Spit it out, what am I missing?'

'Fine. But you need to promise me something.'

'Of course, anything.'

Her friend nodded, apparently satisfied. 'I'm going to tell you what I think and in turn, you are going to take me with you on the hunt. OK?'

Beth nodded. 'Whatever, yes, fine. Now stop drawing it out and just tell me, for goodness' sake.'

'OK, OK, don't get your knickers in a twist. So I am thinking that if your clue is directing you to a boat, and you're looking for boats in Manhattan, you don't have to look any further than your own neighbourhood – this weekend, actually.'

Beth tried hard to figure out what her friend was talking about but drew a blank. Of course, Lower Manhattan was home to the harbour and there were docks and waterfront galore, but that seemed almost too simple.

'Maybe you aren't looking for a boat to be sailing down a street in Manhattan to solve this clue, but you are looking for a sailboat. Possibly one named *Angelina*. And while that might sound like a long shot, I'm willing to bet that there might just be a boat of that name at the Manhattan Sailing Exhibition, conveniently scheduled for this very weekend. In Lower Manhattan, like I said.' With that admission Jodi settled back into her work as if unaffected by the look of sheer, unadulterated joy on her friend's face.

'Oh, wow!' Beth exclaimed, immediately grabbing her iPhone and doing a search for the Sailing Exhibition. 'I would have never suspected that – I would have never known about this at all. Which begs the question: how did *you* know?'

'What – are you saying I'm not a classy enough broad to know about high-brow things like sailing? Well, you're probably right,' she laughed. Then: 'It's Trevor, the guy I told you about before – the one I'm seeing – he's into sailing. And he's thinking about buying a boat. That's why he got tickets and he and I are going this weekend.'

Beth was focused on her phone, but looked up at Jodi's words. 'Ah, no. Do you need tickets to get in? How can I get one? Maybe I can buy them online?'

Jodi waved her hand, dismissing Beth's suggestion. 'No, they've been sold out for ages. Apparently, this is a big deal to the Park Avenue community. I think Trevor has had his for a while, but I'll ask him to see about getting a pass for you too.'

Happy and relieved, Beth reflected on her luck. How perfect that Jodi had not only figured out this clue, at least pointing her in the right direction, but also that she had a ready-made connection that would enable Beth to get a ticket to the event itself.

Which made Beth wonder, how would she have figured out this part of the treasure hunt if she had been unable to get a ticket to the Sailing Exhibition? Obviously, whoever was behind this movie-themed hunt had yet to reveal another part of the clue besides the Tiffany box. The mastermind must surely have had a trick up his sleeve to get her to the exhibition.

She just had to wait and see how.

That evening, after work, Beth decided that she had too much nervous energy to sit around at home so she threw on her comfy boots and grabbed Brinkley's leash. The clues and the hunt were consuming her thoughts, even more so now that she guessed there was nothing she could do except wait and wonder if the boat exhibition was the right direction.

'Come on, boy, let's go for a walk. I need to clear my head.'

The little dog was only too happy to oblige and, reaching the lobby, Beth waved a brief hello to Billy, deciding to tell him where she was off to in the dark, just in case.

'Oh, Beth, hello.' Billy blushed from ear to ear, and ran a hand through his hair. 'I was just ...' His voice trailed off and Beth noticed that he appeared flustered, as if she'd interrupted something.

She glanced briefly over the desk. It looked as though he was in the middle of wrapping something, a small package of sorts. But why did he look almost guilty?

'We're off out for a walk. Shouldn't be more than half an hour or so,' she told him casually, though she was curious as to why the typically unflappable concierge seemed so ruffled.

'No problem. Enjoy.'

'I will.' Beth looked at him strangely as she exited the building. There seemed to be lots of strange goings-on with the men she knew these days.

Oh, well, whatever Billy was up to was clearly none of her business.

Heading out onto the street, she breathed in the night air. All the noise and bustle of the day had left the night in a tired and quiet calm. Brinkley looked right and left and then happily chose his path, walking towards City Hall Park. Beth was happy to let the pooch lead the way; it gave her one less thing to think about.

Thinking back again to Ryan and whether he might be the one behind the treasure hunt, Beth had to admit that Jodi was right about what she'd said the other night – deep down she knew that there was an attraction between them and that she should leave well alone, especially since she was not in the position to be anything more than a friend, and Ryan didn't have that restriction or limitation.

And then, there was Danny. Her Danny. The man that to all intents and purposes was her life partner, her soul mate, the person she had built a life with.

She wasn't willing to give him up or admit that her relationship was in trouble. Jodi was right, she was not good at talking about the bad or difficult stuff, and confrontation over real (or imagined) issues had certainly never been her strong suit. Beth had always argued that it was because she preferred to look on the bright side of life.

But was it that she was too scared to confront reality? Now she wasn't sure.

All she knew was that something was going wrong in her relationship, in parallel to something good and intriguing happening elsewhere and, try as she might, she felt powerless to stop either one.

Chapter 13

The following morning, Billy was just finishing a phone call with Mrs Lovejoy in apartment 15H when a bike messenger rolled up in front of the building, jumped from his bike, propped it up against the glass partition (much to Billy's chagrin) and shuffled into the lobby. He had his messenger bag strapped across his chest and took a bored look at his surroundings before making eye contact with the concierge.

Meeting his gaze, Billy politely put a finger up, indicating that he wouldn't be long.

'Absolutely, Mrs Lovejoy,' he said. 'I have made a note of it here. The agency is to send over a new housekeeper for you to interview this week and if she looks suspicious – oh, I'm sorry, yes, I'm writing it down now. Shifty-eyed. If she looks shifty-eyed I should not let her up.' Billy paused as he listened. 'I certainly understand. Yes, it's always difficult when you suspect someone is stealing from you. Right. Of course, it wasn't overly valuable. Just some plastic bags.

Right. You never can be too careful. But I wonder, Mrs Lovejoy, if she might have just been recycling them for you? Yes. OK, I realize you had a lot of them. And sure, she might not have realised that you were keeping them for a reason.'

Billy looked again at the bike messenger and flashed a grin. He covered the mouthpiece of the phone with his hand and said, 'Sorry, this woman can talk.'

The bike messenger shrugged.

So Billy continued on with his conversation. 'Not to worry, Mrs Lovejoy. I will keep a watch out. And you know I have your best interests at heart. Of course, of course.' Billy listened for another moment. 'All right then. I have to go now, I have someone here I need to help, so thank you. Cheerio!' And he hung up the phone without further ado, rubbing his ear.

'Mother of God, if I get that age and turn crazy, just put me out of my misery. The woman fired her housekeeper for "stealing plastic bags".' He rubbed his temple for a moment. 'Now what do you have for me, lad? I'm assuming I need to sign for something.'

'Just this envelope. It's for Beth Harper.' The messenger looked at his clipboard. 'In 28F.' Billy took the clipboard from the messenger and hastily signed his name. He handed the clipboard back to him as the messenger passed him a manila envelope.

'Thank you. I'll be sure to give it to her when she comes home from work.'

The messenger snapped his gum and put his clip-board back in his bag. 'She's popular, huh? She works at Carlisle's, doesn't she?' he asked.

Billy raised his eyebrows and quickly looked the bike messenger up and down, suddenly on full alert. 'Why do you ask?'

'I delivered something to her there a few days ago. Has to be the same person. Cute little blonde, right?'

Billy raised an eyebrow. 'Why do you want to know?'

The bike messenger put his hands up in front of him to indicate he didn't mean any harm. 'Hey, buddy, no reason. Just curious, that's all. Just saying, she's popular. It's cool.' He began backing away, clearly wanting to get out of the lobby now that Billy had shown signs of overprotectiveness about one of his residents.

The last thing I need is someone thinking I'm stalking this chick. Don't shoot the messenger, bro. Besides, it seemed like she already has a stalker, with these weird deliveries, he thought ominously.

Just as he was about to push through the glass doors and reclaim his bike, Billy called out, 'Wait. Who do you work for?'

The messenger pointed to his partially obscured T-shirt. 'A to Z Messenger Service signs my pay cheques. But we have a bunch of contracts. Advertising, marketing and law firms, individuals, you get my drift. See ya, man.'

And with that, he was gone.

Billy watched him jump on his bike and speed off. The

messenger himself, the name of his company, even this envelope – all were completely ambiguous, vague.

Well, when Beth came back he'd pass it on as asked. After all, he sighed, he was just the concierge. He kept the lobby safe, he signed for deliveries, made sure his residents were taken care of – it wasn't his business to snoop. New Yorkers in general might be pretty paranoid, but Billy wasn't Homeland Security – he wasn't paid to do detective work.

Although, he guessed, he'd be a dab hand at that, too. Nope, this delivery had nothing whatsoever to do with him. He would make sure he passed it on to Beth and whatever happened after that, happened.

'Hello, Billy,' Beth greeted him warmly later that evening. 'How are you today? Staying warm in this cold, I hope?'

Billy smiled and walked out from behind his desk with an envelope in his hand. 'As warm as I can be, with those doors opening and closing all day. How are you doing yourself today, Beth? All OK with you? All good with Danny?'

She narrowed her eyes suspiciously and gave a tentative reply, wondering what Billy was getting at. 'Of course. All good. Why do you ask?'

Billy shook his head and smiled and Beth noticed that he was blushing again. 'Ah, no reason,' he continued. 'A messenger came earlier with this delivery for you. He was a bit sketchy, so I just wanted to make sure you were OK. That's all.' He handed the envelope to her delicately, but she could tell he was more interested than he was letting on.

As was Beth, when she realised that this was exactly what she'd been waiting for.

She took the envelope from him and without hesitation ripped it open, then put her hand in and extracted two items. A ticket and what looked to be a programme or leaflet of some sort.

'Oh, perfect!' she exclaimed delighted.

Billy bit his lip and raised his eyebrows expectantly. 'Something you were expecting, then?'

'Yes. Absolutely. A friend of a friend was sending this over for me. I didn't expect to get it so soon, though.'

'Very good. Right then, much ado about nothing. Sorry, had my radar up. That's all. Some of these bike messengers, you know how they can be; some of them act weird.'

Beth laughed and playfully patted the concierge's arm. 'Ah, Billy, I think you might be getting paranoid like the natives. But thank you for looking out for me all the same. I appreciate it.'

She put the ticket to the Manhattan Sailing Exhibition and the accompanying programme – which described the boats that would be on display, and provided owner biographies and the like – into her bag and headed in the direction of the elevators. 'See you later,' she called over her shoulder as she started typing out a text to Jodi. She wanted to let her friend know that she'd got the ticket and to thank her for obviously communicating the need to Trevor so quickly.

She hadn't mentioned anything that day at work about talking to him, so Beth just assumed she'd pick up her ticket on the day.

Hey, thanks. A messenger dropped the ticket off for the exhibition earlier. I appreciate it. Tell Trevor thanks from me.

She punched the button for the elevator and waited. A second later her phone buzzed in her hand, signalling an incoming text.

???? No idea what you are talking about, was Jodi's reply.

With a furrowed brow, Beth wrote, *The ticket? To the boat show? Arrived earlier by messenger. Assuming it's from your friend Trevor.*

Seconds later, another text.

I haven't spoken to him yet about it. If you got a ticket, it's not from him . . .

As Beth read Jodi's words, a fresh shiver of excitement ran up her spine. She pulled the ticket and the accompanying programme out of her bag and looked at them again. The ticket was straightforward enough – just a simple pass to grant her entry. But then there was the programme.

Maybe this was another part of the clue? Maybe she had to use the programme to figure out what she was supposed to see at the exhibition? Beth, thanks to Jodi, had been assuming there must be a boat named the *Angelina* – but maybe it wasn't that simple?

The elevator dinged in front of her, signalling its arrival, and the doors opened. But Beth ignored it. Instead, she returned to the front lobby. She had to talk to Billy again. With flushed cheeks, she approached his desk. 'Billy. The messenger who delivered this. He was a bike messenger, yes?'

Startled afresh, he looked around. 'Um . . . yes. Bike messenger. He worked for A to Z Messengers, he said. Why? Is something wrong after all? Do you want me to call his employer?'

Beth shook her head. 'No, no, it's OK, don't worry. I just need to know. Did he say anything else when he dropped that envelope off? Anything at all?'

Billy thought for a moment. 'Yes, he said that his company did work for all sorts of companies and private individuals – and he knew where you worked too. At Carlisle's. I thought that was a bit suspect at the time. Is he pestering you, Beth? Is he a stalker? Do you want me to call the cops?'

Beth placed a placating hand on Billy's arm, touched by his concern. 'No really, it's OK, honestly. But he definitely mentioned I was the same person he'd made a delivery to the other day?'

'Yes, he said, and I quote. "She's a cute little blonde, right?" Beth, are you sure you don't want to me to deal with this?'

'No, seriously, it's absolutely fine.'

After she'd reassured Billy again that all really was OK and her honour didn't need defending, Beth made her way back to the elevators, fresh excitement bubbling in her stomach.

It was the same delivery guy. The same one who'd delivered the first clue before. Which meant that the whole package – ticket and programme – had to form part of the latest clue.

Beth smiled happily. The treasure hunt was now well and truly on.

Chapter 14

Saturday afternoon was a day of sunshine and an obscenely cold front. A biting wind blew through the air, which made the temperature feel way below zero. Despite the prospect of a chilly few hours around the waterfront, Beth was in a cab on her way to the exhibition, determined to stay on the hunt.

She felt guilty about the little white lie she'd told Danny, who'd planned to visit his parents in Queens today. While Beth got on brilliantly with Mae and Rick, and usually enjoyed family visits to the Bishop household, once she'd found out about the exhibition she had cried off going along with Danny by explaining that Jodi really wanted her to meet her new man.

Having agreed to meet Jodi and Trevor at the exhibition itself, she reached the marina and immediately spied Jodi, dressed in a beautiful faux mink coat and Prada boots, and holding the hand of a forty-something man whom Beth assumed to be Trevor.

And as she got closer, Beth realised that she did, in fact, recognize him from the night when Jodi had met him at happy hour a couple of weeks back. He had just a touch of grey around his temples and Beth knew immediately that he was a sun lover – he had the smallest of crow's-feet around his eyes – but standing at least six foot one, with a nice tan and classic features, he was quite handsome. Beth hoped that he was a gentleman also. Jodi needed a good man in her life.

'There you are!' Jodi called. 'I was wondering if you had decided not to come after all.'

Beth looked at her watch. 'Ah, come on, I'm not even five minutes late.' She gave her friend a broad grin and then turned her attention to Trevor. 'Hello, I'm Beth Harper. I know we met before – briefly.' She threw a sideways glance at her friend. 'But here's to a more formal introduction.'

She extended her hand and Trevor reached out to shake it. 'Of course. Nice to meet you too, Beth, for real this time. I'm Trevor Jeffers.' He took back his hand and placed it around Jodi's waist. Beth smiled, instantly liking this. 'So,' he continued, 'I hear that our mission is two-fold today. To find me a sailboat to buy, and help you out with what Jodi described as some kind of treasure hunt? Forgive me, but I didn't quite follow all the details ...'

Beth grinned at her friend, more broadly this time, knowing that Jodi wasn't trying to hide the reason that she was there and wasn't embarrassed by her madcap antics either. No matter the hard persona that Jodi sometimes wore, Beth knew that she was deep down a real softie who cared about her friends and loved them dearly.

'Well, it all sounds a bit mad but I'll fill you in as best I can,' Beth said, chatting away about the hunt and the clues as the trio started walking towards the marina where numerous sleek boats waited in the water. 'The so-far-unnamed mastermind behind this adventure provided me with a bit of a roadmap, I suppose, via this programme. And I have been doing a bit of studying on my own in the meantime, deciding which boats to focus on. There are three that are associated with the name "Angelina", so I figure that's as good a place as any to start.' Beth opened up the brochure and began to read aloud the boats she'd selected as good possibilities the evening before, circling them in pen. '*Angelina's Prize, Angelina Asked for It,* and this one is a bit of a stretch, *Devilish Angel.* You two don't have to stay with me either, you know,' she added quickly. 'I know you have other things to do; and I don't mind checking this out on my own.'

But Jodi was already shaking her head. 'Nope, not in your life, honey. I know you think that all of this is sunshine and butterflies, but there too many spots to hide a body around here for my liking. Consider me your shadow today.'

'But I thought you were so sure that Danny planned this?' Beth replied coyly. 'You don't think my own boyfriend would send me to sleep with the fishes, do you?'

Jodi raised an eyebrow. 'I didn't say *I* thought Danny was behind this. You did. Do you still stand by that?'

Swallowing hard, Beth rolled her eyes, trying to be non-chalant. She decided to just change the subject. 'Fine. So you're coming with me. As long as Trevor is OK with that, too? After all, he's the one here to do some business, and I'm playing gooseberry to your date.'

Beth gave a look over Jodi's shoulder to where Trevor was standing, wondering if he happened to share her friend's sentiment, but all she saw was a smile and a shrug.

'Don't look at me,' he said. 'I have nothing but time today. If Jodi says that's the way it's going to be, that's the way it's going to be.' Beth had to appreciate his chivalrous and gentlemanly behaviour and she was liking him more and more. 'Besides, as I've been to this event before, maybe I can play navigator and help you find the boats you want.'

Encouraged by this and grateful that she had someone to bounce ideas off this time, Beth followed Trevor and Jodi onto the gang planks, allowing him to lead the way to the first boat on her list of possibilities, *Angelina's Prize*, a fifty-one-foot sailing boat.

As they approached the boat, Trevor became animated, 'This is a *really* sharp boat – a *really* sharp boat,' he exclaimed. 'And I recognise this. It was designed by Germán Frers and is an Idylle 15.5. This is a complete cruiser too, and will hold one hundred and thirty-two gallons of fuel.' His eyes lit up like a window shopper outside Saks. 'And just look at those solar panels. Get a load of that.'

Beth glanced at Jodi, wondering what she thought of

her boyfriend's excitement towards boats, but her friend wasn't giving anything away. She merely looked at Trevor with happiness all over her face and Beth had to smile. Jodi was smitten.

'Well ... brilliant,' Beth said, having no idea what Trevor was talking about. 'Am I allowed to go on board?'

'Oh, yeah. All of these are open to explore today. Come on, let's go below deck,' he said as he helped the two women aboard.

Having quickly sought out the owner of the boat, Trevor launched into picking the man's brain over amp alternators, watt inverters and suchlike, all things that Beth and Jodi had no knowledge of or interest in. Instead, the pair looked for anything that might tie *Angelina's Prize* to the clue.

'So what do you think we are looking for?' Jodi asked, taking in the stark interior of the boat. While well appointed, there was very little to personalise the craft – and absolutely nothing to indicate this was the right boat.

Beth pursed her lips, feeling helpless. 'Honestly, I have no idea what I am supposed to be looking for – I just feel like I'll know it when I see it. Come on, this isn't it.'

As Beth climbed back up onto the boat's deck, she distinctly heard Jodi mutter the words, 'wild-goose chase' under her breath, but decided to ignore that.

Following a pointed look from Jodi, Trevor quickly finished his conversation with the boat's owner, and directed his charges to the next boat on the list, *Angelina Asked for It*. Beth was impressed at his willingness to help, but it was plain that he was in his element around boats, to say nothing of his adoration of her friend. It was wonderful to see.

But they had little luck with this boat either. Despite learning from the owner that the watercraft was a Gulfstar Sailmaster with a 'centre cockpit and the ability to sleep ten people' – as well as the reason behind the naming of the boat (apparently Angelina, a debutante heiress and the owner's ex-wife did indeed 'ask for it' after she decided to have an affair with the pool boy and did not insist on an iron-clad pre-nup before walking down the aisle), Beth quickly decided that this definitely was not the boat that she was looking for. In fact, the living space of the craft was bedecked top to bottom in NASCAR memorabilia, and she doubted that her secret admirer was trying to point her to the movie *Talladega Nights*.

As they made their way over to *Devilish Angel*, Beth had to admit that at this point she wasn't feeling hopeful about that one either, as the name had only a tentative connection to 'Angelina' in the clue. And the moment that they approached the area where the sailing boat had been listed as being berthed, Beth was sure. *Devilish Angel* had nothing to do with her quest. Indeed, the slip where they were supposed to find it was empty, the owner of the boat having apparently changed his mind about attending.

A stiff breeze hit Beth in the face and sprayed salt water against her cheek as she looked out towards the harbour, disappointed and trying to figure out her next move.

'So what now?' Jodi asked, putting a comforting hand on her friend's shoulder.

Beth shrugged. 'I don't know. I mean, I guessed that I was looking for a boat that was tied to the name Angelina. Like in *Romancing the Stone*. And I re-watched the movie ending – the bit with the boat – at least three times to commit the boat in question to memory and see if there's anything like it here today, but nothing.' She looked at Jodi, and then at Trevor. 'I'm just not sure where to go from here. I honestly don't know what I'm supposed to be looking for.'

The trio started walking back to the boardwalk of the marina, passing boat after boat. Beth kept her eyes to the ground, trying to work over everything in her head and figure out the riddle that her secret admirer (if that's who it was) was trying to tell her. There had to be a connection here at today's exhibition. There just had to be. After all, the messenger had delivered this part of the clue right to her door, even though Beth had already figured out how to access the expo on her own.

She just *had* to be onto something. But what?

'Ha,' said Trevor from behind while she and Jodi walked ahead of him. 'That's a great name.' Both women looked up to where he was pointing at the exact same time and focused in on the words inscribed on the side of a sailing boat. No, this was more than just a sailing boat – this was a yacht. It had three sails, easily spanned over sixty feet and was so blindingly white it compared to the colour of fresh alpine snow.

The Seven Year Itch.

Beth's spine tingled as she suddenly had a memory of a conversation she and Ryan had had not long after they first met. It was when he'd asked her out, and she told him that she had a boyfriend, and had been with Danny for seven years.

And what had he said? He had asked her, with that dimply lopsided smile, if she thought the seven-year itch was real. So all this had to be Ryan ...

'That's related to a famous movie, isn't it?' Trevor asked.

Beth felt a spark of excitement as she neared the vessel, sure that she was on to something, but she quickly felt her spirits crash when Jodi asked a pertinent question.

'But what does that have to do with Angelina and *Romancing the Stone*?' her friend asked. 'Just because the boat is named after another movie doesn't mean that it has anything to do with what Beth is looking for. I think that's a stretch, Einstein.'

Beth's face fell. Jodi was right. If she tried hard enough she could find at least half a dozen boat names here that she could tie to movies, none of which unfortunately helped her solve this riddle.

The trio continued to stare at *The Seven Year Itch*; Beth and Jodi trying to figure out what to do next – and Trevor gawping at the vessel with envy and adoration. So focused were they that they didn't notice when an exotic dark-haired woman crossed the deck of the boat and paused to throw them a greeting.

'Hello there!' she said with a distinct Asian accent and Beth looked up distractedly. The woman was petite in build, standing no more than five foot one, with long, thick dark hair extending to the middle of her back.

'Hello,' Trevor called out. 'We were just admiring your boat. She's a beauty!'

'Thank you. I appreciate that. She's a joy to sail too! Would you like to come aboard and take a look?' The woman smiled, showing her perfect teeth. 'I'm Angelina Yussopov, but you can call me Lin.'

Chapter 15

Beth's eyes widened in surprise as she heard the woman's words. 'What did you say your name was?' she asked.

The beautiful Asian woman smiled, as if she knew what Beth was thinking. 'Angelina, but I go by Lin for short. Do you want to come on board the boat? Take a look around? I'm quite proud of her, but then I'm probably somewhat biased.'

Trevor was already heading up the small plank that connected the boat with the dock, eager to get on board.

Beth, though, remained standing in bewildered surprise. This *had* to be it. Reflecting back, she realised that, since learning about the boat exhibition, she had been so intent on considering the names of the boats in the programme, she had never once thought to look at the owners' names – nor did she consider that another movie reference would indeed be tied into the completion of this clue.

The Seven Year Itch. The film made famous by Marilyn

171

Monroe's white silk dress and that iconic picture of her working her hardest to sexily and flirtatiously hold it down after being caught in the draught from the sidewalk subway vent.

But what it also must mean was that – much like the assistant at Tiffany's – this woman Angelina – Lin – was *in* on the treasure hunt.

Jodi edged Beth forward, breaking into her thinking – pondering – over who Lin was and how she was connected to this. Or, more to the point, how she might be connected to the instigator, whoever that was.

'Wow, she's really beautiful. Just gorgeous,' Trevor was gushing (about the boat, though the same could just as easily be said about the woman) as Beth and Jodi took a look around the deck.

'Thank you,' Lin replied. 'It was a gift. I grew up near the water and have always worked in some capacity near or *on* a boat. My husband gave this to me as a wedding present – we got married last year. We love to sail, travel ... the whole gamut, really. He's in New York on business at the moment, and I figured that I might just take advantage of this exhibition while we were in town. Always nice to meet fellow sailing enthusiasts, you know?'

'Absolutely,' replied Trevor. 'I'm thinking about buying a boat myself. This is exactly what I had in mind too. Maybe you could advise me.'

Lin nodded her approval and turned to Beth and Jodi. 'Of course. But forgive me; I didn't catch your names?'

Beth wondered if Lin really didn't know who she was, especially if she was involved in the pursuit somehow, but she played along with the pleasantries just the same.

After introductions had been made, Lin invited Beth and Jodi to go below, remaining on the top deck with Trevor to talk boats.

Convinced that another clue was located somewhere on this vessel, and feeling that there was deeper meaning to Lin's encouragement to 'go take a look around downstairs', the pair went to see what they would find. Beth was eager to learn who Lin was and why she was party to the treasure hunt – as well as make more progress on her search.

As they did she confessed her thoughts to her friend. 'I have no idea what to look for next. Tiffany's ... expensive boats ... it's not as if I hang around in this type of set, you know.'

'And what set is that?'

Beth rolled her eyes playfully. 'The glam multi-millionaire jet set, of course. Can you imagine something like this being given to you as a wedding present?'

Jodi snorted. 'No, I can't. "He who must not be named" thought he himself was wedding present enough. Jerk.'

Looking around, Beth let Jodi bluster away about her errant ex-husband for a moment. When they reached the cabin in the lower deck, they found themselves in a well-appointed living area, furnished with butter-soft leather club chairs and rich hardwood. Beth felt as if she had just entered an exclusive country club. A large plasma TV adorned one wall and what looked like a Picasso (and could very well be one) hung on another. Beth briefly reflected on the idea of hanging priceless works of art on something that could at some point end up underwater but figured that was Lin and her insurance company's problem.

One thing was for sure, this was how the one per cent lived. Did Ryan come from a well-off background, she wondered? He'd certainly never given that impression in conversations. But these circumstances, and the world in which the clues were set thus far, well and truly killed off any suspicions that Danny might have been responsible. Like Beth, he came from a decidedly working-class background, a million miles from this salubrious lifestyle.

No, Beth realised yet again with a heavy heart, this definitely wasn't Danny's scene. The big question was, could it be Ryan's?

'Would you take a look at this place? Gorgeous. I could totally live here,' Jodi enthused. 'Maybe I can if Trevor buys something like it. Yes, I could get used to this.' She chortled. 'If only that schlep Frank could see me now. Trevor's the whole package, if you get my drift.'

Beth smiled, pleased at her friend's happiness, but in truth her mind was on other things – namely, another clue or some indicator of what was to come next in the hunt.

She didn't have to search long. As she walked from the living area into a zone that housed a well-stocked bar, she suddenly spied a shoe box-sized package on the counter.

It was a plain beige box, wrapped with a white silk scarf, on top of which was a gift card bearing her name. It read simply '*Beth*' in an elegant script.

Her heart immediately hopped into her mouth. 'Jodi,' she called out excitedly. 'You have to come here. Look at this.'

Hurrying into the room, Jodi found her holding the box. 'What's that? Where'd you get it?'

'It was right here. And it has my name on it.'

Jodi shook her head, trying to take it all in. 'But how?' And then the realisation finally dawned. 'So Lin – Angelina – she is involved in this thing too?'

Beth shook her head as if it was full of cobwebs. She looked down at the box. 'Do you suppose I should open it?'

'Well, it has your name on it; I reckon that gives you licence enough. Go on. Open it.'

Without further ado, Beth pulled on the end of the white silk scarf, releasing it from its bow. She set the scarf on the counter and opened the nondescript box. It was full of tissue paper, which she quickly extracted and tossed to the ground, looking deeper to find out what the package contained.

And then with the tissue paper gone, the box revealed its contents. A single Yankees baseball cap. Beth stared at the contents of the box feeling perplexed again.

'Yankees?' she muttered. 'But I told him I was a Mets fan …' She was thinking of that first time she and Ryan went to lunch, when they had joked about his wearing a

175

Red Sox hat in a Yankees bar during a game. She had said that she wouldn't have been offended since she was a Mets fan.

'What was that?' Jodi asked sharply, looking over Beth's shoulder. '*Who* did you tell you were a Mets fan?'

Beth snapped from her reverie and quickly covered her tracks. 'Danny, of course. I was just saying he knows I'm a Mets fan so what's he playing at?'

Jodi picked the hat up out of the box and turned it upside down, as if looking to see if there was anything hidden inside, anything more to this mystery. 'So this is another clue then? It has to be.'

Beth took the hat from Jodi and studied it too. 'I suppose so,' she said, confused. 'But I'm really not sure what *this* has to do with anything.' It seemed once again like another obscure clue. Much like the boat itself. What was she supposed to figure out from this? There was no immediate movie reference here that she could make out. So where, if anywhere, was she supposed to go next?

Quickly she picked up the tissue paper from the ground, cleaning up her mess, and put the hat back in the box. She picked up the white silk scarf, holding it up so it could fall lengthwise and she could fold it. It was a really nice scarf. Hermès, she noted, checking the label. Very fancy. And, once again, expensive too.

But then just as the fabric unravelled, Beth discovered something else. The scarf was obviously a part of the next clue too: there was a message carefully embroidered on the fine material. 'Jodi, look, there's something written on the scarf,' she pointed out excitedly. She read the words out loud. '*It sort of cools the ankles, doesn't it?*'

At this, the two women stood in silence and then turned to look at one another, baffled.

'Don't even ask,' Jodi said. 'I have no idea.'

Beth exhaled heavily. 'Me neither. But I do have an idea of someone who might.'

Emerging back on the deck, Beth and Jodi had no problem finding Lin and Trevor. They were comfortably seated in the shade, sipping prosecco.

'Hello, ladies,' Lin smiled coyly. 'Did you enjoy looking around? Would you like to join us for a drink?'

But Beth ignored Lin's pleasantries. 'I really need to know who left this here for me. Please.'

Lin smiled like the Cheshire Cat and took another sip of her drink. 'Ah, so you found it then.'

'Yes. I found it. But I don't understand. This silk scarf, it has a message on it. See?' Beth held the scarf up to her audience. 'And then this hat.' She opened up the box and displayed the Yankees cap. 'But I don't know ... I don't understand the connection.' She looked imploringly at their host. 'Who knew I'd be here? Why are you involved? Who's behind this?'

Trevor's brow furrowed, but Lin simply continued looking placid. 'I'm sorry, Beth, but I can't provide you with any other information. I was simply asked to provide the location and was told that I would know you when I saw you – and indeed I did – that wasn't difficult at all, considering. But I don't have any other information for you.'

With a deep sigh, Beth sat down and put the box and the scarf on the seat next to her. She supposed she should have expected as much; the assistant at Tiffany's had given her the same spiel. These women, while playing a part in the whole ... charade ... seemed to know just as much (or indeed little) about the grand scheme as Beth did.

She decided to accept Lin's offer of a flute of prosecco. God knew, she needed a drink. As the bubbles hit her tongue, she gave a bittersweet smile – the beverage always reminded her of her and Danny's time in Venice, sipping prosecco in the back of the water taxi. Back when they were still everything to each other.

And then Trevor spoke, lifting her out of her melancholy. 'Wait. Wasn't Marilyn Monroe married to Joe DiMaggio at one point?'

Jodi took a sip of her own drink and wrinkled her nose. 'Briefly. Their marriage was doomed from the start. Barely lasted nine months.'

Beth looked at her friend. 'How do you know that?'

She smiled wickedly. 'I happen to be an expert in divorce, OK? But what does that have to do with anything?' she asked, turning to Trevor.

'Well,' her partner replied thoughtfully, 'I was just thinking. The Yankees hat ... the name of this boat – *The Seven Year Itch*. And heck, even that scarf, wasn't it in that movie that Marilyn wore that sexy white dress?'

178

Beth's eyes grew wide. Was Trevor on to something? Was this indeed yet another movie-related clue?

'Think about it. Marilyn, Joe DiMaggio, that movie, those words written on the scarf – it has to connect to something with that movie *The Seven Year Itch.*'

Jodi smiled broadly. 'Such a smart guy,' she cooed, giving him a proud kiss on the cheek.

But Beth was already working it over in her head. The scarf was indeed similar to the material of Marilyn's dress. And the boat – that was the name of the movie in question. Then the Yankees hat, perhaps a reference to Marilyn's husband, Joe DiMaggio. It all meant something. It was supposed to point her somewhere, she knew that now.

But where?

Then there was that quote, *It sort of cools the ankles, doesn't it?* That was the part of the clue that still needed to be solved.

Maybe it was a quote from the movie? It was certainly the best place to start, she decided.

While she'd seen *The Seven Year Itch,* it had many been years ago and nothing she'd found today, apart from the scarf bearing a resemblance to Marilyn's dress, stood out for her in any way.

She needed to familiarise herself with the film, figure out what the clues meant as a whole and where she was supposed to go next.

She also needed to figure out how Lin might be connected

to Ryan Buchanan, or the Tiffany's assistant, or any of these people that had so far been finagled into helping with all this. For reasons Beth had yet to determine.

But first things first.

'Sorry, but I need to go,' she said, standing up. 'I have a movie to watch.'

Chapter 16

When Beth returned to the apartment late on Saturday afternoon she found Danny once again absent. He was obviously still in Queens. She picked up her phone with the intention of texting him or calling him to find out when he'd be back, but then decided against it.

It was because, she supposed, the action felt duplicitous. She had already told him that little white lie about what she'd been doing that afternoon, and while it wasn't as if she had been out having an affair, she was almost certain now that these clues, this quest ... was connected to Ryan. And so continuing with the hunt felt wrong in itself.

It had to be him, didn't it? Notwithstanding that there were enough hints amongst the clues themselves, who else would realistically go to such trouble for her? And, quite possibly as he'd intended, as she worked to decipher every clue of this treasure hunt, Beth's feelings for her work colleague continued to grow – while her time spent with Danny seemed to diminish.

At this point, Beth was so confused she couldn't think straight.

Picking up Brinkley from the floor, she nuzzled the little dog and settled onto the couch. She reached for the remote control, and summoned Netflix on the TV. 'We're going to watch a movie, boy,' she cooed. 'And maybe, with a little luck, I'll figure out this clue – and what I'm supposed to do next.'

She scrolled through the options menu and then entered in the movie title she was looking for. *The Seven Year Itch.* 'OK, settle in, this is an oldie but a goodie. Haven't watched it for a very long time, but by all accounts it's an absolute classic.'

Brinkley listened to his mistress for a moment before determining he wasn't interested. He yawned and closed his eyes, comfortable and content on Beth's lap. 'Well,' she said, scratching the little dog's head, 'all right, sleep all you want, but you're the one missing out.'

No sooner had the opening credits begun than the front door of the apartment opened and in came Danny. Beth turned to look at him and was immediately struck by his appearance. He looked very dishevelled, and he almost paled when he saw her, as if he hadn't been expecting she'd be back yet.

'Oh, hey ... I didn't realise you would be home,' he said, running a hand through his hair. 'I figured you'd still be out with Jodi.'

Beth paused the movie. 'I just got home a little while ago. I hope that's OK?' she said with a slight barb in her tone, given that he was hardly greeting her unexpected appearance with open arms. 'How was Queens?'

Danny gave a noncommittal shrug. 'Oh, same as usual,' he said. And while he was trying to play nonchalant, Beth could feel nervous tension radiating off him. *Had* he been in Queens? Thinking about it now, she recalled that she'd been so intent on getting out of a potential visit herself that Danny hadn't actually asked her to come along and didn't seem too bothered when she'd cried off.

So had he really been visiting his parents, or was he covering up something? If so, what?

Beth's heart plummeted at what was lately becoming an all-too-familiar scenario. And why couldn't he meet her eyes?

Mustering up some of Jodi's backbone, she decided to come right out and say something.

'Danny, are you OK?' she asked gently. 'You look ... out of sorts. What's going on?'

But he simply waved a hand, brushing away her concern. 'Oh, nothing, I'm fine, just a bit tired. You know how Mom can talk. And I ate so much at lunch my, er, stomach hurts a bit. I'm ... going to grab a shower.'

And with that he was gone, leaving Beth suspicious once again as to why he was so jumpy and evasive. No wonder they couldn't talk seriously about the problems in their relationship when he was avoiding her all the time.

Indeed, he had looked totally unprepared for her to be home too. It was as if he had been intent on being alone when he opened the door and her presence had really thrown him. He looked shocked – and guilty too, she realised despondently. Where had he been?

In Queens ... she didn't think so. But what was she supposed to do, phone his mother to check? Mae Bishop was no fool and would no doubt be full of questions if she realised something was amiss, not to mention that Danny would surely find out she was checking up on him. And the fact remained that Beth wasn't sure if she *did* want to catch Danny out in a lie.

Because if she did, it raised a whole lot of other issues she didn't think she was ready to face.

Sighing deeply, yet unsure what was the best thing to do, Beth decided to retreat into what had always been one of her greatest comforts. She pressed play on the remote control, hoping to lose herself and her thoughts in the movie.

Though she was further interrupted when Danny returned a few minutes later, hair damp from his shower and smelling like soap. Some of his colour had returned and he looked a little more relaxed. It was as if he had needed the shower to regain his composure.

'What are you watching?' he asked, sounding much more like himself.

Beth paused the film again, turned to him and considered the sudden change in his demeanour. His behaviour these days seemed as mercurial as the weather. Where he had been tense and anxious fifteen minutes ago – and had looked almost disappointed that Beth was at home – now he appeared calm and at ease.

'Feeling better?' she asked.

Danny plopped down on the couch next to her. The movement woke up Brinkley, who opened sleepy eyes to spy the other member of his pack. Bidding him welcome, the dog left Beth's lap and climbed into Danny's.

'Hey, buddy,' he said, affectionately stroking the spaniel's head. 'Yeah, a bit. Just this cold and the heat on the train and whatnot. I just needed to freshen up. How did the thing with Jodi go? Was her boyfriend nice? Brave dude,' he added, shaking his head, though he was smiling.

'Danny!' Beth chided, but it felt good to be having a relatively normal conversation. 'He was nice, actually. And he obviously adores her.'

He chuckled. 'Speaking of adoration ... I was talking to your Scottish buddy on the way in. He mentioned he was a bit worried about you, and asked if everything was OK.'

Beth looked at him, surprised. 'Billy? What do you mean?'

'What? You haven't noticed the googly eyes he's always making at you?'

She was genuinely shocked at this. Billy the concierge?

'No way. Of course not. And Billy's not like that. He just looks out for all of us residents, that's all. Some messenger guy made a comment the other day, and I suppose he just wanted to check that everything was above board.'

But then she remembered how flustered Billy had been acting around her lately. And she wondered where all of this was coming from, and more pertinently whether there might be anything to it – especially given what was happening now.

Who's to say a 'messenger' had delivered anything at all? Now Beth was really confused. If what Danny was suggesting was true, and Billy did have a bit of a crush on her . . .

The package he was wrapping the other day, could it possibly have been the same one she'd found on the yacht earlier?

She was still trying to make sense of this strange and completely unexpected piece of news when Danny said, 'So I'm assuming this is a Marilyn kind of afternoon. *The Seven Year Itch*, huh?' He turned to the screen and nodded towards the famous blonde bombshell. 'Are you trying to tell me something? Gonna run away to Scotland with your friend the concierge?'

'Stop it,' Beth joked, though she couldn't help but feel a swell of guilt balloon in her heart. He was obviously referencing their relationship. Seven years together – seven-year itch indeed. It was as if he knew something was up.

Was all this teasing about Billy his way of trying to raise the issue?

Thank goodness he didn't know anything about Ryan then. Not that there was anything to know, Beth corrected herself. Nothing had happened between her and Ryan, or indeed with Billy. Was Danny trying to turn the tables on her? Or was he simply hoping to change the subject? Now more than ever she wondered what was going on with their relationship.

She turned and looked straight into his eyes for the first time in what seemed like weeks. 'Danny, seriously, are you OK?' she asked softly, her tone serious. 'This conversation feels ... strange. What's going on with you lately?'

Danny cast his gaze directly on Brinkley, avoiding Beth's eyes. 'What? Nothing is going on with me. Everything is fine.' He swallowed hard, and this wasn't lost on her. However, she felt that if she pressed him on the subject, it was possible they may in fact end up having a 'big talk'. That would be too much to face when she was having such conflicting thoughts about their relationship, and her growing feelings for Ryan. Never mind the mystery of the treasure hunt.

She turned her attention toward the screen and pressed play. 'I suppose it is a Marilyn sort of day, and no, I'm not trying to tell you anything,' she laughed nervously, finally answering his question.

'Do you mind if I watch it with you?' he asked, and Beth felt immediately sad that he was asking her for permission.

When did that start happening? When did they start tip-toeing around each other? She turned to him and gave him a small smile, wondering if Danny too felt the strangeness hanging in the air between them. And she considered the distance between them on the couch. She was at one end, he was at the other. There was a big gaping divide between them.

Again, when did that happen?

'Of course you're welcome to watch it with me. That would be nice,' she said, meaning every word. Still concerned about the distance (metaphorical or otherwise) between them on the couch, and looking for a way to close it without being awkward, she jumped up. 'I think I'm going to have some wine. Would you like a glass?'

He nodded. 'Sure. That would be good.'

She made her way to the kitchen and selected a cabernet from their wine rack. Opening the bottle and pouring two generous glasses, she came back, handed Danny his glass and curled up next to him, her thoughts in a muddle.

While she felt happy that she had been able to casually close that space – at least the physical one – she still wasn't sure what to do about the non-tangible void that existed in their relationship.

They settled into watching the movie and Beth felt somewhat comforted when Danny began playing with an errant lock of her hair. They hadn't relaxed together like this, in a physical sense, in a long time.

She tried her hardest to push away the thought that by watching the movie with Danny she was inadvertently making him party to this treasure hunt of hers – an adventure likely started by another man. But who? Ryan? Billy, even? Beth felt a bit taken aback, not to mention uncomfortable, at having possibly *two* other men competing for her affections.

Like Bridie always said, 'feast or famine'...

'Did you know that Marilyn Monroe was quite well read?' Danny commented idly. 'She actually took literature classes at UCLA. People always assumed that she was just this vapid sex symbol. I'm sure that drove her crazy.'

Beth nodded as she tried to tune back in to the dialogue of the movie. 'I did know that. It must have been hard. I mean, she was beautiful and sexy and adored by men and women alike, but misunderstood too. You can't help but feel bad for her, especially since it ultimately led to her dying so young.'

'Yes, and she was unlucky in love, to boot,' he said.

Beth thought about the Yankees hat, and the information about Marilyn's marriage to DiMaggio that Trevor had provided earlier. 'Did you know her marriage to Joe DiMaggio only lasted nine months?'

'I did know that. He apparently had a bad temper,' Danny replied. 'And he was incredibly jealous too. Not the best combo if you are married to a world-renowned sex symbol, I'd imagine.'

Beth sat up straighter and looked at him. 'Since when do you know so much about Marilyn Monroe?' she asked with a smile on her face, though it was no surprise. He had always been a fount of knowledge about this kind of stuff, and was a dab hand at pop quizzes, she thought fondly.

'Well, I'm with you, aren't I?' Danny chuckled. 'I'm obliged to know a thing or two about movie trivia.'

She laughed and settled back down next to him. There was something very comfortable about this at the moment. When she was like this – close to Danny, feeling normal – Beth could almost forget about the feelings that had lately been developing for Ryan.

'And did you know that DiMaggio and Marilyn divorced practically right after this movie was made?'

Beth's ears perked up. No, she hadn't known that. She hadn't even known that the couple had been married at the time of this movie. So perhaps things were starting to make sense ...

'Did they really?' she asked in an easy tone, wondering if this connected to the clue somehow, yet at the same time feeling guilty for allowing the hunt to intrude on the cosy intimacy they were now enjoying. She focused her eyes on the TV, waiting for Danny to respond, but he remained quiet. Apparently he too was focused on what was happening on the screen.

Marilyn was wearing the famous white dress – possibly the most recognisable dress in all of film history. As 'The Girl' she meandered over to the subway grate, just as a subway train passed underneath, blowing her dress up around her thighs.

'Do you feel the breeze from the subway? Isn't it delicious?' she asked Richard Sherman, played by Tom Ewell.

'It sort of cools the ankles, doesn't it?' he replied, appreciating the view.

Beth sucked her breath in and tensed. There it was – the words she had been waiting to hear, the very words that had been sewn in to the scarf addressed to her.

And it was right in this most famous scene from *The Seven Year Itch*. She turned to Danny.

'Why did DiMaggio and Marilyn divorce after this movie?' she asked again, hoping he would know the reason. It *had* to connect to this clue.

'It was because of that scene, actually. The studio filmed it in public and DiMaggio was there. The location had been leaked to the press, and paparazzi and fans showed up to watch. About five thousand of them. It made Joe quite mad having other men salivate over his wife, going nuts over her, catcalling at her. He was embarrassed and angry. And when it was over, they went back to their hotel and got into a huge fight. She flew back to California shortly thereafter and filed for divorce. This movie scene essentially marked the end of their marriage.'

Beth listened intently to Danny's words. Of course, everything he said made sense, and she now knew without a doubt that the clue connected to this scene. But she had another question to ask. A question that she guessed would make all the difference.

'Danny, you said that she flew back to California, and that's where she filed for divorce. Where was she flying from? Where was that scene filmed?'

Beth waited with baited breath for the answer, while doing her utmost to try to overlook the idea that Danny was helping her solve a riddle someone else had likely set for her.

And when she heard his reply, Beth knew without a doubt exactly where she was supposed to go next.

'Right here in New York,' he confirmed. 'At the corner of Lexington and 52nd.'

Chapter 17

'Um, miss? I'm looking for these in a size eight, do you mind helping me?'

Beth jumped to attention, only barely registering that a customer was speaking to her. This was not good; she was becoming way too distracted lately and needed to get herself together. 'Of course,' she said, with as much cheer as she could muster. 'I'll get those for you straight away.'

As her customer tried on the size eight Ferragamos, Beth discreetly checked her watch.

It was still a while till lunchtime and the hours seemed to be really dragging by today – she was *dying* to get to the corner of Lexington and 52nd Street. The suspense as to what would happen next in the search (not to mention who on earth was behind it) was teetering on the brink of unbearable.

She had been in a daze all morning really, completely consumed with this next piece of the puzzle as well as

Danny's surprising revelation about Billy. When leaving for work, she'd been relieved that the concierge was on the phone when she passed by, as she guessed she'd be too embarrassed to talk to him.

He'd smiled his usual greeting, and she couldn't see much in his behaviour that suggested that he was being anything other than friendly. She guessed (and very much hoped) that Danny was mistaken because while Billy was lovely, she certainly had no interest in the man, and she couldn't see him going to so much trouble with the treasure hunt.

And for what – just to get her attention?

And then there was the other piece of information she'd gleaned from Danny: the location where Marilyn had made her husband, Joe DiMaggio, green with envy while on set filming *The Seven Year Itch*.

Yesterday, Beth had to delay checking out that location, as Danny would have surely questioned why exactly she had to check out the corner of Lexington and 52nd so late on a Saturday evening. So she had to wait until today – which, maddeningly, coincided with one of her alternate Sunday work shifts.

Still, she and Danny had ended up having such a rare evening in together that, despite the revelation, Beth didn't want to go anywhere.

After the movie he'd suggested they put up the Christmas tree, and with festive tunes in the background, and Brinkley prancing at their feet, it felt almost like old times as they took out the various themed Christmas ornaments they'd collected throughout the years. A bright pink flamingo they'd picked up one memorable weekend in Florida, the Hollywood sign Danny had brought back for her from a work event in LA, the roulette chip from a spontaneous fun-filled trip to Vegas, a glittering pair of ice skates from the Christmas markets in Bryant Park, where a couple of years back the two of them had gone ice-skating at the out-door rink. The little happy couple snow globe she'd bought for their very first Christmas in this apartment; each and every ornament served almost as a road-map of the good times they'd had together, and the festive ritual seemed to relax them both as a couple and almost reaffirm their relationship.

Though Beth noticed that Danny seemed almost ... melancholy when, as was their habit, they finally positioned the star atop the tree and stood back arm in arm to admire their work. As he was nowhere near as sentimental as she, she was surprised to see his eyes shine a little when after-wards he bent down and kissed her softly on the lips. Once again she got the sense that there was something going on with him these days, or at the very least that she was miss-ing something.

And it made her worry afresh.

Now, deciding to focus on her customer in an attempt to banish these worrisome thoughts, she was happy not only to sell one, but two pairs of Ferragamos to the client. Another nice commission, she congratulated herself.

A little while later, she spied Ryan making his way through the department, heading in her direction.

'I was hoping I could persuade you to go to lunch with me today. It seems like ages since we've talked,' he said.

Beth felt a blush creeping to her cheeks, somewhat against her will, but doubted that she would be able to pull this off – handle her treasure hunt errand, and go to lunch with Ryan, especially when she and Danny had begun to reconnect a little. It just seemed too conflicted, not to mention inappropriate.

'Well, I actually have to run a bit of an errand today, and I'm not sure if I'll have time for lunch.'

'Another errand? Or are you just trying to give me the brushoff? Beth, you're killing me here.' He put a dramatic hand over his heart. 'Tell me, what did I do to invite such rejection?'

She made a face, feeling caught between a rock and hard place. She was beginning to feel hungry at this point, and would have to eat lunch, of course. But she needed to get on with the treasure hunt. Now that Beth understood where she was supposed to be, she didn't want to put off finding the next clue any longer. She couldn't.

'It's just I really do have this thing I need to do. A long story,' she added, in case he was curious about what she was up to. 'But I am hungry too; all I had was a coffee for breakfast. What did you have in mind? Maybe I can fit in both?' she suggested.

'A multi-tasker, I see,' he teased. 'Nothing special today.

Just craving some deli food. I was thinking Toastie's, not sure if you know it?'

Beth searched the recesses of her mind for the location of such a deli, but couldn't place it. Though it was hard to throw a stone in Manhattan without pegging a deli at some point.

'I don't think so. But a sandwich would be perfect, as I can eat on the run. Where is it?'

'Oh, not far. This place has become one of my favourites since I got here. It's on 54th Street, between here and Third Avenue. Is that good for you?' He was directing *that* smile at Beth, and she couldn't decide if his words were laced in double entendre, or if his suggestion was mere coincidence.

'Actually, that's quite serendipitous,' she said, convinced now more than ever that he, and not Billy, was the mastermind in question. And it merely made this all the more confusing. 'The very area I was heading to, actually.'

Having knocked off at the same time for lunch, Beth and Ryan arrived at their destination in no time – Ryan springing for a cab further down Lexington Avenue so they wouldn't have to 'deal with the cold and the Christmas crowds'.

As the cab made its way to their destination, Beth watched all the festive hustle and bustle on the streets outside, and realised that it was now less than a week until Christmas. Time had seemed to fly by lately, and what with

Danny blowing hot and cold, as well as this treasure hunt keeping her so preoccupied, she felt she barely had time to breathe.

The cab pulled up to the corner of 54th and Lexington, and Beth easily spied the deli that Ryan was so eager to go to. As he helped her from the cab, he nodded in the direction of where they were headed.

'So where is your errand? Do you want to do it before or after lunch?'

Beth needed to think of a way to shake him – he might be playing dumb about where she was headed, but she really needed to do this part on her own.

'Just a couple of blocks away. Why don't you go ahead and order? I shouldn't be long.'

Ryan smiled mischievously. 'You got it. Just tell me what you want.'

To determine what this clue means, she thought. But she ordered a sandwich just the same.

After outlining her order for a pastrami on rye and an iced tea, she watched as Ryan headed in the direction of their lunch place, thankfully not giving Beth a backward glance.

Maybe he understood that she simply needed privacy for this, or perhaps he was merely pretending that he wasn't interested. She looked briefly over her shoulder, but yes, he was definitely gone and she was now on her own.

Approaching the corner of 52nd Street, she quickly figured out exactly where she was supposed to be headed. A small group of tourists were amassed around what had to be the world's most famous subway grate.

Beth moved closer to the group and realised that she'd happened across a tour in progress. She stood close to the back of the crowd, listening to what the tour guide had to say.

'So, the iconic scene from *The Seven Year Itch* was originally scheduled to be shot here, on location in Manhattan on 15 September 1954,' said the pretty young tour guide in charge of the group. 'It was slotted to begin at one a.m.; however, the location was leaked to the press and thousands of fans and media personalities showed up, just to get in on the action. The crowd was going absolutely wild – watching Marilyn's skirt blow higher and higher – much to the chagrin of Joe DiMaggio, Marilyn's then current and bitterly jealous husband. He was present in the crowd and it was absolutely driving him mad with envy that the crowd was so intent on ogling his wife's nether regions. Their marriage was already on the rocks, apparently, but this put it over the edge. And the couple divorced shortly thereafter.'

Beth tapped her foot, thinking hard. So the guide had confirmed Danny's story. But what now?

'Ultimately, the footage shot that day was all for naught, though. It was completely unusable as film editing techniques of the time didn't allow for the noise in the background to be removed. So the director, Billy Wilder, ended up having to shoot the entire sequence at

20th Century Fox Studios in LA at a later date. Just a bit of movie trivia. However, if you would like to take this opportunity to stand where Marilyn stood, please do. There isn't an active subway line under this grate; it was inactive even when they were filming here. Instead an effects man was tasked with standing under this grate, using a fan to blow up Marilyn's skirt from below. I only tell you this so any ladies wearing skirts today know there is nothing to fear,' joked the guide.

The crowd began to disperse, going about posing and taking a look down into the depths below the grate. Beth smiled at the touristy craziness of it all. After all, while Marilyn Monroe happened to stand on this particular section of earth over half a century ago, at the end of the day it was still just a subway grate.

Finally, when she had the opportunity and the way was clear, Beth approached the grate, wondering if she should be looking for something specific. She stood over the ironwork and looked down – nothing to see but darkness. She placed her feet where she imagined Marilyn might have and tried to summon the imagery of that scene – the heat, the sexiness, the excitement. She closed her eyes and could even have sworn that as she did, she felt a breeze sweep through the area – cooling her ankles. Her imagination, no doubt.

But when she opened her eyes again, she was no further ahead – she didn't know anything that she didn't know before.

What am I looking for? Beth thought, peering up at the

buildings around her. OK, so an iconic movie moment might have happened here, but this corner was just like any of the hundreds in Manhattan.

But just then her line of thought was interrupted.

'Excuse me, miss? I think you dropped something,' said a voice behind her.

Beth spun around to meet a stranger's face – a young man, probably no more than nineteen or twenty, wearing what appeared to be a hotel bellhop or concierge uniform. He held a jacket in one hand and Beth could just make out a name tag reading 'Steve' attached to one of the garment's lapels. However, what captured her attention was not his uniform, but what he held in his other hand.

A book.

'I think you dropped this,' the young man called Steve said again, holding the book out to her.

'No, I didn't. It's not mine,' Beth protested politely.

But Steve was already shaking his head. 'No, really, I saw it fall out of your bag. This is *definitely* yours,' he insisted, smiling.

She stared at the book for a beat longer and looked up to meet the guy's eyes. 'You said you saw it fall from my bag?' she asked dubiously.

He shook his head with conviction. 'Absolutely. Fell right out of your bag. Right onto the subway grate.'

Beth thought about what he was telling her. She knew without a doubt that the book didn't fall from out of her bag. For one thing, she didn't have a book in there, and for another, she guessed this must be all part of the treasure hunt.

She was suddenly on high alert. What with Lin on the boat and the assistant at Tiffany's, this wasn't the first time someone had known to expect her at a location. This bellhop might be part of the plan, too.

In any case, Beth felt at a loss for what to say. OK, so this book – wherever it came from – definitely didn't belong to her, but how was this a piece of the treasure hunt?

'But, I don't understand. I mean ...'

'You don't have to understand. You just have to have faith,' the bellhop said then, smiling.

Beth stared at him intently, her brain synapses firing all at once, as the nerve endings beneath her skin tingled with recognition. Where had she heard those words before?

'Faith in what?' she asked, feeling as if she was reading from a script – or at least working to ad lib a script that she hadn't yet been provided with.

Steve shrugged happily, as if she had taken his cue exactly the way she was meant to.

'Destiny,' he said simply.

Beth sucked in her breath. *Destiny?* She accepted the book without further hesitation and opened it quickly, without looking at the title. A five-dollar bill was tucked inside.

'Hold on, there's money in here. This must belong to you,' she said in confusion, but Steve was already shaking his head.

'No, that wouldn't be possible. After all, you dropped it, remember?'

'OK,' she said absently, feeling a little like she'd stepped into a scene from a movie herself, it was all so surreal. She picked up the banknote from where it sat, folded, between the book's pages.

On it there was writing in pink marker. It said, '23'.

Heart pounding, she looked excitedly up at Steve, wondering what would happen next. 'This is a clue, isn't it? It will point me where I need to go next. Is there anything else?'

Steve gave her a wink. 'I think it might, but that's all I can say ... Beth.'

She smiled broadly. 'You know my name. Of course you do. And you're Steve.'

'How did you know that?' he asked, frowning suddenly.

Beth pointed to his jacket. 'Your name tag. On your jacket. Where do you work?'

'Oh.' With some relief, Steve looked down at where she indicated. But suddenly he seemed eager to get away. 'Speaking of which, I need to get to work. Good luck.'

And then he was gone, walking off in the other direction from where she'd come.

Beth was left standing on the corner of Lexington and 52nd Street with a book, a five-dollar bill and a mysterious number: 23.

How to put it all together? Then she closed the book, caught sight of the title for the first time, and suddenly knew exactly what it all meant.

Melissa Hill

Love in the Time of Cholera.

Beth thought back to what she had said earlier, when Ryan had suggested they head to this area for lunch, and her eyes widened.

Serendipitous indeed.

Chapter 18

Ryan sat across the table from Beth and watched her happily dig into her pastrami sandwich. She was definitely enjoying it, and he loved a girl who could eat and who wasn't afraid of doing so in front of others. Whatever 'errand' she had been on had brightened her mood, and while she had seemed a bit tense on their way here in the taxi, she now looked as if she was walking on air. Ryan couldn't help but smile. He *really* liked this girl.

Looking up from her sandwich, Beth bit her lip and raised her eyebrows at her lunch mate. Immediately, she grabbed her napkin and covered her mouth as if she was afraid she had food on her face.

'What is it? Oh, no, am I being a slob?' she asked, her cheeks turning pink. Ryan couldn't help but be enchanted by her. She was so ladylike – even when she was self-conscious – and so easy to be around. Make no mistake, he really had a thing for her. Of course, that was complicated in itself. Primarily, because she already had a guy.

He let out a laugh and shook his head. 'No, nothing on your face. And really, you're the last woman I would ever call a slob.'

Beth put her napkin down and made a face. 'Then what are you grinning at?' she asked.

'You,' he answered simply. Then his smile faded and his tone became more conversational and less adoring. He didn't want to scare her off, after all. 'So you took care of your errand then? What did you have to do?'

But she shook her head and waved a hand at his question. 'Oh, nothing. Just something I had to figure out.'

'Sounds intriguing,' he chuckled, eyes twinkling. 'What did you have to figure out? Despite what you think, I'm not just a pretty face, you know. Maybe I could help?'

Her face was a picture. 'Well, actually it's kind of private. Maybe I'll be able to tell you about it sometime ...' she added. Then she returned to tucking into her sandwich and took a polite bite, chewing thoughtfully for a moment or two. 'Can I ask you a question?'

He peered across the table, now sensing a definite change in her tone – the playfulness was gone, and he really hoped she wasn't going to try to warn him off again. He was already too heavily invested for that. 'Of course. Anything.'

Beth paused for a moment, as if she was trying to figure out how to say whatever it was that she wanted to articulate. She opened her mouth to speak once, and then shut it again, as if reconsidering. He could tell an internal struggle was going on and he waited, wondering exactly what she'd say. Deep down he couldn't help but hope that it was some revelation that she had left her boyfriend – Danny, his name was – and that perhaps she needed somewhere to crash that night? Of course, she would be more than welcome at his place ...

But that's not what Beth said.

'So, do you believe in destiny?' she asked.

OK, tricky one, he thought. This didn't seem to be directly involving her guy or their relationship, but he supposed there was a chance that it could.

He smiled confidently. 'Of course I do. Why do you ask?' While he thought he might know what was going on in Beth's head, he would rather let her do the talking – there was much to be learned.

'Well, I was watching this movie last night and it's just – that's just a word that popped into my head,' she said, revealing nothing more. 'It's a powerful idea, don't you think?'

'It is. Powerful, that is,' Ryan agreed, intrigued. 'So has destiny knocked on your door lately?' He couldn't help but flirt – with Beth it was so much fun.

For her part, though, she had been on her best behaviour. And he wouldn't expect anything different from a woman like her. She was loyal to the core – after all, she had been with her guy for seven years. However, Ryan couldn't help but think that maybe chinks were appearing in her armour recently and he was hoping for a seven-year itch indeed. There was something going on in her life, that was for sure – especially at home – and Ryan was determined to wait in the wings. When the time was right she would understand who really got her; who would sweep her off her feet. Not that Danny guy, who was obviously taking her for granted.

And with every day that passed, he knew he was getting closer. The pieces of the puzzle would eventually fall into place and Beth would understand that she had moved on from her relationship – out-grown it, even – and it would be time to start something new.

Preferably with him.

At least, that's how Ryan saw things working out. But there was still the fact that he didn't know all that much about Beth; he was still establishing his relationship with her, which obviously put him at a disadvantage in comparison to her boyfriend. Yes, he knew her favourite movies and certain things about New York that she loved – she talked about that stuff quite regularly – and he was dedicated to hoarding each and every detail away. However, it went without saying that Danny probably knew anything and everything about her too – even if it was clear at the moment that the guy wasn't giving her the attention she deserved.

Which, of course, helped in creating a level playing field for Ryan. But it still wasn't enough. He had to win Beth over.

She nodded knowingly at his question. 'You might say that. Actually, I've always thought destiny was just another form of magic. There is something special about it, something that makes it a little outside of this world. As if greater forces are at play, almost. I guess you never know when it's going to intervene in your life, or where and when you're going to be met with it.'

'Like at Carlisle's?' he prompted, remembering how their paths had originally crossed. And his words got the exact reaction he intended: her cheeks turned pink.

'Or at the corner of Lexington and 52nd ...' she shot back, eyes shining, before blanching as if she'd suddenly said something she shouldn't. Ryan loved it when he could get her to flirt back. He knew she tried to fight it. You could almost see her catch herself. And while he didn't like the idea of Beth feeling guilty or chastising herself over her incredibly innocent behaviour, he couldn't help but admit that seeing that guard come down occasionally gave him the motivation he needed to continue his pursuit.

Ryan also didn't feel the slightest bit guilty at the idea of working to pull her away from Danny. After all, it seemed like the guy had it coming. You couldn't ... *shouldn't* ignore a girl like Beth – who was so passionate and fun, and full of joy and optimism – and expect her to stick around regardless. From what she had told him, he secretly suspected that Danny might have something going on in his life too, perhaps a piece on the side? If that was the case then he definitely deserved to lose her.

Why wouldn't any guy who had been with Beth for that long – seven years – put a ring on her finger and take her off the market? Idiot. The guy deserved to lose her. And it seemed like Beth knew deep down that things weren't going to work out either. Otherwise, why would she be so happy to hang out with him?

'I think that destiny, fortune, fate, whatever it comes down to – however we make our path – I think it's important to pay attention to the signs.'

Ryan had a hunch he knew where she was going with this. Sometimes Beth had a way of talking around herself, but that was part of her charm. She had this ethereal quality about her, as if she lived on a slightly different planet from everyone else, a happier and considerably less cynical, planet. He wondered what it would be like to kiss her.

Patience, Ryan, patience, he chided himself. There's time for that. Don't overplay your hand. You can't spook her by doing anything too soon. You push things and you will lose her – send her rushing back into Danny's arms out of guilt alone. That wouldn't do.

'You mean serendipity?' Ryan ventured, catching her drift, and Beth nodded. 'As it happens, I agree with you,' he continued. 'I think you do have to know the signs, and understand the clues.' Much to his delight, he saw her smile a little. 'But I think for those moments you have to have your eyes open. You have to realise *when* you are being met with destiny. Those certain moments – crossroads, even – the really special ones where you know your life is about to change, they don't come around too often.'

Beth's smiled faded at this and her gaze appeared far away, as if she was somewhere else, thinking of another time and place. Ryan wondered what he'd said wrong and couldn't help but be worried. Right now he wanted her back in the moment.

'Beth?'

She snapped out of it and smiled guiltily. 'Sorry, I was just thinking of something. Lost my train of thought.'

'It's OK. I know you've had a lot on your mind lately.'

She nodded and finished her sandwich. 'Yes, I have this ... project of sorts that I have been working on. It's been challenging at times,' she offered, briefly meeting his gaze, before sharply looking away again. 'But I think it's going well.'

Ryan wiped his hands with his napkin and took a sip of his soda. 'Well, you know that I am here for you, Beth. Whatever project you're working on, if you need help with anything – anything at all – just ask.' He added with a wink, 'I'm at your service.'

Chapter 19

Since returning from lunch, Beth had felt energised and refocused. She now knew exactly what to do – or, more to the point, where to go – once her shift was over. But having to wait to do so was killing her, and heading back to Carlisle's with Ryan after their lunchtime excursion, she thought impulsively of saying that she didn't feel well, that she had eaten something funny at lunch and had to take the rest of the day off.

Then she could continue on in her quest and pursue the next clue that she had been given.

However, there was just one problem. No matter how much she stared at herself in the ladies' restroom mirror, she couldn't will herself to look like anything other than the picture of perfect wellness. Indeed, she was glowing with excitement. Her lack of grisly pallor was displayed in rosy cheeks, bright eyes and a clear complexion – the epitome of health and happiness.

There was no way anyone – especially Jodi, who would be the one covering for Beth if she threw a sickie – would believe her story. She might be able to fake it to the human resources department upstairs, but her friend would see right through her. Instead, she decided that she would just have to wait it out. Only a couple more hours to go until the end of her workday. And then, on to the next stage of the trail.

Where it was all ultimately leading, Beth had no idea, but she was very much enjoying the ride.

Working away on the sales floor, she felt buoyed by her most recent discovery and how easily she'd worked this part out. She couldn't help bouncing a little on her feet to burn off some of the giddiness that had settled in her stomach.

She'd actually created an in-store display last Christmas based on this very scenario, so the set-up was more than familiar to her. As the saying went, this one was in the bag. She knew *exactly* where the clue given to her today by Steve the bellhop was pointing her, almost as if 'X' marked the spot.

A five-dollar bill with writing on it; the book, *Love in the Time of Cholera*: it all pointed to the movie *Serendipity*. One of Beth's absolute favourite New York Christmas movies.

Shakespearian in its delivery – and indeed reminding Beth a little of her own life at that moment – the movie was based on a variety of near misses and plot reversals. Set here in New York, Jonathan, played by John Cusack, and Sara, played by Kate Beckinsale, meet by chance in Bloomingdale's department store at Christmastime (real-life parallels, much?). Irrespective of the fact that both are in relationships with other people, there is an immediate attraction and connection between them. But Sara doesn't think it's the right time for them to be together. So she comes up with an idea to test fate. Jonathan writes his phone number on a five-dollar bill and Sara, in turn, writes her name and number on the inside jacket of a book, *Love in the Time of Cholera*. If they are meant to be together fate will ensure they find the book and the five-dollar bill respectively and be led back to one another.

But Jonathan isn't satisfied with this, and comes up with a more immediate test of fate. He insists that they enter the bank of lifts at a hotel and see if they happen to end up on the same floor. And while the audience sees from the individual perspective of each character that indeed they both choose the same floor, Jonathan is delayed as a child gets in the lift and pushes every single button, preventing him from arriving in the same spot at the same time as Sara.

And with that Beth was incredibly clear on where she was supposed to go next.

To the same hotel in the movie. The Waldorf Astoria.

The '23' marked on the five-dollar bill was pointing her exactly where she was supposed to go. The same floor that Jonathan and Sara had both picked in the movie.

'You look like you're a thousand miles away,' said Jodi, interrupting Beth from her train of thought and bringing her back to reality. 'What's up with you? More clues? What's it this time?'

Beth nodded briefly in answer and immediately got back to work, doing a bit of cleaning up and filing around the cash wrap. 'Yes, another one, actually. And I know where I'm going this time. Didn't even need help with this one,' she beamed.

She quickly gave Jodi the synopsis of the *Seven Year Itch* connection, and how Danny had inadvertently pointed her in the right direction. But the moment that she mentioned that Ryan had wanted to go to a deli near the location she was supposed to find, Beth knew that Jodi was on high alert.

'What? Ryan just "happened" to want to go to the same place that you needed to go to in order to solve the last clue?' Jodi rolled her eyes. 'Oh my God, I can't believe I didn't see this before. What a friggin' idiot I am. You suspect that *he's* behind this, don't you? Why did you tell me that you thought it was Danny? So I'd help you out? Because you know well that if I'd thought for a second that ...'

Jodi shook her head, frustrated, her words trailing off and immediately Beth felt guilty. It wasn't as if she was one hundred per cent sure yet that Ryan was the instigator, nor had she misled Jodi intentionally. And even so, despite one or two potential indications here and there, there was no *clear* indication that Ryan had planned it all, especially given Danny's recent revelation about Billy. Remembering this set Beth on the defensive.

'No, I don't know that for sure, actually. I still have no idea who's doing this. Besides, it was only pure chance that he wanted to go to that deli. That's all it was. Serendipity.'

But Jodi wasn't convinced. 'Wrong. That is just the kind of movie-talk nonsense you're calling on to justify all of this to yourself. You have used that excuse to rationalise this whole crazy thing, that's what I think. Unless you believe in your heart that Danny has put this all together as a surprise for you – as something romantic because you are his girlfriend, and the relationship needs a boost – then I insist you abandon this insanity immediately. I'm serious, Beth. If Ryan is behind this then he is way overstepping his boundaries, and by being party to it you are only encouraging him. That's not right at all in my mind and, frankly, he should know better, as should you. And, well, if it's not him, then this is just plain creepy because you have a stalker. That's what I think.'

Beth bit her lip. Was Jodi right? Should she abandon this? Because if she really looked at this analytically the way that her friend wanted her to, she had to admit that she didn't truly suspect that Danny was behind this. What would be the point? Why would he go through the trouble of putting together this elaborate scheme when it appeared that they were growing apart by the day?

She thought hard, willing the pieces of the puzzle to fall into place.

Could it truly be Ryan, then, or Billy, or was someone else entirely at play?

But of course, that led to more questions – specifically, as Jodi pointed out, Beth's willing participation in this venture. If Ryan was behind it, then for decency and morality's sake she should stop. If Billy was behind it then she definitely didn't want to continue. And by some chance, if it was Danny, what was his motive?

Never mind the reasoning behind it if it was someone else entirely . . .

Even though she had thought the words 'secret admirer' in her mind, Beth hadn't really seriously considered that option yet, and now she felt like a fool.

But no, this couldn't be a stranger, some random person, putting this together, she realised. It had to be someone who knew her; especially given the New York movie references, which seemed specifically tailored for her, and all three men were aware of that passion.

Beth swallowed hard. More confusion. More uncertainty. More questions.

She was between a rock and a hard place with this one.

'Jodi, I *have* to continue with this. You just don't understand.'

But Jodi was already shaking her head. 'No, I do understand, I've been there before. You seem to keep forgetting that, for some reason. You are feeling a bit let down by Danny lately, I get that. You are looking for something exciting in your life. This "treasure hunt" falls into your lap. You lie to me, your best friend, and get me to help you with this, while I operate under the notion that it's Danny who's behind it. But you have other ideas – that this crush of yours—'

'He's not a crush,' Beth insisted, annoyed. 'I told you before, he's a *friend*.'

'Whatever,' Jodi continued, unconvinced. 'You start pretending or drawing conclusions in your mind that maybe Ryan is behind this. And you justify in your head that this is just for fun. But, Beth, if Danny isn't doing this and Ryan is, it's inappropriate. He's out of line and not respecting you when you say you're not available. I mean, unless—'

'Unless what?' Beth snapped, not meaning to sound as harsh as she did. She didn't lose her temper with people, especially Jodi, but right now her buttons were being pushed.

'Unless you are done with your relationship with Danny.'

'No, I'm not. I'm not finished with Danny. It's just a rough patch. That's all. And we will work it out … somehow. And this treasure hunt …' Her voice trailed off as she realised that she didn't have an excuse. And any comeback she had now seemed illogical. At least it did when Jodi made it all sound so black and white.

Beth bristled internally. What right did Jodi have to make her feel guilty? Just because her friend couldn't see the magic and romance in anything didn't mean that Beth had to cut it out of her life. In that instant, she decided she would continue the treasure hunt, but she wouldn't let Jodi know. If Jodi didn't want to help any more – well, fine, she didn't need her help.

However, there was one thing that continued to trouble her and nag at her insides. And she couldn't deny that it did present somewhat of an issue.

Where her next clue was pointing her – the Waldorf Astoria. A hotel.

If Ryan was the one behind this, what would she do if he was there? At the hotel waiting for her? She frowned. No, that *would* be crossing the line. And she would leave. Simple as that. And that would be the end of this treasure hunt.

But what if . . . Beth allowed her mind to trail off, considering other options.

What if it was just another stop? What if there was another clue waiting for her at the Waldorf? She realised that she had to find out.

She couldn't *not* find out. Whoever had set this whole thing up realised that too; knew Beth well enough to know that she wouldn't rest until she got to the bottom of it, which was reassuring enough in itself.

No, Beth was going to the Waldorf Astoria, whether Jodi liked it or not.

Chapter 20

Jodi had insisted on taking the subway all the way to Beth's stop in Lower Manhattan after they had ended their shift at Carlisle's mid-afternoon, and had even got off the train with her – walking side-by-side practically to the front door of her building – even though she was supposed to be heading in the opposite direction, off the island to the Bronx.

Beth knew what her friend was doing. She was babysitting her. Making sure that she didn't pursue the next clue and go to the Waldorf. Right then, Jodi was walking next to her, eyeing her suspiciously. 'So what are you going to do this evening?' she asked.

Beth shrugged. She was trying her best to look casual, nonchalant. 'I don't know, make dinner, take Brinkley for a walk. And then watch a movie.'

'What movie?' Jodi enquired with a sharp tone, as if daring her to say *Serendipity*.

Well, Beth could play that game, too. 'I don't know,

Maybe I'll just settle in for a nice night of *Rambo* or *Full Metal Jacket*. Something with lots of blood and guts. That's what I feel like at the moment.' She looked darkly at her friend, but Jodi simply laughed it off.

'Sure. *Full Metal Jacket*. That sounds like you. You might want to try out *Platoon* too, if you are on that kind of kick.'

Beth waved her off. 'So is this going to be a habit? You walking me home from work. I'm off tomorrow, do you need to pick me up the day after? I'm just wondering how much babysitting I require, that's all.'

Jodi stopped in her tracks and Beth turned to face her. 'I'm not babysitting. I'm protecting you from yourself.'

'You're protecting me?' Beth exclaimed. 'I didn't realise that I was in danger.'

'Maybe not physical danger,' Jodi chided. 'But I have a feeling that this whole thing is going to land you in trouble. I don't know how, but I just have a feeling that something really bad is going to come from this. So, like I said, I'm protecting you from yourself.'

Beth started walking again. She saw her building ahead of her and decided that a different approach might work with Jodi, in an effort to get her off her back. She knew that Jodi liked to be in charge and she was likely to be much more accepting if Beth simply acquiesced. Or at least appeared to. If she continued to butt heads with her like this, well, then she was likely to have Jodi follow her up to her apartment and stand guard outside the door.

'OK, fine. I understand that you're just concerned about me, and that you simply care about my welfare. You're a *good* friend.'

Jodi's eyes narrowed. She was clearly suspicious about Beth's sudden change in tune. 'So you give up? No more treasure hunt?'

Beth nodded but said nothing.

Jodi crossed her arms over her chest and considered her friend. She caught Beth's quick glimpse over her shoulder, as if plotting an escape route and smiled. Beth was a bad liar, especially when working to fool someone like Jodi, who had an internal lie detector that could sniff any untruth out.

'OK, fine. I only do this because I want to protect you, you know. I care about you. That's all.'

Beth nodded and reached forward to give her friend a hug. 'I know, and I appreciate it. So now, if I have your permission,' she teased, 'I'm going home. See you at work, OK? Have a good evening and thanks for walking me home.'

The women said their goodbyes and Jodi watched as Beth went through the motions of walking the remaining distance to her building, saying hello to Billy, and then disappearing inside.

Jodi turned round, heading back towards the subway. She knew exactly where Beth would go next: back uptown to the Waldorf Astoria. That meant she would have to head to the subway and return the way they'd come.

Jodi considered the neighbourhood. Quickly she spied

a bar on the opposite corner from where the stairs to the subway platform were located. She could go in there, have a drink, and wait for Beth to enter the subway, and then she could call her out on her lie and maybe embarrass her into giving this up once and for all.

Feeling that she had a plan, she walked towards the bar, checking behind her every few feet just to make sure that Beth hadn't immediately circled back, thinking Jodi was already gone.

But no, the path was clear.

Jodi walked into the bar, ordered a JD and Coke, and sat next to the window, which looked out onto the street. Now she just had to wait. She stared in the direction from where Beth would eventually come. She took a long swig of her drink and settled in.

Beth stood in her doorway, feeling that she had been able to read Jodi's mind. She crossed her arms, determined to wait it out.

She smiled in the usual way at Billy, but there was no denying that she now felt hugely uncomfortable around him. Still, just then she needed his help. 'Billy, there is somewhere I need to go, but Jodi doesn't want me to. Can you go out onto the street and see if she is walking away? Just act as if you are doing your normal concierge thing,' she added airily, referencing the way so many New York doormen would walk the path regularly in front of their buildings as if they were sentinels to the property.

223

Billy considered the request, eyes twinkling. 'And what is this *thing* that Jodi doesn't want you to do, lovey? I hope it's nothing that's going to get you in trouble.'

Beth tried to see if she could read anything into this response other than friendly interest. 'No, nothing that is going to get me in trouble,' she replied evasively. 'No danger that I know of. Jodi is just being Jodi. Will you check, please?'

Billy opened the door and casually looked down the block. He looked down the opposite way, waved to someone he obviously knew and then turned back towards the building.

Opening the doors, Beth was all over him for an answer. 'Well? Was she there?'

He shook his head. 'No, I didn't see her anyway. The street was clear. She probably already went down to the subway.'

Beth considered Billy's words, but couldn't shake the feeling that something didn't feel right. Hell, these days it was impossible to take anything for granted. But she worried now that if she decided to go back uptown via the subway, her plans would be hijacked. She guessed that was exactly what Jodi was planning on, and wouldn't even put it past her friend to be waiting close by, probably on the platform, hoping to catch her in the lie.

So, she would just have to do something that Jodi hadn't planned on.

'Billy,' she requested sweetly, 'I need a cab.'

Within minutes he had secured a cab for her and she was heading in the direction of uptown, leaving her friend – wherever she might be lurking – in the dust.

She had also taken the opportunity to swear Billy to secrecy, although she wasn't sure how long that could last against any subsequent assault from Jodi. Nevertheless, she would have to chance it. Beth hoped that if Jodi truly was looking out for her she would take her at her word, and just go home.

Circling her thoughts around, Beth began to refocus on her mission. She pulled out the book and five-dollar bill that she had been given earlier that day and considered the two items again.

Yes, the Waldorf was exactly where she was supposed to go. This was a clue that she felt very sure about. She wondered, though, what she would find when she got there. Jumping a little in her seat, her stomach fluttery with excitement, Beth placed the two items in her lap and took a deep breath, composing herself. Even though she still had considerable uncertainty about who could actually be behind all this, she had to believe that eventually it would all make sense.

Just like a classic movie with a plot that featured countless twists and turns, Beth had faith that the path would lead her to answers. She was committed to seeing it through.

The cab slowed, and the driver turned round from the front to face Beth. 'Sorry about this traffic. You said the Waldorf, right? I'll get you there as quick as possible.'

Beth smiled politely and shook her head. There was no way to control Midtown traffic at rush hour. 'No worries, I'm not in a hurry,' she said, even though she sort of was, but she had to keep it in perspective. It was her own internal deadline that was making her agitated – it wasn't like there was any emergency.

She looked out the window at Park Avenue to find something to entertain her thoughts; to distract her from wondering what was waiting at the hotel for her. Chances were it wasn't Billy, she reassured herself with some relief, given that she'd just left him.

However, almost as if serendipity was playing its own kind of trick, Beth suddenly got more than she bargained for.

On the path, no more than twenty feet away from where she sat in the cab, was Danny.

He was walking briskly, avoiding the tourists and crowds of Christmas shoppers that seemed to be crushing the space around him.

Beth's expression dropped when she noticed he looked incredibly stressed, completely out of sorts, as if something terrible had just happened. She could see it in his face. The cheery twinkling fairy-lit trees along the avenue seemed even brighter against the grey misery of his demeanour.

Forgetting her own mission at that moment, Beth had eyes only for Danny. What was wrong, what had happened? She hoped it wasn't more bad news from the office, and that all those extra hours he'd been working had ultimately been for naught ... She started to roll the window down so she could call out to him, make him stop so she could get out of the cab and find out why he looked so upset and preoccupied.

She could go to the Waldorf another time – tomorrow – whenever. 'Just a minute,' she said to the driver. She had just got the window down halfway, and she started to stick her head towards the opening to call after Danny, but someone beat her to it.

'Wait!' cried a woman's voice from nearby. 'Hold on.'

Beth pulled back from the window and watched as a beautiful, dark-haired woman rushed after her boyfriend. She had an arm up in the air and seemed desperate to reach him – to get his attention. Beth's brow furrowed and she looked around in confusion, suddenly realizing that this part of town was quite some distance from Danny's workplace. What was he doing here?

Her attention was very quickly dragged back to the scene in front of her. The dark-haired woman had been successful in getting Danny's attention. She had reached him and grabbed his arm, pulling on him, trying to get him to face her. And Danny's face was just ... ashen, Beth thought; it was hard to describe how he looked. And not only that but he seemed dishevelled, not at all as groomed as he usually was, his shirt hanging out as if ... As if he had got dressed in a hurry or something. What on earth ... ?

But notwithstanding how he looked, it was also crystal clear that he knew this woman.

Who was she? Beth studied her. Dark and Mediterranean-looking, she had long, silky hair and wore a pencil skirt and high heels. Beth focused in on the woman's face. She handed him something and she and Danny were talking now – no, not talking, *remonstrating*. Something was going on and it was heated. Beth tried to remember the last time she and Danny had communicated like that, openly and unrestrained, the way these two people were interacting. It reminded Beth of something, it was like two lovers in the throes of a passionate discussion. A dramatic outburst on the city streets – followed by making up somewhere private.

Beth felt as if she was holding her breath.

Danny was clearly upset and Beth wished that she could hear their words. How did they know each other? Was she a workmate of his? What was going on?

And then the realisation hit Beth. Danny was ... involved with this woman. She swallowed hard, trying to understand it, trying to make sense of it. Suddenly his behaviour over the last few weeks made perfect sense.

'Oh God ...' she gasped out loud.

'Miss?' the driver suddenly said, interjecting into her thought process. 'Do you want to get out here or what?'

But Beth turned away from the window and shook her head violently. 'No, no. I don't.' Her fear and confusion escalated as she turned back. She had to get away from here – she wasn't ready to deal with this. She wasn't sure when she would *ever* be ready to deal with this.

Danny cheating on her ...

And right then, she came to the crystal-clear realisation that Danny didn't plan this treasure hunt – he certainly wasn't behind it. Evidently he had moved on, was making plans for – or more to the point, *with* – someone else, and Beth wasn't included.

'Sorry, no, I don't want to get out,' she managed to the cab driver. 'Keep going. Please. I have to get out of here.'

As the cab continued on its journey, and Beth scrambled to get her thoughts together, suddenly she felt very sure of one thing.

As her world was crumbling around her, she would continue on with this hunt, she decided, swallowing the lump in her throat and hardening her heart.

Anything that would offer her a respite from this terrifying new reality.

Chapter 21

The cab driver practically had to snap his fingers in front of Beth's face as a signal that they had arrived, so fraught with confusion was she.

'Miss, we're here, the Waldorf,' he said. 'Miss? Miss? You OK?'

Beth came to attention and stared blankly at the man talking to her from the front seat. She was still trying to process what she had just seen. It didn't make any sense.

Or did it?

'Sorry, what?' she mumbled, honestly forgetting what she had originally set out to do.

'We're here, at the Waldorf. It'll be fourteen dollars.'

Beth shook her head in an effort to get rid of the cobwebs that cluttered her brain and reached for her purse. Pulling a twenty out of her wallet in one absent motion, she handed it to the cabbie, not asking for change, and getting out of the car before he had time to thank her for the tip.

What was it she'd just seen? Danny – with a woman ... No, it couldn't be; Danny wasn't like that. He wouldn't cheat on her.

But then she thought again about his recent strange behaviour. She had been well aware that, of late, things had been off with how he acted: those long nights at the office, the fact that he'd jumped all over her that time she'd offered to go through his pockets, not coming near her until he had a shower. Indeed, if Jodi had been here at that moment, assessing the situation with her, she would have been screaming 'cheater' at the top of her lungs.

Standing on the path in front of the hotel, the reality once again hit Beth and left her weak and breathless with horror.

Oh my God, he truly was having an affair. This wasn't just a rough patch in their relationship. Danny, her boyfriend of seven years, was cheating on her.

With that woman. That stunning-looking woman who looked to be Beth's opposite in every way. Stylish, beautiful, poised ... everything she wasn't.

Feeling crushed afresh, she chided herself then, unable to believe that she had felt so guilty about her steadily growing feelings for Ryan. Now, in light of all this, she found it so embarrassing that she felt stupid for worrying. When she was dealing with all of this internal conflict, Danny had already taken the lower road. He'd betrayed her, kept secrets from her, cheated.

Cheated ...

Yet still, even with everything that Beth had just seen, her subconscious was telling her not necessarily to believe her eyes. Maybe she wasn't seeing the whole picture. *Talk to him. Maybe there's more to it.*

But how could she talk to him? How could she tell Danny that she'd seen him on the street with some woman? It would open up a can of worms that Beth wasn't sure she was ready to deal with.

Now, she peered up at the façade of the hotel, festooned with twinkling holiday wreaths and garlands. Just a taxi ride ago she had wondered, but now Danny's name was definitely crossed off the list of possible suspects behind this treasure hunt. After all, why would he bother doing something fun and romantic if he was falling in love with someone else?

Falling in love, thought Beth, and a sob caught in her throat. He had fallen in love with me at one time, too.

She thought back to that time in Venice: to their locking their love on that bridge; tossing the key in to the canal below. To that moment when she thought it would be the two of them – for good. So much for the love of a lifetime.

But what did that matter? What did any of it matter now? Against her will, a tear escaped from her left eye, and then her right. She put a hand to her face quickly, afraid of what bystanders on the street would think of her standing in front of the Waldorf crying.

It was almost like a piece of a movie-reel, Beth thought.

A tearjerker, to be sure. And she was the loser in all of this – she was the one who was going to be left on her own. She was the one who wouldn't have a happy ending.

She swallowed hard and took a ragged breath when suddenly her subconscious chimed in again. Maybe this – the reason she was here at all – was leading her to another, better ending?

Beth faced the hotel once again and steeled her features into an expression of resilience. She supposed there was only one way to find out.

Casting Danny from her mind, and instead calling upon Scarlett O'Hara's famous mantra to 'think about that tomorrow', Beth stepped forward towards the building, determined to find the answer to this latest clue.

As she approached the ornate entrance to the famed New York hotel, she looked up at the art deco angel standing sentry above the doorway and was immediately struck by a sense of history – and also longing – as she pushed her way through the revolving door, and was deposited into the opulent lobby.

There was nothing that quite epitomised the luxurious, classic and iconic New York like the Waldorf Astoria, Beth thought. A study in elegance and luxury, with soft lighting from table lamps, dark wood, potted palms, and sumptuous seating, this place had featured in so many of her favourite movies – had been the focal point for so many wonderful New York love stories: *Serendipity, Maid in Manhattan, Catch Me If You Can* – the romance of it was cemented in her mind. And at this time of year in particular it was even more magical.

She'd always thought that if she ever got married, she'd want it to be somewhere like this, she remembered, as she headed up the marble staircase into the lobby, the cheery sparkle of the huge chandelier above, and twinkling Christmas trees on either side almost mocking her anguish.

She'd decided long ago that such a major romantic moment in her life would surely have to take place in New York rather than back home in Ireland. Looking around, and trying to picture herself making a grand cinematic entrance up these stairs in a beautiful white dress, she realised how empty that thought – that fleeting hope – seemed now.

Of course, marriage had not been a recent focus of Beth's, not outwardly anyway, though it had been in the back of her mind, a thought that was always present, even though she and Danny hadn't spoken about it seriously, not in quite a while at least.

But now, that very faint hope of being married to Danny seemed dashed altogether. It didn't even seem possible. She had to admit that it had been increasingly hard to picture herself in a white dress, walking down the aisle wearing her grandmother's beautiful vintage shoes, towards her groom in this city. The vision was obtuse and unformed and, unusually for her, Beth could no longer even summon it in her head, almost as if her mind was putting a block on allowing her to consider a future with Danny. It wasn't even allowing her to think about him. Not after what she had just seen on the street. Not now her heart felt as if it was broken in two.

Keep going she told herself. Don't think about it.

Taking a deep breath, she once again looked around the lobby, taking stock of the layout and focusing her thoughts on the task at hand. Dominating the main lobby was the famed, ornately carved, bronze Waldorf Astoria clock, set on an octagonal base of marble and mahogany and topped with a Statue of Liberty. It was a popular place for photographs, and a regular meeting place, much like the clock at Grand Central. Today, for Beth, it was a good starting point.

She pulled the book, *Love in the Time of Cholera*, out of her bag and opened it up to where she had placed the five-dollar bill like a bookmark.

Twenty-three. *As in floor* twenty-three. *I'm sure of it.*

Walking purposely, she continued on to the bank of beautifully ornate lifts that had famously featured in the movie *Serendipity*. Smiling a little as she began to feel closer to the energy of the wonderful love story that was set in this place, she reached out and pushed the 'up' button, waiting for a lift to arrive; her chariot to the upper floors.

She tapped her foot and tried to remain focused. *Do not think about Danny, do not think about Danny, do not think about Danny ...* Saying it over and over in her head like a silent mantra – a prayer to the God of Broken Hearts, the Goddess of Spurned Lovers – seemed to help.

Finally, a ding resounded above her, announcing that a lift had arrived. It was the same one that Jonathan had taken in the movie. Entering the car, Beth almost had to fight the urge to hit all of the buttons on the control panel – just like the child who had shared the car with the character in the film – foiling his efforts to meet Sara on floor twenty-three.

Instead, she focused on her destination. Twenty-three. She pressed the button, the doors closed in front of her, and a feeling of nervous anticipation entered her stomach.

Beth was once again focused on her mission, and the giddiness that she had been experiencing since first setting out on her treasure hunt soon returned. She was in her element. Romantic anticipation, a beautiful puzzle featuring her favourite city in the world – and a secret admirer who apparently knew her well, realised her passions and understood exactly what made her tick.

Real life could wait for later.

Chapter 22

Danny sat on the freezing cold bench on 58th Street, over-looking the East River.

The afternoon sun was clouded over, and the beginnings of snow danced around the atmosphere. A child walked by with her mother, laughing delightedly as snowflakes fell into her open mouth. And here he was, in the same spot where he had sat and talked with Beth so long ago.

Though it was almost seven years ago now, he could remember it as though it were yesterday.

The lights had twinkled on the Queensboro Bridge and reflected off the nighttime waters of the East River. It had been Beth and Danny's second date and they'd walked slowly on the sidewalk that ran beside the water, talking softly, taking in the scene before them – learning about each other.

And Danny was pretty sure he was already smitten.

'Dinner was really fantastic. I just wanted to thank you

again,' Beth had said, smiling up at him. 'I didn't think that you could get such great Italian food anywhere – outside of Italy, of course.'

'Glad you liked it.'

They had just come from Bella Notte, a great trattoria he knew. Their reservation had been for seven thirty and they had been the last diners in the entire restaurant to leave – and had done so only because it was apparent that the staff wanted to go home.

'I feel bad that we kept them there for so long, though,' Beth said, as if reading his mind. 'I just lost track of time,' she laughed.

'Me too. But, we don't have to keep walking if you don't want to. This is "the City that Never Sleeps", after all. We could go get a nightcap somewhere if you like?' he asked hesitantly. He had already given Beth his jacket, but he was afraid that she might still be chilly. You could tell that summer was almost over and fall was settling in over the city.

But Beth shook her head. 'Oh, no, I love the weather at the moment. I'm not cold, don't worry. But I will admit that these heels are killing me. Do you mind if we sit?' She pointed to a bench about twenty feet ahead. 'That looks perfect.'

Danny took a look at where she'd indicated and then cast his gaze out across the river. He smiled. A perfect spot indeed, one of the best places to sit in all of Manhattan. In fact you might call it picture perfect.

'I think that's a great idea,' he agreed, leading Beth to the bench and sitting next to her – close enough that their arms were touching, but still far enough away to build anticipation yet feel the electricity that seemed to be sparking between them.

Once sitting comfortably, he looked out over the river, taking in the cityscape in front of them. It was hard to believe it with all of the urban light pollution around, but tonight, when you looked up in the sky you could actually make out stars.

'Would you look at that?' Beth whispered in that gorgeous Irish accent, seeing the stars too. 'This has to be the best seat in the house ... in all of Manhattan, maybe,' she giggled. 'Someone really should put this in a movie. The rest of the world should see this.'

Danny smiled, wondering if she was joking or not. Because someone *had* actually put this in a movie. But he guessed, taking in her happy and innocent expression, that Beth wasn't joking; it was just likely that she had never seen Woody Allen's *Manhattan*.

'So tell me,' Beth said, turning to him then. 'We covered a lot of important stuff up until this point, I know you're from Queens but your parents are originally from Philadelphia – where the best cheesesteak is to be found at Jim's, not Pat's nor Gino's despite what Rocky Balboa thinks ...' She grinned, and he remembered he'd been pretty adamant about that. 'And you work in marketing, love to travel, but you missed out on telling me one very important fact.'

He looked at her, curious. 'And what's that?'

'What's your favourite movie? Like your favourite movie *ever.*'

He nodded and thought for a moment, understanding that this would be important to a girl who'd told him the movies was the main reason she'd moved to New York.

'My favourite . . .' He thought about telling her there and then about *Manhattan*, but no, he didn't want this moment to look staged. Not when it was so truly genuine – that they had happened upon this venue by complete chance.

'Well, I like *Goodfellas*. And *Wall Street*. Both classic New York flicks, you know.' Beth scrunched up her face and he chuckled. 'What, not on your list of all-time favourites?'

'Well, they are both good enough, I suppose. Cinematic treasures and all that,' she agreed. 'I can certainly appreciate Paulie Cicero's garlic slicing techniques, but I'm a fan of the less violent stuff myself.'

Danny laughed, recalling how the character in *Goodfellas* prepared dinner while in prison – with a razor blade. 'Ah, I see . . . so I have a bleeding heart romantic on my hands? I'd never have known,' he teased, and she nudged him playfully. 'So tell me your favourites then.'

Beth took a deep breath. 'Just about any movie set here in the city, to be honest. I especially adore *West Side Story*, and anything from the thirties with Clark Gable in it – the ultimate leading man. Oh, and *Roman Holiday*, of course.' She clapped her hands delightedly. 'Someday I want to go to

Rome and eat gelato on the Spanish Steps and pretend I am Audrey Hepburn. And as for modern movies, well ...' she sighed dreamily, 'I know it's not in New York but I don't think anything can beat *The Notebook*.'

'*The Notebook*. Oh, man,' said Danny, laughing. 'Of *course* you love that movie.'

Beth's mouth flew open. 'What?' she asked warily, though her eyes were smiling. 'What's wrong with *The Notebook*?'

Danny put his head dramatically in his hands. 'Sob fest. Melodrama. Cheeeesy. That's all I'm going to say.'

'It's romantic!' she argued. 'It's touching and wonderful and ... perfect.'

Danny put his hands up in surrender. 'Oh, OK – fine, fine. You can get away with all that. *Only* women can get away with admitting to liking that movie.'

Beth smiled. 'At least you know when to end an argument. I'll give you credit there. Smart man.'

'OK, so now that I know straight up that we're going to be watching a lot of chick flicks,' he said smiling, 'I'm wondering something else.'

'What do you want to know?' Beth answered, her expression open and honest, as if she'd happily tell him anything. Danny took in her face, and he couldn't help but allow his eyes to travel to her lips. He wondered what it would be like to kiss her. He considered doing it right there and then, but stopped himself. They'd only just met, were only just getting to know one another, and he didn't want to scare her off. Still, the temptation was strong. There was just *something* about this girl. Something that made him want to be around her all the time.

Danny took a deep breath and thought for a moment about how to pose his question. He didn't want to make it look like he was probing in such a way that a red flag would be set off in Beth's mind.

'So, what's your five-year plan? Where do you see yourself?' And as the words crossed his lips, he had the overwhelming urge to punch himself in the face.

Five-year plan, Danny? Five-year plan? What are you doing? Negotiating a corporate merger? Jesus! his subconscious chided.

Beth's eyebrows rose. 'My five-year plan?'

Right, completely unromantic, I get it, Danny thought.

'Well, I suppose, to rise up the ranks at my job – I really like it at Carlisle's. Maybe make my way up to management someday, though I have to say I do love it on the sales floor. I get to talk to lots of different people from all walks of life, help them – I love being around shoes, being creative with the displays – and the commission is pretty nice, too. Best of all I get to live the dream by spending my days in New York. I adore that most of all, and I feel like it is important to enjoy your life as it is, rather than always be focused on the next milestone.' She paused for a moment, gauging Danny's reaction and continued on when he murmured a quiet agreement and smiled. 'And, well, I know this sounds silly ... but I've always really wanted a dog. A cavalier King Charles spaniel. We have one at home in Galway – Charlie – and I really miss having her around, but the place I'm in at the moment is just way too small for a pet. And finally ... I really want to travel – see as much of the world as possible.'

Danny nodded, pleased to find something else they had in common. 'I love dogs and as for travel, me too. Where would you like to go?'

'Oh, everywhere. Give me a globe and spin it. I'd go anywhere my imagination – and my budget – could take me. Unfortunately, that means I haven't done much at this point other than get from Ireland as far as here. So while my ambition is rich, my bank account needs to catch up,' she smiled. 'But like I did in following my dreams and coming here, I can focus on it – and keep working hard – and I know I'll get there eventually. Nothing wrong with wishing, my grandmother used to say, but you must also do your best to help make your dreams come true.'

And, just like that, Danny knew without a doubt that he wanted to sweep this wonderful woman away. There was something in his heart that wanted to grant Beth Harper every wish she had. Make her every dream come true.

'I think it's a worthy goal,' Danny agreed. 'But I want to know, taking the globe spinning out of the equation, if you could go one place right now, where would it be?'

Without thinking Beth said, 'Home. Back to Galway to see my family. I haven't been for a while and I miss them.'

Danny was nodding. 'I've always wanted to visit Ireland.

Seems like it's a great place.' He held back from adding that perhaps one day they'd go there together – it felt too forward.

'It is. But other than that . . .' Still thinking, Beth tapped her mouth with a finger. After a moment, she spoke, 'I would probably have to say Italy – Venice, especially.'

Danny smiled. 'Amazing city.'

'You've been?' she gasped.

'Yes, many years ago. When I was still a kid. But even though I was very young, I could still appreciate the city. It's unique.'

She nodded with faraway eyes. 'I bet it is. How wonderful that you were able to have that experience, even as a child.'

Danny hesitantly put his arm around her, wondering if she would allow it. She did. 'Ah, I have a feeling that you will, too,' he said, as she relaxed into him. 'Lots of time for that.' What Danny didn't say was that he was now one hundred per cent committed to having her see Venice with him. He would take her there someday; he was sure of it. Just like he hoped they'd visit her hometown together some time, too.

Beth and Danny sat in silence for a long time, looking out over the river, utterly content in each other's company.

It was a special moment and they both knew it, had talked about it many times over the last few years. Like the song went, it was their New York minute.

Now, in the bitter cold, the memory drifting away like

the falling snow, Danny looked at the empty space next to him. And try as he might, he couldn't conjure Beth's image there. This definitely wasn't the scene out of *Manhattan*.

He stared out over the river, remembering the words that he and Beth had spoken that night. They had just been learning about each other, and he recalled feeling so hopeful – there was so much opportunity. They had so much time.

He felt something seize the chords around his heart and his breath catch. But this wasn't the same kind of feeling that he'd felt that night with Beth. That was based on excitement – like heading over the first hill of a roller coaster and having your heart jump into your throat and adrenalin surge through your veins like a drug. This was different; this was ... regret. Regret about the past and for the future – his and Beth's. Except he could no longer picture Beth in that future. He could no longer visualise those stars over the Queensboro Bridge.

What did the relationship hold for them now? Adele had made things very clear to him barely an hour ago.

About the new addition that was going to further complicate his life.

His eyes watered. There was no hiding this from Beth now. Had it really been only an hour ago since he'd first learned the news? Danny wondered. He looked at his watch. Yes, an hour. Such a momentous, life-changing conversation. Though it was hardly a conversation at all. Adele had done most of the talking. Whereas Danny had listened

245

for a little but had become so overwhelmed he'd walked right out of there, unable to focus on anything other than what he'd just discovered. It was almost surreal.

How flippant we were as humans, to think that we were in control of things, he thought, once again casting his face up into the light of the fading sun – wishing it would warm him; turn up the heat on his cold heart. That's what it was, after all, he was convinced of it. A cold heart – for all he wasn't telling Beth now, for all that he had to tell her, and what he was going to put her through.

Danny reflected on yesterday when he and Beth watched that movie together and put the tree up.

That had been nice. It had felt so normal – so right. Beth had seemed to enjoy herself, though there were times when it was obvious that she was distracted, that she too had something else on her mind. Maybe that guy – Ryan. Danny felt his pulse start to speed up as he thought of the man and his goddamn dimples, but then he shook his head, banishing the negativity that was building in his thoughts.

It was probably good that she was distracted just now. He hadn't expected her to be at home when he arrived back from his folks' house, and Beth knew that. She knew something was up. He'd almost been tempted to come right out and tell her then, but he hadn't wanted to ruin the first comfortable moment they'd had together in an age. At least he was able to distract her – and indeed himself – with some movie trivia. At least in the end they just had a lovely evening together, normal, easygoing, just like old times, though going through the Christmas ornaments, painful reminders of the wonderful memories they'd shared, had almost broken his heart.

Once the truth came out there weren't going to be any more of those.

Danny felt a sob start to well in his throat. Out of frustration. Out of confusion. Out of regret. Sitting here now, in the place that held so many memories of good times shared with Beth, he knew deep down that, despite his best attempts, their happy life was about to come to an end.

And he knew he wasn't ready for that just yet.

Chapter 23

Waiting for the lift to reach the twenty-third floor was sheer agony for Beth. She didn't know what she should be looking for, or what to expect, but then an errant thought crept into her mind and she remembered what she had contemplated earlier that day at work.

If Ryan was the one behind this, would he be waiting for her here?

Admittedly, her palms started to sweat at the thought. Especially as her circumstances, it seemed, had changed so much in the last half-hour. If Ryan *was* here, what would she do?

Was seeing Danny on the street like that a sign of sorts? Serendipity ...

But no, it wasn't as simple as that, she reminded herself. While she had immediately jumped to conclusions about what she'd seen on Park Avenue, was she one hundred and fifty per cent sure that Danny was actually cheating on her?

She wanted to say she *felt* sure, but that still didn't give her the right to jump into Ryan's arms, only to discover that she had jumped to incorrect conclusions about Danny.

'Two wrongs don't make a right,' she said to herself with conviction – another one of her grandmother's wise sayings – as the elevator car slowed, approaching her final destination. If Ryan was here it was still a no-go.

'But first things first,' she reminded herself anxiously. There was no point in worrying about what she would do if Ryan – or indeed anyone else – was here until she at least made some headway on this clue.

Beth pressed her lips together and wiped her hands on her sides. She didn't necessarily understand *why* she was so nervous just then, she just knew that she felt some sort of trepidation, as though whatever she discovered would lead her to a tipping point of sorts.

She didn't know what made her feel this way, but she suspected that she was very close to solving this entire mystery. It was as if her own inner movie soundtrack was bringing symphony music to a crescendo behind her.

A moment later, the lift dinged, signalling her arrival on the twenty-third floor. Beth felt a lump form in her throat and she realised that her stomach was jumping around out of sheer anxiety. It was a feeling akin to heading over the first, menacing hill on a roller coaster and she had to take a deep breath, if only to try to regulate her pulse and quell the excitement (panic?) that was building in her chest.

The doors opened, and Beth could have sworn that she

was moving in slow motion. As the opening expanded to its limit, she stood for a moment, breathlessly looking at the scene in front of her – the twenty-third floor's lobby – as if she was waiting for someone to jump out and yell, 'Surprise!'

But instead, she was met with silence. Absolute, complete and mind-numbing silence.

The doors started to close, and Beth realised that she had to act. She could delay no longer. She threw a hand out and the doors parted again as the machine registered her movement.

This time, Beth got out without further ado. The lift doors closed behind her and it departed to find a new passenger. But what was she supposed to do now? What was she looking for?

Taking a few tentative steps forward, she peered around the area. In keeping with the rest of the hotel, the hallway was elegantly decorated, the carpet plush and spotlessly clean. But nothing looked out of the ordinary. Everything appeared normal. There wasn't an object out of place.

Curiously, Beth looked back at the other lift, wondering if suddenly those doors would open and she would understand the hunt's intent, and what she was doing here. But no, the other one stayed silent, closed. There was no secret to be had.

At least not in this area.

Beth began walking along the hallway to where the bedrooms were located, realizing that standing around like this definitely made her look suspicious. And she guessed that if anyone happened to see her – and deduce that she wasn't a guest here – they would report her to security in less than a New York minute.

She straightened her posture and began walking with purpose. There was no reason to 'creep' around the hallways at the Waldorf – not unless she wanted to be escorted from the building. And that is something I definitely need to avoid, she thought, imagining the scene and how embarrassed she would feel if she had to face being 'perp-walked' out the front doors.

Beth wandered down the quiet hotel hallway, her steps barely making a sound against the plush carpeting. She passed each individual door, with the hotel's signature carving above the room numbers, wondering who was staying in each room, contemplating if it was anyone famous or well-known – movie stars, maybe. So many had stayed here over the years she knew: Marilyn Monroe, Elizabeth Taylor, Grace Kelly, Katharine Hepburn – pretty much all the greats of Hollywood's Golden Age.

She paused a little, soaking in the building's long and prestigious association with something so close to her heart. Whoever had organised for her to be here today would surely have known that, too; understood that someone like Beth would appreciate the weight of that history more than most.

At this, her mind wandered ever so slightly, but still she felt on high alert, focused on her quest, searching for a clue.

Keeping an eye out for any type of indicator that would tell her she was on the right path.

But so far, there was nothing.

Beth made a complete sweep of the twenty-third floor, but when, a few minutes later, she returned to the bank of lifts, she was no further along in her quest.

She sat down for a moment in the regal-looking chair that was positioned across from them, waiting for a sign, for anything.

But nothing happened. It was so quiet Beth could have heard a pin drop.

She rubbed her temples, trying to regain some clarity, when just then she heard a noise in the hallway from whence she'd come. A door opened, and a moment later closed with a resounding thud. She looked up to see who would emerge from the hallway. No doubt it was someone leaving their room and heading for the lift.

However, thirty seconds passed and then a minute, and Beth was still alone. What's more, the silence had returned and she couldn't detect any footsteps or other sounds coming from the hallway. When she realized this, the hairs on the back of her neck stood up.

Her inner tuition told her that something had just changed. That the game had begun. That she was *meant* to hear that door open and close.

It was a sign.

Beth stood up and headed back down the hallway. She turned left and found the corridor deserted, but she also knew without a doubt that this is where the noise had come from before.

Purposefully, she took off down the seemingly endless corridor, passing the doors to rooms on either side of her, knowing for sure that what she had heard came from further, deeper down the way.

As Beth neared the end of the corridor, she was faced with a set of double doors, the kind that usually signalled a suite. Even though she had passed this same location just minutes before, now she realised that something had changed, and she had no doubt that the door that she had just heard open and close had been this one.

Because on the floor, just outside the doors, lay a glove. A single, black cashmere glove.

She knew that this was no coincidence. This *was* serendipity. And she meant that in the truest sense of the word.

In the movie, Jonathan and Sara try to buy the same pair of gloves from Bloomingdale's, and, a little while later at the Waldorf, they split the pair of gloves up, each taking one. The gloves were the central part of the fate aspect of the plot, in which they agree that if they can reunite the gloves, they are meant to be together.

But then at the hotel, they lose each other in the lifts, and don't reunite (with each other, along with their singular glove) until the end.

What Beth was now looking at was the exact kind of black woollen glove, and even though it was highly likely that any random hotel resident could be wearing a pair of cashmere gloves in New York at this time of year, she knew in her heart and soul that this wasn't dropped by accident. She bent down to pick it up and looked around. She was still alone. So there was only one thing left to do. She had to knock on the door.

Whoever had dropped this glove had wanted her to find it. They knew that she was here. And no doubt, further answers – or clues – were about to be revealed.

An inexplicable chill ran up Beth's spine and her thoughts returned to Ryan. What if he was behind that door – in a suite in the Waldorf – arguably the most romantic movie-themed hotel in New York? What would she do then?

Beth didn't know, but in true Hollywood movie heroine tradition, she was going to find out.

Taking a deep breath, she held up a hand and made a fist. Reaching forward, she knocked delicately on the door and returned her hand to her side. She heard the faintest sounds coming from the other side of the door. Someone was on their way to answer.

Beth swallowed hard once again and realised that her mouth was dry.

It was time for the big reveal.

Chapter 24

The moment the suite door opened, Beth knew that she didn't have anything to fear, at least right then, from Ryan or indeed Billy.

Because the guy standing there was a complete stranger.

He was an older, greying, but distinguished-looking man. He had on a deep navy suit – obviously well cut – and was adjusting the cuffs of his dress shirt, as if he had just thrown his jacket on and was rushing out the door to go to a glittering event downstairs in the Grand Ballroom. She noticed immediately the large cufflinks – sapphires, she was sure.

In short, his whole demeanour told of wealth.

'Yes?' he said with a heavy accent that Beth guessed was Middle Eastern, or maybe Russian. 'May I help you?' Rather than look annoyed at the interruption, though, the man's ice-blue eyes danced a little, as if he was intrigued by his visitor.

Beth swallowed hard as her heart jumped in her chest. It was only when he shifted his weight from one foot to the other that she realised she was staring at him with an open mouth, silent. Her brain was struggling to make sense of too many things at once. But one thing was for sure – she needed to say *something*.

'Er, I'm sorry. But I was just passing,' she lied, 'and this glove was sitting outside your door. I thought that maybe you or someone from this room dropped it by accident.' Beth felt proud of herself. Even with the mental conundrum she was currently facing, she was impressed that she had been able to come up with a semi-believable fib off the cuff like that.

However, instead of answering her, the man merely smiled at her, as if he was goading her, knowing full well that she was making up an excuse for knocking on his door.

'A glove, you say, yes?' he asked again, seemingly accentuating his accent.

'This glove,' Beth said, holding it up for him to see. 'Right outside your door – here – on the floor.' She pointed as if the man needed this sort of instruction to understand what she was talking about.

But maddeningly, he simply nodded and continued to smile, as if he was well aware of where she had found the glove. Probably because he put it there, Beth thought. She waited for him to answer her, but clearly the guy would have easily beaten her in a game of poker, because she folded first. 'So, is this yours? Do you have the pair?'

The man smiled. 'You are assuming there *is* a pair.'

Beth's brow furrowed. Another riddle obviously. *Of course there is a pair, like shoes, gloves always come in pairs.* She shrugged. 'Well, with all due respect, that's the way gloves normally come.'

'Hmm, yes. Well, I would agree. Gloves do usually come in pairs. However, I have no idea if in fact this glove has a match, as it is not mine.'

Beth's was taken aback. If not his, then who did the glove belong to?

'Then, perhaps whomever you are travelling with dropped it?' Beth offered, attempting to peer around the man and see if anyone else was in the suite.

But he blocked her view. 'I'm sorry, but my wife does not own this glove. She already has a pair; it's cold outside, no?'

Beth felt as if this entire situation was turning into one big circus. What was this guy playing at? Clearly he was involved in this, and if he was anything like the others he was supposed to be helping her, moving her along to the next destination, the next stage in the hunt. So why did he continue blanking her and pretending not to know anything while looking at her like the cat that ate the canary?

Beth sighed. She was tired, it had been a horrible day, and she really thought that this was it – she was going to get somewhere at the Waldorf. Right then she was only seconds away from screaming out in frustration, but instead, she simply decided to call his bluff.

'Right it's cold outside. I know. December in New York can be like that. But look, you and I both know I was supposed to find this glove, OK? I heard your room door open and close from all the way down by the elevator. That's where I was sitting. That's why I'm at this hotel today in the first place. I have a five-dollar bill with the number twenty-three written on it and that's how I knew I was supposed to be on this floor. And because of the book, too and—'

She stopped talking abruptly, primarily because she realised just how crazy she was beginning to sound. If by some chance this man wasn't involved in this treasure hunt, then he was likely only seconds shy of calling hotel security on her. She shook her head. 'Sorry about that. I have a tendency to ramble sometimes.'

The man's face softened, the way someone would upon witnessing the precociousness of a small child. 'It's OK, I heard.'

Beth's eyes narrowed and she immediately went straight back on high alert. So he *was* involved. *Somehow.* 'What do you mean, you heard? From who—'

But the man cut her off. He was playing coy with her. And he wasn't going to answer her either, that much she understood. 'You know, I think your best bet would be to return that glove to hotel lost and found. That's what I would do.'

Beth opened her mouth to speak when suddenly she heard a woman's voice calling out from inside the suite.

'Yuri? Who is at the door?' The voice also held an accent, but one that was different from the man's, and Beth leaned in to see if she could get a look at who was speaking. For some reason the voice seemed familiar. But maybe she was going crazy. God knew, after today she had every reason to be.

But the man, whose name it seemed was Yuri, immediately went on the defensive. Evidently he hadn't counted on someone else interrupting their conversation. He took a sharp step back from the door, as if indicating the subject was now closed and their discussion over. Beth was sure that he was about to shut it in her face. 'Lost and found. Try there. That's what you should do,' he reiterated as Beth continued to stand in place.

'Lost and found?' she repeated, trying to make the entire situation add up, especially when she was pretty sure she really did recognise the voice from inside. 'But—'

'OK. Good luck.' And just as she'd anticipated, the door closed with a resounding thud, leaving her once again alone in the hallway, holding the stray glove.

She sighed, defeated afresh.

After considering her options, of which there were admittedly few, Beth decided her only hope was to follow the man's – Yuri's – directions, and head back down to the lobby. Did the Waldorf even have a lost and found department? And if so, just what was turned in? Diamonds, furs, tiaras? Or single black cashmere gloves, perhaps?

She shrugged in confusion, and pressed the button for

the lift again. As she rode down she realised that the anxiety and anticipation that she had felt while riding up to the
twenty-third floor had not yet left her. If anything, it was
worse.

Beth didn't feel any further along in the hunt, though
she knew she must be somehow. The glove had been placed
there on purpose – likely by the Russian man – and she
was even beginning to believe that as much as the man had
looked spooked when their conversation was close to being
interrupted, she was supposed to have been privy to that.
She was supposed to have witnessed it all.

The name Yuri, the woman he was with, the fact that
he'd directed her to lost and found – these were all part of
the riddle, and an answer to . . . something . . . was playing
on the edge of her brain. Tempting her, cajoling her, teasing
her; close – but still frustratingly out of reach.

Reaching the ground floor, she wandered back out into
the main lobby, scanning the area and wondering what
would constitute the Waldorf's 'lost and found'.

Spying the concierge desk behind a black marble mono-
lith, she turned in that direction, all the while keeping her
eyes peeled for anything or anyone who might be party to
this whole thing, and associated with this clue.

Unfortunately, no one nearby was wearing a single black
cashmere glove and waving at her with purpose, so by the
time Beth reached the concierge station, she figured that
turning in her findings was her only course of action.

She sighed heavily and thought about just how she was

supposed to explain – to the Waldorf Astoria concierge, of all people – that actually no, she was not a guest here, she just happened to be cruising the hallways of the twenty-third floor and had found this single glove. Then she had been encouraged by a guest, whose name was Yuri and who had no doubt actually placed the glove outside his hotel suite door for her to find, to turn in said glove to the hotel lost and found.

And, oh yeah, on top of it all, I'm on a mysterious treasure hunt and do you happen to have my next clue for me, please? No, it's not an episode of The Amazing Race, *honestly. There are no cameras that I know of. I have no idea who is behind all of this and what it's about. I just need help.*

Beth rolled her eyes as she mentally ran through her spiel. *They're going to have me locked up,* she thought.

She sidled up next to the desk. A broad-shouldered man, apparently the concierge, was turned away and talking on the phone. Beth went through what she was supposed to say once more in her head, trying to figure out a way to make it sound somewhat less crazy, but she lost her train of thought when the concierge ended his call, hung up the phone and turned to face her.

Immediately recognising him, Beth's eyes widened. 'Oh my goodness. It's you!'

Maybe explaining all this wouldn't be as tricky as she'd thought.

Chapter 25

Sipping on her second drink, Jodi felt mounting dread in her chest. She stared intently out of the bar's front window, considering every passerby who entered the subway. None of them was Beth. But all the same, she just *knew* her friend was getting one over on her. And she was going to get herself in trouble.

She decided that she could no longer sit here – drinking, waiting for something to happen. She scrolled through the contacts in her iPhone and found Beth and Danny's home number. Without a further thought, Jodi pressed dial.

Holding the phone to her ear, she listened, mentally willing Beth to pick up. She wasn't sure why she felt so strongly about this, but she was certain her friend was heading into dangerous territory with this treasure hunt, especially now that she knew that Beth didn't suspect it was Danny behind it. Jodi didn't want to see Beth compromise herself with a guy like Ryan after a seven-year relationship. That was something that you couldn't get around, that you had to live with the rest of your life – just like Frank, the nasty rat that he was. And while it seemed nothing had happened yet, Jodi felt confident that this treasure hunt – if created by Ryan or even some other secret admirer – would lead to something bad.

Jodi listened intently: Beth's home phone rang once, twice, three times. She wasn't there – Beth had given her the slip.

Suddenly, though, the ringing stopped.

'Hello? Harper/Bishop residence,' chimed a young woman's voice.

Jodi's brow furrowed. That definitely wasn't Beth.

But then she realised who it was. 'Courtney? Is that you?' She knew that a young neighbour and her family took care of Brinkley while Beth and Danny were at work.

Gum snapped on the other end of the line. 'Speaking. Who is this?'

'It's Jodi. Beth's friend. Is she there?'

The girl answered immediately. 'No, she hasn't gotten home from work yet.' There wasn't the slightest hesitation, which suggested she was telling the truth.

'Are you sure?' Jodi pressed, wondering if maybe Beth had popped in and back out again, without Courtney knowing.

'Yes, I'm sure. I've been here for the past hour or so playing with little Brinkley. She hasn't gotten home yet. Neither has Danny,' she continued, as if anticipating Jodi's next question. 'Maybe they, like, met up after work and went for dinner or something?'

Jodi bristled. She doubted that very much. And what's more, now she had confirmation that something very bad was about to go down. Beth had gone back on her word that she was done with the treasure hunt, and it annoyed Jodi even more that she had also intentionally given her the slip. Lying and sneaking around wasn't the Beth she knew. Further proof that this thing had corrupted her friend.

'I don't think that's the case, Courtney,' said Jodi bluntly. 'I'm pretty sure where Beth is – and I also know exactly who will tell me.'

And with that she said goodbye to the teen, threw back the rest of her drink – hiccuped – and grabbed her tab.

A few minutes later, Jodi threw open the glass doors of Beth's apartment building. Immediately zeroing in on her target, she walked with determination across the lobby, heading directly to Billy's desk, where he was on the phone to a resident.

'Yes, Mrs Lovejoy, I can absolutely look out for that package for you. And no, Mrs Lovejoy, I will be sure that the UPS man doesn't tamper with it. Ach, I hope you don't think they do that? There are standards they have to adhere to,' the concierge was saying, holding up a finger to Jodi to indicate that he would be right with her.

She tapped her foot impatiently. She was aware of Mrs Lovejoy – the woman was nuts, from what Beth had told her. Goddamn talkative too.

'Mrs Lovejoy, of course – yes. Yes. Yes.' Billy looked at Jodi and winked but as an answer she simply narrowed her eyes at him and gave the hand motion for 'wrap it up'. When Billy continued on, she realised she couldn't wait any longer, and she promptly reached across the desk and put her finger on the receiver button – ending Billy's call.

'What the hell …?' he exclaimed. 'Don't you know that you are going to get me in serious trouble with that woman? I need to call her back.'

But Jodi held fast. 'Nope, not right now you aren't. Not until you answer my question. I saw Beth walk in here a while ago. But she's not at home. Don't try to tell me she is because I just talked to the dog sitter and she never made it upstairs. So where did she go?'

Billy pursed his mouth.

'Tell me, Billy,' Jodi growled, her upper lip curling.

'I can't,' he blurted, looking uncomfortable. 'She swore me to secrecy. She said I can't tell you.'

Jodi took a deep breath. 'So, Beth said specifically that you couldn't tell *me*?'

He nodded. 'Yes. She said that if you came here asking about where she went, then under no circumstances should I tell you.'

'Uh-huh, I see,' said Jodi, considering her options.

At that moment, the phone rang and Billy seemed happy to have something else to do other than suffer under Jodi's withering glare.

'Hello, Mrs Lovejoy, ah, I'm so sorry, yes, the phone

slipped, no, I didn't mean to hang up on you. I'm terribly sorry, I—'

But Jodi snatched the phone away before Billy could say another word.

'Mrs Lovejoy? No, this isn't Billy. He's indisposed just now. This is Jodi Cartwright, I'm a friend of Beth Harper; she lives in your building. Yes, on twenty-eight, that's right. Hey, Mrs Lovejoy, I actually need a favour from you.' She paused, listening to the woman on the other end of the line. 'No, don't worry, I don't have to come up to your apartment. This favour can be done right over the phone.' She nodded. 'Uh-huh, the phone. Right. I know you love to talk. Mrs Lovejoy, I need you to ask Billy a question for me.' Another pause. 'Why won't I ask him myself? Right. Good question. Because he won't talk to me about this. But he will talk to you.' Jodi looked up at Billy, who was looking decidedly uncomfortable, and smiled. 'Sure. So I need you to ask Billy where Beth went off to. I'm pretty sure he put her in a cab. I need to know where she went.' She smiled winningly at the Scotsman, feeling triumphant. 'OK, I'm going to hand you back to Billy now. I just need to find out where she went. No, she's not in danger, so you don't need to call the police. All you need to do is ask him the question.' Jodi smiled as she listened. 'Well, that's very nice of you. Yes, I try to be a good friend. Yes, maybe I will stop by to introduce myself one day. Sure, I absolutely love cats. Great. Talk to you soon.'

She pushed the phone back under Billy's nose. He took

it with visible reluctance, realizing that he was about to be harassed not only by Jodi but no doubt by Mrs Lovejoy too.

'Hello, Mrs Lovejoy,' Billy said his voice terse, while Jodi smiled triumphantly. 'I'm sorry about that. Yes, I know Jodi. No, I'm not supposed to tell her where Beth went. Why? I don't know. Beth just said – yes, it does indeed seem that she found a loophole.' Billy paused and frowned. 'I see. Well, that's nice. You like a girl with some spunk – and smarts.' Billy fell silent and Jodi leaned forward. She knew that Mrs Lovejoy was asking Billy the question that she needed an answer to right at that moment.

Of course, she should have figured out the answer, but she had to be sure. This treasure hunt was progressing rapidly; she had no idea what could have changed in the short amount of time that had passed since she last saw Beth. Maybe another 'gift' had turned up?

'The Waldorf Astoria,' Billy confessed wearily. 'She left about thirty minutes ago.'

And with nary a backward glance or indeed a goodbye, Jodi rushed through the doors, hailed the first cab that she saw and was off.

Billy felt as worn out as if he had just worked two ten-hour shifts. Trust Jodi to get the upper hand on him.

He bit his lip, hoping that Beth had had enough time to do what she needed to.

Chapter 26

'Ah. I see you figured it out,' said Steve, the Waldorf employee who had originally provided Beth with the book and the five-dollar bill on the street earlier.

'You!' Beth exclaimed happily. 'I saw your jacket. But I didn't know you worked here.' She smiled, revelling in the happy coincidence before she realised her error. This wasn't a coincidence, of course. None of it was. The glove in the hallway upstairs, the Russian gentleman who had instructed her come down to the lost and found, and now Steve, who conveniently happened to be waiting here for her.

It was all carefully scripted, she thought. *And the mere fact that I am hitting these 'markers' means that I must be getting somewhere, doesn't it?* She felt her spirit soar – she was exactly where she was supposed to be.

'Apparently,' Beth continued, 'I am pretty good at this. And yes, yes, I'm sure that you are sworn to secrecy by whoever has arranged all this, but I need to report that I found something – apparently lost on the twenty-third floor. This black cashmere glove. It needs its mate.'

Going along with the script, she winked at Steve and smiled, feeling very clever and confident.

But his face gave nothing away. 'You said you found a glove? On the twenty-third floor?' he repeated.

Beth nodded and placed it on the marble countertop. 'Yep. Seems odd – a cashmere glove just lying around like that – very out of place. And so I knocked on the door. The glove was lying outside one of the hotel room doors – a suite. The gentleman who answered, well, he suggested that I come down here and turn it in. He said it wasn't his, but I think that he is involved in this, just like you are,' she added with a knowing grin.

Steve picked up a clipboard that was on his side of the desk. 'The suite on twenty-three? Yes, Mr Yussopov. Nice gentleman.'

Beth's eyebrows rose when she heard the name. The woman's voice inside the suite had called him Yuri. And Steve just revealed his last name.

Yuri Yussopov. She had a full name, and, again, it was sounding familiar. Beth thought hard. How did she know that name?

Steve reached across the counter and picked up the glove. 'Thanks. I appreciate you turning this in.' Then he just smiled and turned back to whatever he was doing.

Beth suddenly felt confused. 'What? I don't get it. You're

269

just going to take it? There isn't another glove? I don't understand.'

He smiled again. 'Actually, it *was* reported missing.'

'By whom?' she enquired anxiously.

'By someone who thinks that you're the most important thing in the world,' Steve said slowly, with particular emphasis on the last half of the sentence.

'Sorry – what?' She blinked, hoping to catch what he was trying to tell her.

'Someone out there thinks that you're the most important thing in the world, Beth. Does that make sense?'

Beth narrowed her eyes. She was almost sure Steve was quoting something. A line from another movie? It had to be.

You're the most important thing in the world. If it was another movie quote, then it was an incredibly obscure reference. Beth racked her brain. It definitely wasn't from *Sleepless in Seattle*, or *You've Got Mail*, or *An Affair to Remember* – none of the easily identifiable New York movie classics. Maybe something more modern? *Something Borrowed, Sex and the City* or *Definitely Maybe*?

But again, nothing jumped out.

'That's it? That's all I get?' she implored. 'But that makes no sense ...'

Evidently feeling that he had toyed with her enough, Steve cleared his throat. 'Actually, there is something else. My instructions were to give you this.' He slid an envelope that had a noticeable bulge in it across the desk to her. On the front, there was some nondescript handwriting. Simple block letters that read 'Beth'.

'The person who believes that you're the most important thing in the world left this for when you turned in the glove.'

Now what . . . ? Beth reached for the envelope with shaking hands. She swallowed hard and felt Steve's eyes on her, studying her.

'This is pretty awesome, actually,' he said, apparently to himself, and for the first time Beth looked up at him, wondering his age. Just then, he had sounded like a kid. A chink in his armour, perhaps?

'How old are you, Steve?' she asked. She'd thought that he might be around twenty, and his answer surprised her.

'Seventeen. Just turned. This is just a part-time job for the holidays.'

'As a concierge?' Beth asked sceptically, suspecting Waldorf concierges usually had a few more years' experience and grey hairs on them.

'Not quite,' he answered. 'Bellhop. I just knew that I needed to look out for you. Needed to be around when you came looking for lost and found.'

Satisfied by this – if not terribly illuminated – Beth nodded. If she only had a vague idea of the script that needed to be followed by the supporting characters in her journey it would help, and now she had confirmation that someone really was pulling a lot of strings and incorporating quite a few people into this quest.

'So how did *you* get involved in this, Steve?' she enquired, hoping to take advantage of the teenager's youth to get him to say something he shouldn't. But he wasn't going to be tricked.

'Let's just say that helping out with your treasure hunt will put some money in my pocket that will help me buy something nice for my girl this Christmas.'

Beth narrowed her eyes, trying to figure it all out. She was hoping there was some hidden meaning to everything that Steve was telling her now. All of the supporting roles she had come across thus far in this story did have meaning, and she was becoming surer all the time that nothing and no one involved in this quest was placed there by chance.

So if it was Ryan, how did he know Steve, or the Russian guy, or the woman from Tiffany's? Especially as a supposed city newcomer. Beth's thoughts swiftly switched back to Billy then, and how the very nature of his job put him in touch with people from all walks of life.

Something to consider?

Steve cleared his throat, and in an obvious effort to get the attention away from himself he pointed to the envelope. 'Don't you think it's time to open that?'

Nodding, Beth mentally filed away her thoughts. She would have to mull over all the angles again later and track back through all of the clues so far. Maybe that would help her achieve some clarity.

But for now, here was another mystery. 'Let's see what

you have for me now,' she said softly, focusing on the envelope.

She opened it quickly. Whatever was hidden within was round and hard. Peering inside the paper envelope, she quickly discovered her latest prize.

A single red marble.

Chapter 27

Heading back towards the apartment, Danny felt as if he had the weight of the world on his shoulders. He wondered if Beth would be home yet. He really hoped not. Today if she was there, there would be no way to hide how he was feeling.

She wasn't stupid. One of these days he knew that she was going to press him for answers. And he just wasn't ready yet. He'd been waiting for the right moment just to sit her down and confess everything, but he'd really thought he'd had a bit more time. And that whole thing he'd witnessed at Carlisle's with the guy Beth worked with had thrown everything off . . .

But today had changed things completely, and Danny now knew he could avoid it no longer.

As he rounded the corner of Gold Street, he saw Jodi suddenly rush out through the doors of his building. She was alone, but her bustling demeanour suggested that she was being chased by the devil himself. Danny stopped in his tracks, wondering if she'd seen him, and for a moment he considered ducking back around the corner to avoid her.

He really didn't feel like exchanging pleasantries – actually, knowing Jodi, *un*pleasantries – or playing a game of twenty questions with anyone, especially not now.

But she didn't notice him approaching at all. Instead, she was solely focused upon hailing a cab, which she did impressively quickly considering it was still rush hour.

Without further delay, she jumped into the back of the cab, and the car jolted forward a moment later as if Jodi had just thrown a directive at the driver that ended in, 'And step on it!' Which she probably had.

Danny wondered what her rush was. And why she'd been at his place anyway.

He closed the remaining distance between himself and the front entrance, and through the glass doors he could see Billy standing behind his desk, his head propped on his hand, looking worried. The moment the front door opened, the Scotsman jumped to attention. However, upon seeing Danny, he appeared to deflate even further.

'Hey, Billy. You OK, man?'

Billy shook his head. 'Forgive me for saying so, but no, it's been a horrible day,' he said in his drawling brogue.

Danny's brow furrowed, wondering what was up. 'Wasn't that Jodi I just saw running from the building? Where's the fire?' He gave a small smile, trying to inject some levity into the conversation, but if anything the man appeared even more frustrated.

'Yes, it was Jodi. And apparently the "fire" is at the Waldorf Astoria. That woman should be locked up,' he added, his tone heavy.

'The Waldorf?' Danny asked, his mind working. 'Why?'

Billy, his vow of silence already craftily broken, shook his head. 'I wasn't supposed to say anything but ... Beth is there. Please don't ask me what she's doing, or why she's avoiding Jodi or anything else, because I've already been involved in enough shenanigans for one day.' He sighed tiredly.

'OK.' Danny considered Billy's words and thought it all through. He had been close by the area earlier with Adele. Only a block or so away from the hotel on Park Avenue, on the same route that any cab containing Beth would have likely taken.

'When did she go there?' he asked, trying to look cool, even as his skin prickled and his concern grew.

'About an hour ago. Caught a cab like it was do or die. I don't know anything else,' the doorman added quickly.

About an hour. Danny had left Adele round about that time. And she'd come out after him on the street when, in his agitated state, he'd left his cellphone behind.

If there was a chance that Beth had even caught a glimpse of that ... it would be terrible. There would be questions. Especially when he and Adele continued what had been a rather fraught conversation right out on the street in full view.

Was it possible that Beth might have seen that ...?

Danny felt palpable fear surge through his stomach, and his knees felt weak. Today had been way too much. All of this was coming to a head now – he could feel it. Everything was surging forward like a tsunami, and it was likely that it was going to knock him down, drown him, tear him apart.

It was only a matter of time.

He distractedly left the lobby, forgetting even to bid Billy a good evening. He had this feeling, intuition almost, that Beth might had seen something, witnessed something that she shouldn't have on her way to the Waldorf – and he couldn't face the implications or inevitable questions, not yet.

Talk about timing ...

He wondered if, rather than face her later, he should head out to his folks' house in Queens, just in case. But no, his mom would naturally query an unplanned visit, and wonder why he wasn't at home with Beth, especially when he'd been using the 'flat out at work' excuse to them, too. His mother was way too intuitive and, indeed, confrontational. Nothing would get past her, and she was much more likely than Beth was to tackle him straight out about anything untoward. So going home tonight was out.

Instead, he would just retreat to the office on Madison for the night and (again) blame his absence on the big work account. It was only a partial lie. Once the current campaign had wrapped up, maybe he could focus some time on landing a new client. After all, he hadn't exactly been 'on' lately at work, that much was for sure. And as much as Danny didn't like to spend the night there – not when there were more inviting and comfortable options available to him – he didn't want to be around anyone else right now. His office offered a safe haven. It would provide him space away from all of this, and he wouldn't have to face Beth tonight when she returned.

Tomorrow, though, was another story.

Chapter 28

Beth emerged from the hotel deep in thought after bidding Steve goodbye, at least for now; she wasn't sure if he would make an appearance again sometime before this journey was over. As far as she could tell, she had to connect the tiny red marble with the quote: 'You're the most important thing in the world.'

And while she was searching her extensive mental encyclopaedia of movie knowledge, right now, nothing was ringing a bell.

But before Beth had time to think about it any further, she was pulled from her silent deliberation when she heard her name being called, angrily.

'Beth! What the hell?'

She turned round to be faced with a very irate Jodi, who was currently emerging from a cab a little way down – slightly unsteady on her feet, and looking a bit sweaty.

But Beth didn't have to wonder too hard why her friend

was upset. Jodi had obviously figured out that she had given her the slip. And of course her destination had not been too hard to figure out either.

She raised a weary hand as her friend closed the distance between them, hoping to calm her down from the outset. 'Don't be angry, OK?' she began before Jodi could get a word out. 'You have to understand. I had to do this. I couldn't just let it go. I was – *am* – unable to ignore it. Please don't be mad at me.'

But Jodi wasn't hearing Beth's excuses. 'No, don't even go there. You have no idea what you are doing. You're treading down a bad path and you are willingly walking into a spider's web. If Danny didn't set this up and Ryan did, then you have to know ... it's emotional cheating Beth – it's—'

Beth cut her off. 'No it's not. And you don't know the half of it, actually. I don't know if it is Ryan, and even if it is, I'm not going to feel bad about this. You have no idea what has happened, Jodi. My entire world has been upended.'

Jodi rolled her eyes dramatically, unwilling to listen to Beth's justifications any more. 'Oh, please. Your entire world has been upended since the last time we saw each other – about say, an hour ago? Seriously, what type of idiot do you take me for? You can't honestly expect me to—'

But Beth wasn't going to be steamrolled. 'Danny's cheating on me, Jodi. I saw him here on the street earlier with my own eyes. He was with a woman. Along the avenue a while ago, not far from here. She was running after him – I think they were arguing and—' Her voice caught in her throat, and for the first time she allowed the tears to flow freely down her cheeks. It was as if uttering the words out loud had made it all real.

At once, Jodi's expression changed, softened, as Beth felt all the betrayal, frustration and confusion finally come to a head. She sobbed unashamedly.

'Wait, wait, wait. Hold on. Slow down, tell me what you saw.' Jodi quickly pulled her into an embrace, beneath the awning of the hotel, not caring that they were attracting the attention of curious onlookers. She reached into her purse and found a Kleenex and handed it to Beth so she could dry her eyes.

Beth struggled to catch her breath and when she did, told Jodi what she had seen from the cab's window. When she was finished, she found Jodi studying her, obviously churning over the details in her mind to try to make sense of the story.

'So you just saw them – in a quarrel of sorts, you said? How did you know that they were together?'

'I just … knew.' Beth shrugged, guessing that Jodi suspected that her claim was based on little more than circumstantial evidence.

'So you didn't see them kissing or embracing? You didn't see them being physical with each other … maybe holding hands? Acting like they were together?'

'I saw her running down the street after him. He looked

to me like he'd just got dressed in a hurry or something ...
Look, Jodi, I know what you're thinking. You suspect I'm
just making an assumption, but it all makes sense, especially
taken with his behaviour lately. Him being protective over
me touching his stuff, and needing to shower the moment
he walks in the door.' She provided her friend with a brief
synopsis of what had been happening at home recently, and
as Jodi's scowl deepened Beth realised that she was coming
around to her line of thinking.

'Frank did that too,' her friend whispered, her face
solemn. 'He'd come home. Shower before giving me a kiss
or coming close to me. Like he had to wash the guilt off,
and he did, you know. He'd been with that skank – every
time he did that, he'd been in bed with her before coming
home. He always blamed it on a busy day, just being a cop.
Of course, when I caught him in the park that day with
her, well, it all made sense.' She turned her attention back
to Beth's situation. 'Are you going to confront Danny? Tell
him what you saw?'

Beth wiped the last tears from her eyes and looked
around the street, as if noticing where she was for the first
time. 'I don't know. Where do I start? How do I ask him
about it? If I ask him, then I might have to explain what I
was doing there in the first place and where I was going at
this time of day. Don't you think that complicates things
too?'

Jodi shrugged as if Beth's concern was no big deal. 'So
you don't mention that. Don't give him any ammunition to

turn the tables; just ask straight out what he was doing with that woman. This is about him, not you.'

But Beth was already shaking her head. 'No, no, no, I'm just not ready to do this.'

'Beth, you have got to be *kidding* me! You *have* to talk about this with him. You have to ask him. Demand to know who she is. If he's been screwing another woman while still in a relationship with you then that relationship is over and you need to get out of it as quickly as possible and move on. If he betrayed you on that level you have to kick him to the kerb. Immediately.'

Beth crossed her arms. 'Jodi, please. Let me do this on my own time and in my own way. I'm not you, OK? I don't do things the same. I need to think this over. Process it a little; maybe even give him the time to come forward and confess ... I don't know. But first and foremost, I need to determine how this plays out.'

Jodi furrowed her brow in confusion, and then understood that Beth was talking about the treasure hunt. 'You mean this little charade you're still pursuing?' she said wearily. 'Not your relationship.'

'Yes – and yes. I am thinking about the treasure hunt. And I'm also thinking about my relationship with Danny. Look, I promise you, I will deal with this; I just have to do it on my own terms. I can't walk into my apartment all guns blazing, making accusations, throwing his clothes off the balcony. That might be the right thing for some people – and I'm not saying it's wrong – it's just that Danny and I are different. That isn't how we do things. And if this is it,' her voice broke a little, 'if it is the end, then we will work it out our way. Jodi, I loved Danny – I . . . I love him still. And our history together is important to me.'

Her friend nodded, conceding. 'And what if he is in love with this other woman?'

'Then a new act begins for him. And for me, too. But at the moment, I have a feeling that *my* next act is tied up in this treasure hunt. So I have to go on with it. I'm not going to pretend to you that I won't be chasing down this next clue, Jodi. I'm determined to finish this, possibly now more than ever. I'm going to let it lead me all the way to the end, wherever that might be. So please don't ask me to stop.'

Beth's voice was laced with such determination that Jodi must have finally decided that she wasn't going to fight her on it any more. 'You and your crazy Hollywood talk. This isn't a movie, Beth, this is your life. But OK, fine. If you think that you need to do this because it might lead you to the next "act" in your life – whatever the hell that means – then I guess I understand. And I support you.'

'Thank you.' She smiled, allowing her friend to pull her into one more hug. 'I love you.'

Jodi held her tight. 'And I love you. You're my best friend. Don't forget that.'

'Ditto,' Beth nodded.

Jodi guffawed. 'Quit it, Patrick Swayze.' But she wasn't finished lecturing just yet. 'OK then, if you're truly set on pursuing this crazy nonsense, not only am I going to support you, but I am going to help you too. All the way to the end. If it's a serial killer, might as well make it hard for him. So,' she continued, now all business. 'I'm assuming you found something else inside that hotel?'

Beth looked at her friend with a smile, her eyes glistening with relief as she realised Jodi was back on side. She nodded.

'Then where to next?'

Chapter 29

As soon as Beth was able to compose herself again, she and Jodi began walking up Park Avenue, heading nowhere in particular, discussing the most recent clue.

Admittedly, while Jodi's movie knowledge was nowhere near on a par with Beth's, the pair were at a loss as to what it all meant and they decided to stop trying to over-think it and instead turn the search to the ever-reliable internet.

Unfortunately, plugging in the quote, 'You're the most important thing in the world to me,' to an iPhone search browser returned a slew of results – few of them focused on movies.

'So we have bloggers talking about what type of French toast they love the most, a bunch of teenagers posting on message boards about Justin Bieber, a dog rescue group, a Facebook page titled "The most important thing in the world", and a bunch of other crap,' Jodi summarised with a roll of the eyes. 'Where do we go from here?' She looked at Beth, who was lost in thought.

The two women were slowly strolling along the glittering tree-lined avenue and, completely in sync, unconsciously turned left on East 59th Street, and wandered towards Central Park South.

'Honestly, it's hard to believe that you've been making any headway with these clues – they seem so vague. You must be a lot smarter than me or something, that's for sure. For you to be putting them together, well, it's like you're a modern-day Sherlock Holmes.'

Beth grinned at her friend. 'I suppose that makes you my Dr Watson, then.'

'I guess so.' Jodi paused then, seeming to think over whether or not she should share her next words, then apparently decided to go for it. 'You know, whatever happens with Danny, just know that you have a friend. That I'm here for you if you need me. Whether it's a place to crash, someone to drink a bottle of wine and eat Ben and Jerry's with, or even get out of town to clear your head, no matter what, I'm here for you honey. OK?'

Beth nodded, willing herself not to cry again. She had already done way too much of that today. 'I know you are. Thank you.'

It was times like this that she really missed having her family close by. Up to now, and for a very long time, Danny had played that role and was a substitute family of sorts but now . . .

At least with a friend like Jodi she knew she was never alone.

Jodi hadn't finished speaking. 'But just understand that I tell you this because I really didn't have anyone else when Frank and I split up. My whole world had been Frank – to the exclusion of old girlfriends, all the people I lost touch with over the course of my marriage. And then, when that crashed and burned, I had to start all over. I know better now. If I ever get serious again – with Trevor, for instance – there's going to be better balance. You need friends. Men, well, they come and go, but not girlfriends. They are important. Every girl needs them – just to keep her sanity. And I'm glad I met you when I did.'

'Me, too.' Seeing Central Park yawn before them, Beth put her arm around Jodi's waist, touched by her friend's kind words. It was true that Jodi had plenty of bark most days, but she didn't ever bite. She was a softie to her core. 'Come on then, Watson. Let's put our heads together and solve this clue.'

As they made their way into New York's famous park, Beth's mind was busy working overtime trying to decipher the riddle.

Her thoughts continued to drift from Ryan to Billy, focusing on conversations they'd had, trying to recall any movie dialogue they might have exchanged. And while she realised she had talked with each man quite a bit about movies and New York, there was no particular thing that stood out. Certainly nothing in relation to this latest clue, anyway.

To Beth's left, Jodi had her eyes focused again on her iPhone, throwing out possible suggestions about the clue's meaning. 'Are you absolutely sure it's a movie quote? According to GoodReads there's this book called *Nobody's Baby But Mine* that contains some variation of it.'

But Beth was already shaking her head; she knew for sure that she had never once discussed books with Ryan – maybe briefly with Billy. She loved reading, certainly, but literary knowledge was much more Danny's domain. While he often described books as being akin to movies being played out in the reader's mind, for Beth, seeing the characters and locations onscreen, along with the accompanying music to manipulate her emotions, was a far better experience and, perhaps more importantly, one to be shared.

Sitting at home on the sofa, tucked up in a blanket with Bridie, enjoying their mutual passion for the classics was one of her earliest and most enduring memories of her grandmother.

But more to the point, she knew she had never read the particular book Jodi had mentioned.

'No, the answer isn't a book, I'm sure of it. All of the clues so far have been taken from movies: *Romancing the Stone*, *The Seven Year Itch*, *Serendipity*, *Breakfast at Tiffany's*. I doubt the theme would change this far into the hunt.'

Jodi nodded and went back to looking at her phone. 'There are movie variations on the quote too, in *The Matrix* and *V for Vendetta*.'

At this Beth barked a laugh. 'I don't think so. Anyway, all the films involved so far have been set or shot here in the city. Neither of those has any New York connection.'

'*Ghostbusters* then?' offered Jodi lamely.

'When was something like that said in *Ghostbusters*?' Beth asked, dubious.

Jodi just shrugged and rubbed her eyes. 'I have no idea. Google just provides a bunch of crap – I don't think there is a connection – whoever programmes these search engines needs to be fired. What about the red marble, then? What do you think that means? Man, I need a drink.'

'I don't know. This is a tough one. None of it makes sense. But that's a good idea. After the day I've had I think *I* need a drink now too. Let's go to the Boathouse.'

Jodi smiled. 'Sounds good to me. The bourbon I had earlier is wearing off.'

'Lush.'

The two rounded the path towards the popular Central Park eatery, and settled into a table on the busy outdoor drinks patio adjoining the main restaurant, directly alongside the lake. It was cold but the restaurant had helpfully provided cosy blankets for patrons to bundle up against the winter chill.

A waitress took their drinks order – another bourbon and Coke for Jodi, and a hot chocolate for Beth – and the two sat back in their seats, enjoying the peace and stillness of the lake, in the twilight of the day. Earlier on, it had looked like snow was threatening, but Beth could no longer see the sky to ascertain whether or not it was on the way. She hoped not.

Snow in Central Park at Christmastime had always been one of her favourite things about this city, but it had always symbolised magic and romance. None of which she was feeling just then.

'Roll on summer,' Jodi grumbled, draping the blanket around her shoulders 'This winter's been murder; it's like Mother Nature is trying to kill us off. 'Course, the tourists love this winter wonderland stuff. Ugh, try living here.'

Beth nodded, and looked out over the lake towards the Bethesda Fountain just visible on the opposite end from where they were sitting. The fountain, dominated by a bronze eight-foot-high winged statue at its middle, The Angel of the Waters, was a famous Central Park landmark.

In the warm summer months, the imposing fountain was a beautiful display of water, but just then it was frozen, a solid artistic ice sculpture right in the centre of the park.

The waitress returned and put the drinks down in front of the two women and Jodi wasted no time in taking a large swallow of hers.

'Man, that tastes good.' She sat in silence for a moment and turned to Beth. 'So, tell me the truth, *do* you think Ryan is behind this?'

Beth couldn't help but blush. She hadn't yet confessed

to Jodi Danny's revelation about Billy. It was all a bit embarrassing, to be honest, and truth be told, she really hoped it *was* Ryan behind the treasure hunt rather than the Scotsman. 'I don't know,' she replied honestly. 'I think that yes, there seems to be some correlation in the clues to some of the conversations we've had, and I suppose he has been sort of ... wooing me for a while.'

'And your head is turned too, I can see that,' said Jodi, but Beth noticed that there was no judgement in her voice now.

She shrugged. 'Maybe just a little. But I don't know, it's a lot to think about at the moment. As I said, I just have a feeling that this adventure might prove important – one way or another. I need to play this out first before I figure out what to do with what else is going on in my life.' She cast her eyes down to her steaming mug, suddenly feeling weary. 'But, if it's OK, I don't want to talk about all this any more. Let's change the subject.'

One thing at a time, she thought, hoping Jodi wouldn't press the issue. Thankfully, after several seconds of silence, her friend spoke again.

'So like I was saying. I'm soooo over this cold – I need to get Trevor to whisk me off to Barbados or something,' her friend babbled. 'Mmm, a frolic in Caribbean waters sounds like heaven, just me and him splashing around like teenagers.'

Beth, who had just taken a sip of her hot chocolate, suddenly stopped mid-drink. She held the warm liquid in her mouth for a moment, realizing that Jodi had just stirred a memory of something. Gulping loudly she turned to stare at her friend with a look on her face that was part enlightenment, part confusion. It was not lost on the other woman.

'Beth? You OK? Something go down the wrong way?' Jodi reached forward and slapped her hard on the back, in case she was choking.

'No, no, it's not that,' Beth croaked. 'It's something else. What you just said.'

Jodi's gaze widened in confusion. 'What I just said? About getting Trevor to take me to the—'

'No, no, not that. About splashing around in the water.'

Now on full alert, Beth turned again to look across at where the Bethesda Fountain proudly stood overlooking the lake. What Jodi had just said had sparked a memory involving the fountain. But not just a memory – an actual scene. From a movie. A very famous clip from another New York romantic film she recognized.

'Oh my goodness ...' she gasped, her hand flying to her mouth. 'How did I not think of it before?'

Jodi sat up straighter in her chair. 'What? Oh. You've figured it out, haven't you? The movie, I mean. What is it?'

Beth smiled triumphantly. '*One Fine Day*,' she told her, delighted. 'I remember it now. Michelle Pfeiffer's character Melanie says that line, "You're the most important thing in the world to me," to her son, Sammy. He just wanted to go to his soccer game, which was to be played here in Central Park.'

Jodi listened to Beth's synopsis. 'I honestly don't think I have ever seen that one. And what about the marble?'

Beth extracted the red marble from the pocket in her purse where she had placed it and set it on the table. 'It was Jack's – the hero – played by George Clooney. He let Sammy play with it and the little boy stuck it up his nose.' Jodi made a face and stuck out her tongue in disgust. 'Oh, Jodi, it wasn't *this* marble – at least I don't think so,' Beth added hurriedly. 'But in any case, it was one of the warnings that Melanie had given Jack earlier in the day: that her son liked to stick things up his nose. But Jack wasn't paying enough attention and that's exactly what happened. Sammy stuck a red marble just like this one up his nose.'

Jodi was nodding as she listened but then shrugged. 'OK, so that's all very well and good, but now where do we go? Bellevue Hospital? Lenox Hill? The ER? Not very romantic.'

But Beth was already shaking her head and standing up. She took some money out of her purse and placed it on the table to cover their drinks.

'No, not the ER. *One Fine Day* is one of those movies that did a particularly great job portraying New York as a backdrop. I remember watching it back home and being captivated – not by Clooney but the location. New York itself is as much a character in that movie as any other – it held a starring role. And there were lots of other famous city locations featured in it – Carnegie Deli, the Lincoln Center, Elizabeth Arden. But I don't think the answer is at any of those places, Jodi,' she said, eyes shining with anticipation as she realised she'd got this clue figured out too. 'I don't think I'm supposed to go to any of those places, because the hero and heroine, Jack and Melanie, realise that they are falling for each other in one very pivotal scene.'

Jodi knocked back her drink and gathered her things, sensing Beth's urgency and guessing that they would soon be departing the Boathouse.

'OK, OK, so you got me – where?'

Beth smiled and pointed across the lake.

'Over there. The fountain. Jack and Melanie splash in the puddles of water around the fountain with their kids. It was the turning point in the story.' She bit her lip. 'And call it a gut feeling, but I think that it's going to be *my* turning point in this adventure too.'

Chapter 30

'Beth, wait up – I can't run in these shoes,' Jodi called out as she struggled to keep pace with her friend while tottering unceremoniously in Lucy Choi heels. Beth was effortlessly running around the lake in boots, headed straight towards the Bethesda Fountain. 'Why do we have to rush?' Jodi moaned.

But Beth wouldn't be delayed. She ran as quickly as her legs would take her and as she rounded Terrace Drive, the Bethesda Fountain was presented before her. Her eyes frantically searched the space – the crowd – hungrily as she gasped for air after her sprint.

She was on high alert for something – anything – to indicate that she was indeed in the right place.

She knew she had just solved the clue. But, like before, what she was supposed to be looking for next, she had no idea. However, as with the rest of this hunt, Beth felt certain that she would know it when she saw it.

She stopped for long enough that Jodi had a chance to catch up. Out of breath, her friend approached from the right and followed Beth's gaze, searching the open terrace.

'OK, Sherlock, *now* what are we looking for?'

Beth took in the scene. There was a small festive-themed art exhibition of sorts taking place in one area of the terrace, couples drinking coffee on the benches, people walking their dogs and enjoying the last remnants of the day. But, truth be told, nothing out of the ordinary stuck out or grabbed her attention. It was essentially just a pretty typical evening in Central Park. 'I have no idea, Jodi. I just feel like I will know it when I see it.'

At that moment, Beth's phone beeped, signalling an incoming text.

Weird timing. Or convenient timing, perhaps? But as she grabbed her phone and looked down she saw it was just Danny.

'Just' Danny, she repeated, feeling numb. Funny how the brain modified its internal language.

She looked at the message. He was telling her that he was going back to the office; that he had to work late. Again.

Right. Again. If anything was *convenient*, it was Danny's message. She hated the fact that her imagination immediately conjured up the worst-case scenario. That he was going back to his girlfriend's place. Maybe to make up after this afternoon's drama.

She typed a terse reply. 'No problem. Have a good night,' and pressed send without another thought.

But within seconds, another text came through – again from Danny. *What are you up to – working late maybe? I'm so sorry again, that I have to bail, but I'll make it up to you, I promise.*

Make it up to her? That was just the kind of thing a cheat would say, wasn't it? Talk about a cliché. Beth focused on the screen and had to work hard at batting away some of the replies that came to mind, but then she realised it was neither the time nor the place for this. She kept her response neutral. *Finished work. Just out for a walk in Central Park with Jodi. No problem. Talk to you later.*

She hit send, secretly hoping that he wouldn't respond, but still feeling her spirits sink when indeed her phone remained silent. She guessed he was probably happy she didn't fuss. He could enjoy his time with the dark-haired woman and sleep easier tonight.

Jodi stood by, watching her friend's face and taking clear note when it fell into despair.

'Was that Danny?' she asked quietly.

Beth nodded. 'He's working late. Said he had to go back to the office.'

Jodi let out a sound that sounded disturbingly like a dog's growl. 'Jerk. I would love to give it to him for you, sweetie. But don't mind him – this has nothing to do with him. Let's stick to the plan. Put him out of your mind.'

Beth swallowed hard and knew that her friend was right. It was true: this had nothing to do with Danny. She wouldn't let his deceitful antics sully the treasure hunt.

The pair continued to wander around the perimeter of the fountain. Beth could almost feel the nervous tension radiating off Jodi's body – almost as if she was waiting for a silent assailant to lunge upon them, or maybe she was just still angry about Danny's behaviour.

But Beth didn't feel any of that anxiety. She was focused squarely on putting the pieces of the puzzle together.

'So like, how does this work then?' her friend asked. 'Are we looking specifically for something to do with the movie? Because remember, I've never seen *One Fine Day*, so I don't know how much help I can be.'

Beth shook her head. 'No, that's not really how it has worked up to now. So far I've shown up at a location to which a clue pointed. And it's there that I'm provided with another signpost. Think about when we were on the boat yesterday. The reference from *Romancing the Stone* pointed me – or should I say *you* pointed me – to the location of the boat. And it was there I received the clue to *The Seven Year Itch*. So it's likely that by figuring out this clue's location, I should come across another pointing me somewhere else.'

Jodi yawned. 'Seems like waaay too much work to me.'

'Not if you love this stuff as much as I do. I think it's great fun, and very sweet too.' She thought again about Ryan and how much in character this was. He was such a flirt by nature, and she supposed that's exactly what this was – a form of extended flirting; wooing, even.

But where will it all lead?

Beth and Jodi circled the fountain twice. Darkness had fully set in, the streetlights were on and people were beginning to leave and head back out to the city. Beth started to wonder if her timing with this one might be off. And then another thought occurred to her. What if she was in the wrong place?

'Beth, it's getting late,' Jodi said. 'Maybe it isn't your night for this one.'

But Beth wasn't satisfied just yet.

Now that the crowds at the terrace were thinning out, she was able to get a better view of the space – and the first thing that caught her eye was the small exhibition. It seemed to be a collaboration of various festive craft stalls and art exhibits, and many of them had finished selling their Christmas wares and tourist trinkets, and were closing up shop for the night.

However, one artist who continued to sit with his paintings, seemingly in no rush to leave, caught Beth's attention. Suspecting that this guy might be key somehow, she made her way over to his stand.

'Hey there,' said the man as she approached one of his canvases. Beth saw that he was showcasing a number of hand painted reproductions of various famous works. There were some that she recognized on sight, *The Starry Night* by Van Gogh, *Water Lilies* by Monet, and various others. But nothing in particular – certainly nothing in relation to the *One Fine Day* movie – jumped out at her.

'Did you paint all these?' she enquired of the young man,

who had a sallow complexion and swarthy appearance, as if he had grown up on some Mediterranean island. When he spoke he had only the subtlest hint of an accent – he had obviously been in the States long enough to lose it. So, longer than she had, anyway.

He smiled. 'Yes. I did. Not as good as some of the greats, I'm humble enough to admit, but not bad either, yes?'

Beth smiled and considered the paintings one by one. She noticed that Jodi was at the other end of the display, also studying the young man's work.

'Here you go, Beth. If you still need a Christmas present for me, this is what you should pick. More my style,' said Jodi, pointing at one particular canvas.

Beth approached to see what she was looking at and she had to laugh. 'Yes, that would fit right in with your décor. Perfect.'

The young man, who had been watching the pair, smiled and waved his hands around with great flourish. 'Ah yes, Coolidge's unsung masterpiece *Dogs Playing Poker*.' On the canvas were various breeds of dogs sitting around a poker table, throwing chips in, dealing cards.

Beth looked at the painting again, and then looked at the two canvases on either side of it. *The Son of Man*, originally by René Magritte, was there too. Famous for its ambiguous corporate appeal, the painting depicted a man in a suit with a bowler hat and an apple covering his face. And then, another painting she knew immediately on sight – *San Giorgio Maggiore at Dusk*, originally by Monet.

It was perhaps the view she remembered most from that time in Venice with Danny all those years ago. In the famous painting, Monet had skilfully captured a Venetian sunset across the lagoon waters. She had to admit, it was a very good copy – this young painter did indeed have some skill.

Noticing her interest, the man approached. 'You like this one?'

Feeling emotional, Beth nodded and felt tears pricking the back of her eyes.

Quickly she placed a smile on her face, determined not to succumb to all the wonderful memories from that trip. Danny kissing her cheek in a gondola and holding a camera with his left hand, his arm outstretched to capture the moment on film. His green eyes crinkling around the edges and that dimple that she loved on his left cheek, one that only appeared when he was about to burst out laughing, which had been the case then. Thinking back, she recalled the moment and remembered what had been funny – two gondoliers in the canal next to them had been serenading Beth. One of them had subsequently fallen off the back of his gondola into the canal, only to emerge from the water, blowing kisses their way.

A veritable movie-reel of memories continued on – she and Danny on Rialto Bridge, dancing amongst the pigeons to the café orchestra on St Mark's Square, in the Biblioteca di San Barnaba – the library in which a scene from *Indiana Jones and the Last Crusade* had been filmed. It was actually Danny who'd informed Beth of that piece of trivia, and while it wasn't an overly romantic movie, she'd had a hard time keeping her heart from pounding at the thought of swashbuckling Harrison Ford. And she had an even more difficult time not breaking into giggles as she imagined Danny trying to pull up the manhole cover that in the movie the dashing Dr Jones had crawled out of in front of the library following an escapade in the city's sewer system.

So many memories of their relationship in the good times that were once so treasured, and now were irrevocably tainted.

She pointed to the painting, a lump in her throat. 'This one – it's one of my favourites by Monet. I adore Venice and I've always especially loved this painting.'

The young man nodded. 'Yes, me too. I grew up there.'

Beth's eyes widened. 'In Venice? Oh, wow. I've been only once, but it was very special. Why did you leave?'

The artist shrugged. 'Venice, yes, it's beautiful, a great city. But I am young, artistic. And this is the City that Never Sleeps.' He smiled and ran a hand through his hair. 'New York is a great place to go to art school, and this – it helps pay the bills.'

A migrant herself, Beth could, of course, appreciate that.

'Well, you're very talented.' She took a step back and looked at the painting and then considered the others that surrounded it. *The Son of Man* and *Dogs Playing Poker*. Then an idea struck her. It couldn't be? Could it? Or was she just seeing potential clues in everything now?

But she decided to chance it. 'These three paintings,' she

asked. 'Why did you group them together? Seems like an odd choice – unless . . .'

Suddenly the young man's eyes turned mischievous.

'What is it?' she urged, feeling as if she was being left out of a joke.

'Nothing, I was just waiting to hear what you were going to say,' said the young man.

She pursed her lips. She didn't want to put words in anyone's mouth, but she had to ask. 'Do you like movies?'

And the young man's grin widened. 'Love them.'

Beth felt excitement growing in her stomach, and her heart rate speeded up. She was on to something, she knew it. 'These three pictures – they were all featured in a movie actually. Did you know that?'

Yes, this was a little different to the other clues, but here was a New York movie reference right in front of her, and Beth would be a bad detective if she didn't ask outright.

'I did know that. But I am waiting to see if you have it correct.'

Was she being tested? Beth didn't know, but she was going to play along. Realizing that something was happening, Jodi sidled up alongside her.

'What's up? Are you on to something, Beth?' she asked.

'I think I might be. OK, so *Dogs Playing Poker*, *The Son of Man* and *San Giorgio Maggiore at Dusk* were all featured in one movie, *The Thomas Crown Affair*. Am I right?' she said, waiting with bated breath for the student's reply.

'We have a winner!' said the young man theatrically. 'Yes, you are correct. And that's a great movie, by the way.'

Beth stood in front of him expectantly, waiting for a reward, anything to indicate she was on the right path. But the young man just kept smiling at her and after several seconds it was clear that there was nothing more to it. That it was just a happy coincidence that she had stumbled upon a bit of movie trivia here. She was truly looking for clues where there were none.

Her smile began to fade as the young artist finally decided it was time to pack up shop for the night. He began to put his paintings away carefully one by one, a clear indicator to Beth that he was ready to go.

She spun on her heel and looked out across the now deserted Bethesda Terrace. 'This doesn't make sense, Jodi. There has to be something more – we must be missing something.' She turned back to the young man. 'Isn't there something else? Aren't you supposed to tell me something? Isn't there a clue here?' she pressed, desperation entering her voice.

But from the look on his face alone, it was clear the young artist had no idea what she was talking about.

Jodi put a comforting hand on Beth's arm and tried to pull her away from the artist's stand – especially as the guy's face had by now changed from warm and friendly to concerned that Beth just might be one of those crazy New Yorkers.

'I don't think he has anything else for you, sweetie. It

Melissa Hill

was a coincidence. The movie stuff, it was just by chance.'
Jodi turned her attention back to the young man who was
regarding the scene with curiosity. 'Thank you very much
for your time. You do beautiful work. Merry Christmas.'
And she went about escorting her confused and somewhat
dazed friend towards the nearest park exit.

'Time to go home now, Beth. It's been a long day for
both of us. I'll see you at work the day after tomorrow,
OK? Just try not to think about it too much and enjoy your
day off.'

Beth nodded glumly, and even as she allowed Jodi
to bundle her into a cab, giving the driver directions to
her Gold Street apartment, she couldn't overcome her
disappointment.

For the first time in this quest, she'd failed.

Chapter 31

Beth lay wide awake in bed most of the night, working the clue over and over in her head, racking her brains trying to figure out if there was somewhere else she was supposed to go, something that she'd missed.

She even summoned *One Fine Day* on Netflix and watched it through from beginning to end, staying up until the wee hours of the morning and considering every possible New York location at which the movie had been filmed, searching for potential relevance.

She was so sure that she had got it right again: that the answer to the clue lay with the Bethesda Fountain. That was the turning point in the movie – it had to be where she was supposed to head. Maybe, if nothing else worked, she would return tomorrow and scope it out again.

Finally catching some sleep around three o'clock in the morning, she rested fitfully until her phone buzzed at eight, signalling an incoming text. While she expected some sort of excuse from Danny again that morning, she was surprised when instead it turned out to be Ryan. He was wondering if she was able to steal away for a bit and grab some brunch. Obviously he wasn't on shift in Carlisle's today either.

Not expecting to see Danny any time soon – he was sure to keep up the 'working late at the office farce' – Beth agreed to Ryan's proposal. She had nothing else planned for her day off.

Though she wondered now if this out-of-the-blue request meant that she had indeed missed something yesterday, and that as a result Ryan needed to drop some hint – inadvertent or otherwise – to help spur her on in her search.

Jumping from bed, she agreed to meet him outside the building in half an hour. Her decision to allow him to come that close to her apartment was based on the knowledge that Danny was likely waking up in his lover's arms right now.

The notion made her reckless. 'I can't think about that now,' she told herself as she carefully applied her lipstick in the bathroom mirror. 'Don't think about it, you'll drive yourself crazy.'

So she turned her thoughts to Ryan, and took extra care as she styled her hair and chose what to wear. She selected a fluffy red cashmere sweater and a great pair of skinny jeans, and, even in light of her restless night's sleep, she had to admit she looked pretty good.

As she stepped into the crisp cold of the morning outside

her building, she turned to the left and immediately saw Ryan strolling her way from the direction of the subway. She waved at him and couldn't deny that her heart sped up just a little as he returned the greeting.

'Well hello, gorgeous, fancy meeting you here,' Ryan grinned, dimple in full view. He reached forward and enveloped her in a friendly – albeit borderline intimate – hug, and then took a step back, a look of obvious admiration on his face. 'Wow, you look beautiful today, Beth. How on earth did your guy even let you out of the house?'

She knew he was joking – laying it on thick – but she still felt a small pang of guilt bubble up in her throat. Of course he had no idea what had happened yesterday. Should she tell him? Was it a kind of betrayal to spill her secrets? To implicate Danny without talking to him first?

Beth didn't know. She was completely unsure of proper protocol here, but then the image of Danny and that woman entered her mind and she remembered her vow of entering the 'next act' in her life.

'Well, Danny has no idea how I look, actually. And frankly, he probably wouldn't care,' she replied airily. 'So where are we going for brunch?'

Ryan was obviously curious, and Beth saw something hungry in his gaze. 'Hold on, you don't get off that easy,' he said. 'What's happening?'

She shrugged and tried to look evasive. 'Oh, it's a long story. I'll tell you once we get in out of this cold. But you have to keep it a secret, OK?' Suddenly realizing she was nervous to be standing out in front of her building gossiping about Danny, she had the urgent desire to leave – get out of there – before she saw anyone she knew: Billy, Mrs Lovejoy, Courtney, anyone who might question what she was doing. 'Come on, let's catch a cab.'

And just as Ryan helped Beth into a cab, a bike messenger pulled up to the front of the building with a package.

Regardless of any initial worry or hesitation she might have had, Beth was soon telling all over brunch. She related to Ryan everything she had seen on her way to the Waldorf yesterday, which elicited appropriate expressions of shock and indignation.

Of course, it also caused Ryan to do something else – something she wasn't prepared for just yet – move his chair closer to her and put his arm around her. It wasn't a pushy gesture – more sympathetic – and he was just trying to comfort her, she knew, but there was still something that was very intimate about the action.

Beth wasn't ready for that sort of thing yet. Even though she felt the electricity between them, she reminded herself of her beloved grandmother's mantra that two wrongs don't make a right.

She couldn't overlook that – not just yet, no matter how tempting it was to get closer to Ryan. Beth noticed that he kept looking at her lips, and was now barely disguising his attraction to her, but she also knew that was because of the information she had just provided. She had introduced the possibility of trouble in her relationship and Ryan was seeing it as an invitation.

And why shouldn't he? she supposed. He'd surely noticed the sparks between them as well.

'Beth, dump him,' he said suddenly, his gaze lingering on her face. 'You don't deserve to be cheated on. The guy should have his head examined. You know that, don't you? I swear, if I had a girlfriend like you—'

Her heart skipped a beat.

'If I had someone like you,' he continued, shaking his head 'it would be downright impossible for me to even *look* at another woman. Honestly, leave him.'

Beth blushed and looked down into her lap, unsure how to respond, when she felt Ryan put a finger under her chin and direct her gaze to his. 'I mean it.'

She swallowed hard. *Oh God, is he going to kiss me?* He was getting closer, leaning in; he *was* going to kiss her. And right then Beth realised that she wanted to be kissed. Indeed, she could feel the attraction pulsating throughout her body.

But then, something dawned on her. The next act of her story. It couldn't start like this.

Two wrongs don't make a right …

Yes, this treasure hunt was romantic – in and of itself, being the kind of thing commonplace in a romantic movie plot. But Beth had seen enough such movies, and knew enough about the rules to understand that happy endings didn't happen for cheaters, or heroines who started one relationship without finishing another.

311

She had to do this the right way. If Ryan was in her future, she didn't want a cloud hanging over them from the get-go. Karma mattered.

Beth placed a shaking hand on Ryan's chest and pulled away. She had been seconds away from feeling his lips on hers, and as much as she thought she wanted it, it wasn't time.

'I'm ... sorry, no.' She scooted her chair back and felt her soul deflate ever so slightly at the pained look that found its way onto his face.

'No?' he repeated. It was both a statement and a question. And he needed an answer.

'It's a no ... for now, I suppose. I mean ... I want you to understand that I have to settle things with Danny. I haven't even spoken to him about this yet—'

'Because he was with her last night,' Ryan argued, his tone short.

She bit her lip. He had a point. 'Look, that may be the case, but I owe it to him not to do anything rash. I keep telling myself that two wrongs don't make a right and—'

'Remember what we talked about at lunch the other day?' he interjected. 'You do understand that seeing him – with her – that was a sign, a signal from destiny, fate, whatever. You deserve to be happy, Beth. That's the moral of this story.' Ryan smiled as he realized his words seemed to be striking a chord. 'OK,' he acquiesced. 'I can wait if you can. I'm not going anywhere.'

'Thank you. It's just ... well, I suppose, it's hard to explain but—'

'No need to explain. I guess I wouldn't expect anything else from you, and the last thing I want is to push you. Just let me know when you're ready and I'll be here, OK?'

She looked across the table at him, hardly able to believe that what she'd suspected all along was real. It truly wasn't just flirting on his part; this gorgeous man truly did have feelings for her. And maybe he was right; maybe destiny was at play.

Although it pained Beth to admit as much, hadn't she known deep down for some time now that her relationship was Danny was dying? So maybe this was the universe's way of telling her to move on. Being in the right place at the right time yesterday, witnessing what she had ... clearly there was a reason for all that. And despite the pain of it now, Beth truly believed she was supposed to get her happy ending.

But before that, she would just have to let Danny go.

She definitely wasn't looking forward to that part: the bit in a movie following a big bust-up or revelation, where the heroine typically goes through a soul-searching transitory period, usually via a montage set against a heartrending soundtrack of her packing her old life away, before she's ready to begin anew.

But thank goodness, Beth thought as Ryan smiled reassuringly at her, like most movie heroines, in the end she too would have the true love of her life waiting in the wings.

Chapter 32

Afterwards, Ryan shared a cab with Beth on the way back to her apartment.

'Well, I suppose this is it,' she said as she gripped the door handle of the cab.

'For now,' he said, his meaning clear.

Beth felt her mouth go a bit dry; the tension was radiating off them both. She had been so silly to try to pretend to Jodi that this heat wasn't present before, to brush it off as a simple flirtation.

One step at a time, her conscience warned her. There was still Danny to consider.

'Are you sure you don't want to do something else today?' he asked. 'There's this great new exhibition at the Met and—'

'Thanks, but no,' Beth replied, her mind elsewhere. 'I need to get this over with first.' Now that she'd come to terms with the fact that her life with Danny was really over, she knew she needed to confront him and talk about what happened next. And she wouldn't be able to concentrate on anything else until she did that. It would be difficult, of course, if he continued to avoid her, but either way she couldn't in good faith enjoy being with Ryan until then.

She smiled and gently touched the side of his face. 'Thank you for brunch.'

'Any time. I mean that,' he said softly, his gaze boring into hers. 'Whenever you need me, I'm here.'

Swallowing hard, Beth opened the door and got out of the cab – feeling instantly sorry to leave his company. She was about to wave goodbye when he reached out to grab her hand.

'Remember, just follow the signs, OK?' he said his voice gentle yet, to Beth, heavy with meaning. 'There's no such thing as coincidence. I'll be here at the end, no matter what happens, I promise. I'll wait.'

She stared back at him as he lowered his head and pressed his lips on the top of her hand, giving it a light kiss and, even while she savoured the sensation, his words echoed in her brain.

Follow the signs. No such thing as coincidence.

Was he talking about the treasure hunt? Or her relationship?

When Ryan let go of Beth's hand, she closed the cab door and gave a small wave, struck by his words and their possible meaning. Suddenly she wondered if she had been right all along last night in the park at the fountain.

Is that what he was trying to tell her?

Feeling in a daze as she made her way back to her building, Beth checked the time. She had been at brunch for only a couple of hours, and had the distinct feeling that, once again, her world had shifted on its axis.

Walking into the lobby, she immediately noticed that Billy was working again. He must be pulling overtime. Giving him a tentative smile when he looked up at her from behind his desk, she took a pre-emptive approach to the conversation. 'You're here; I must have missed you earlier.'

Billy snorted. 'Likely wished it, no doubt. What did you do? Sneak in last night and out this morning?'

She shook her head. 'There was no sneaking involved this time. I went out earlier; you just weren't at your post.'

'In any case, after sneaking a few shots of Johnnie Walker last night, let me assure you that my nerves are now calm. Never ever put me up against your friend again, though. That's just cruel.'

Beth laughed. 'I'm so sorry.' Then her tone changed. 'Danny hasn't come home, by chance, has he?' she asked. 'I think he ended up staying at the office last night.'

'Aye, I know, I saw him come in last night and leave just as quick. But no, not a sign of him this morning.'

Beth breathed a bit deeper, not sure whether to feel disappointed or relieved that he wouldn't be there when she got home. 'OK, well thanks, and again, sorry about Jodi.'

She prepared to head up to her apartment when Billy suddenly called her back. 'Ah, hold on just a sec. A package

came for you earlier. It must have been while you were out.'
The doorman turned round and headed towards a storage
room just off the lobby where he typically left residents'
deliveries.

'A package, you say?' Beth repeated suspiciously.

Billy emerged from the storage room with a brown
paper-covered bundle about two by three feet across and
rectangular in shape. 'Yes. Here you go. And funnily
enough, it was delivered by that same bike messenger from
the other day – the one that I was a bit cagey about.'

Beth's radar went up. 'The same bike messenger from
the other day?' The young guy who had made the delivery to her at Carlisle's. And the same one (supposedly)
responsible for delivering the anonymous tickets to the boat
exhibition ...

'The very fella,' Billy confirmed, his face not giving anything away.

Beth reached for the package. It must have been delivered after she had left to meet Ryan. Had this all been
co-ordinated? Had Ryan perhaps wanted to get her out of
the apartment for when the messenger showed up?

Or had the parcel been delivered by a messenger at all?

Beth's pulse quickened and she had to resist the urge to
tear the parcel open there and then. Instead, she bid Billy
goodbye and calmly made her way up to the twenty-eighth
floor. By the time she reached her apartment her heart felt
as if it might explode.

Fumbling to put her key in the lock, she finally was able

to get through her front door, throw her handbag on the ground and place the parcel on her dining-room table. Taking a deep breath to steady herself, Beth clenched her shaking hands for a second before reaching forward and ripping open the paper.

When she was finished unwrapping her treasure, she stared at her discovery and her breath caught in her throat.

It was the young artist's painting she had admired yesterday, the rendition of Monet's *San Giorgio Maggiore at Dusk*.

Right then Beth knew for sure that she had been right. She *had* solved the clue last night. And this was how her secret admirer wanted to make sure she knew she was on the right track.

She smiled triumphantly as she considered her latest reward.

Ryan was right. Follow the signs. There were no coincidences.

The Thomas Crown Affair. Beth thought hard about the latest movie riddle the painting's arrival had presented.

It was obviously a reference to the 1999 remake – not the original with Faye Dunaway and Steve McQueen, but the one with Rene Russo playing savvy Catherine Banning and Beth's fellow countryman Pierce Brosnan as Thomas Crown. The two films, while of the same name, were vastly different.

The original had portrayed Thomas Crown as a common bank robber, but in the 1999 version the character was played as a rich, cultured art thief. As well as a very slippery and smart art thief. Beth considered the painting. She put her right index finger on the canvas and felt the paint that had been used by the young Italian artist bubble up.

His work was very good for an imposter of sorts, she thought, while, of course, it was easy to see that this wasn't a real Monet. But Beth couldn't understand why she suddenly felt so internally discombobulated.

Imposter, she thought again. That was the word that was making her uneasy. But why? Obviously, she had solved the clue and figured out the right movie – exactly as she had been meant to. And this painting was supposedly pointing her in the direction of her next step.

She propped the painted canvas up against the wall in her living room, allowing a curious Brinkley to come forward and give it a cursory sniff. Realizing it was nothing edible, the dog quickly lost interest and hopped up on the couch, sighing contentedly and closing his eyes for a snooze.

But Beth was the exact opposite of her unconcerned dog. Energy coursed through her veins. She truly didn't understand why she felt a sense of foreboding, but she figured the only way to rid herself of this feeling, and settle her mind, was to solve this clue.

She went to her bedroom to retrieve her laptop and as she entered the room she momentarily smelled Danny's familiar scent. He always wore Chanel Pour Homme. The fragrance was in the air as if he had just left the room, but she knew that not to be the case.

Beth felt vaguely put off by the feeling and, as she picked up her laptop from the nightstand, she even looked back, confirming in her own mind that he wasn't actually in the room with her.

The spooky feeling was heightened further when she felt the hairs on the back of her neck standing up. Her intuition was trying to tell her something, that much she knew, but what, she didn't have any idea. The synapses in her brain were obviously not connecting.

Trying her best to brush off the feeling of discomfort she was suddenly feeling, Beth returned to the painting in her living room.

She picked up her phone as she booted up the laptop and called Jodi on her cellphone. She had to tell her friend what had happened and what she had found.

Jodi finally answered on the fourth ring. She sounded sleepy, as if Beth had just woken her up.

'Are you still in bed? Did I wake you?' Beth asked, looking at the clock. It was almost midday, though she did know Jodi was on the later shift that day. Then she stifled a smile when she heard a man's voice in the background. Obviously Trevor had come over last night when Jodi reached home – the reason her friend was still in bed.

'I'm still in bed,' said Jodi groggily. 'But I wasn't asleep. What's up?'

Beth got straight to the point. 'I was right about the paintings,' she said, and filled Jodi in on the rest of the story. When she finished, she admitted, 'However, something's still not sitting right with me.'

Fully alert now, Jodi mumbled something to her bedmate and focused on Beth. 'OK, so talk to me. What's not adding up? You have confirmation that the movie in question is *The Thomas Crown Affair*. That's good. And it's an easy clue. I've seen that flick so I know that it's all pretty obvious. The whole movie centres around the Metropolitan Museum of Art. Easy.'

Beth knew that, but it was something else. It all felt *too* obvious to her, plus there was something more that she was reading into this clue as well. As much as she searched her memory, she couldn't remember talking about *The Thomas Crown Affair* to Ryan at all. It was true there were other coincidences at play here, yet he himself had told her there were no coincidences. There was the mere fact that the painting had shown up while Ryan was taking her to brunch and making a very open effort about wooing her. And yes, obviously this entire hunt was focused on New York movie locations, but the clue continued to trouble Beth.

'I thought about that, too. However, it's not like the painting is actually there at the Met. The original one, I mean – that was just in the movie.' She typed the painting's title, *San Giorgio Maggiore at Dusk*, into her laptop.

'Are you in front of a computer?' she asked Jodi.

'I can be. Give me a second.'

A moment later the two women were comparing the findings of their respective internet searches.

'So the original is owned by, and apparently housed at the National Museum in Wales,' said Beth. 'That doesn't do me any good.' She sighed. 'Again, simply going to the Met and wandering around feels way too obvious to me. I know the clue has to do with not just any painting but this one.'

Jodi made some agreeable murmuring noises on the other end of the phone. 'Right, no, I get you. It makes sense. But what if ... ?' her voice trailed off.

Beth felt eager to hear what Jodi was thinking. 'What if what?'

'Hold on. I'm just checking something out. Something just occurred to me.'

Beth peered at the screen of her computer, wondering if Jodi was seeing something on her end that she apparently wasn't seeing on hers. There seemed to be a considerable mountain of information out there about this painting – tons of essays on it, history on it, what Monet had been thinking and contemplating while he was working on it. But there wasn't necessarily anything that was current and timely.

'So think about it this way,' Jodi said then. 'If you feel very sure that this painting is part and parcel of the next step in the trail, then just learning a bunch of history about the painting isn't going to suffice.'

Beth pressed the phone to her ear. Jodi shared the

thought that just occurred to her but it sounded as if her friend was on to something else too. And her suspicions were confirmed when suddenly Jodi let out a little squeal of satisfaction on the other end of the phone.

'Bingo,' she said.

'What, what is it? What did you find?' Beth flipped through Google pages – nothing was standing out.

However, Jodi sounded determined to torture her a little longer, allowing the suspense to build. She wasn't about to divulge her knowledge easily.

'So you know how sometimes art collections, or individual works travel?' she said to Beth eventually. 'Obviously not everyone can drop what they are doing and head off to the Louvre or the Vatican Museum or the National Museum in Wales at a moment's notice, yes?'

Beth was having none of this drawing out the explanation. Jodi had this thing figured it out and if she knew what was good for her she seriously needed to tell her *now*. 'Jodi, please, what is it? What are you looking at? What do you know?'

'Do yourself a favour and leave the general web search. Instead click on "News" at the top of the page.'

Beth returned to the search bar and immediately found what Jodi was talking about. With shaking fingers, she clicked on 'News'.

And there it was. The answer. A single news story.

The headline of the *New York Times* article was dated almost two weeks ago and read: '*Venetian History Exhibit at the Metropolitan Museum of Art Features Famed Monet Painting'.*

And that painting was *San Giorgio Maggiore at Dusk*.

It was currently on display here in New York for the holiday season. Part of a display featuring the history of Venice.

There's this great new exhibition at the Met ...

Ryan had talked about that very same exhibition earlier, had even asked her if she wanted to come along! Did he realise that she was having trouble figuring out the clue, and that the penny would drop if she saw it at the exhibition.

And when that happened, he would be right by her side ...

It really *was* Ryan, Beth realized. He had arranged this whole thing; the current clue as well as his words this morning merely hammered that home.

'Jodi, you're brilliant,' she gasped breathlessly, feeling true admiration for her friend as another feeling blossomed in her chest. And Beth knew exactly what the feeling was.

She was about to discover all the answers. She just knew it.

The hunt was coming full circle.

'You can say that again, Sherlock. Get yourself together. Dr Watson will meet you there.'

'Follow the signs ...' Beth whispered to herself, as she got ready to head to the Met.

Chapter 33

Beth wasn't sure how Jodi was able to accomplish it, but her Bronx-based friend had actually beaten her to the Metropolitan Museum of Art by the time Beth's cab pulled up in front of the famous building located at 1000 Fifth Avenue. But then again, she'd probably just come from Trevor's on the Upper East Side.

Jumping out of the cab, Beth glanced down the street and realized that they had literally only been blocks away the evening before, while in Central Park searching for this clue. Indeed, Bethesda Terrace emptied out onto East 72nd Street, and here she was ten blocks north of that.

Ten blocks – and something big is going to happen in there. I just know it. I feel it in my bones, Beth thought. She peered up at the building.

Once I walk those stairs and go inside, there is a good chance I might come out a different person. My destiny lies within the museum.

Her hands shook at the thought.

Destiny. She could almost hear the movie soundtrack swell in the background.

'Come on, Beth, what are you waiting for? I already bought our tickets. The suspense is killing me,' cried Jodi as she jogged down the stairs, watching her step carefully as her heels were not made for jogging. She rushed forward and thrust an admission pass into Beth's hand and then grabbed her by the elbow. 'Seriously, let's go. I would have thought you would be moving faster. After all, this is *your* treasure hunt and—'

'Jodi, hold on a second,' said Beth, pulling back from her friend's grasp. She stood unmoving, staring up at the museum's façade. 'I need to catch my breath – just for a second.'

Her friend turned to her with a quizzical look on her face. 'Are you having second thoughts about going in? But if you don't, you won't be able to locate the next clue.'

Beth bit her lip and considered Jodi's words, unsure as to whether or not she should tell her she was now almost certain that it was Ryan. 'I think this might be it. I think this is the finale.'

Tilting her head in confusion, Jodi said, 'What do you mean, the finale? You mean the end of the hunt? What makes you think that?'

Beth swallowed hard. 'I just have a feeling that this is it. That whatever is waiting for me in there is going to change things. Ryan said it himself – there are no coincidences. I

326

think I know what I'll find in there; I think I've known it for a long time.'

Jodi folded her friend into a hug. 'You don't have to go in then. Not if you're scared. Not if you don't want this.'

Beth accepted the embrace but shook her head. 'It's not that I'm scared. That's not it. It's something else. Excitement? Yes. Trepidation. That, too.'

'You sound like a bride on her wedding day,' Jodi smirked, and Beth sucked in a breath. The butterflies in her stomach increased the speed of their wings and Beth steeled herself.

'That's it. It's now or never. Show time.'

Beth and Jodi walked through the entryway of the first floor of the museum and headed to the information desk to snag a map.

'This place is huge,' Jodi commented. 'It's been years since I've been here. How's that for a born-and-bred New Yorker?'

Beth fixed her stare on the map. 'A lot of the permanent galleries are on the first floor. That much I know.'

Scanning her eyes across labels indicating 'Egyptian Art' and 'Impressionist Gallery', she turned her attention to a list of special exhibitions outlined in the margin and quickly found what she was looking for. 'There it is: "Legends of Venetian History". It's back here – in galleries 950 through 960.'

'Furthest point in the building,' Jodi muttered glumly,

looking at her feet. 'Figures. I should have worn ballet flats.'

But Beth couldn't concentrate on her friend's footwear concerns – she was completely focused on her goal and took off in front, making a beeline for the furthest galleries on the first floor.

The museum was busy with tourists and extra crowds in town for the holidays.

'This place is packed. Now I remember why I don't go to tourist hotspots in New York. Case in point, don't you think?'

Beth agreed that it was indeed busy, but she also knew that somewhere amongst that crowd was the answer to her puzzle. She just had to make it to the Venetian exhibition and, once she was there she was sure that she would find whatever she was looking for.

Or whomever, her inner voice clarified, reminding her of the belief that this clue would provide her with all the answers she needed about this entire adventure.

Giddy with anticipation, Beth noticed that her palms were sweating and she had a brief flashback of the kiss that Ryan had placed on the back of her hand that morning.

There are no coincidences, the same little voice in her mind reminded her once again – repeating it like a mantra. However, the voice went silent the moment that the doorway to the far galleries appeared before her. Beth stopped in her tracks and Jodi bumped into her back.

'What are you stopping for?' she asked sharply. 'Come on, we're here.'

Outside of the gallery entrance stood a museum docent, handing out programmes to the special exhibition. Beyond, Beth spied colourful and beautifully ornate Venetian masks – the same kind as the one that was in her bedroom – and she couldn't help feeling once again melancholy as memories flooded her brain. Venice. How ironic. The city and its themes were almost a constant backdrop to her and Danny's relationship – for good and bad.

No coincidences, she reminded herself once more. She was on the right path, she just knew it. She took a deep breath and continued on behind Jodi, who took two programmes and handed one to Beth. Beth opened the small booklet and flipped through it. She scanned a list of the art that was on display and soon found what she was looking for.

San Giorgio Maggiore at Dusk was the showcased work in gallery 955.

She pointed at the map. 'This is where we have to go. Here.'

Jodi nodded, taking in her surroundings. Her eyes were wide as saucers she looked at all of the beautiful masks on display. 'This stuff is amazing.'

Beth nodded and swallowed hard. 'It's representative of the city. Probably one of the most beautiful places I have ever been in my life. I'll never forget it.'

A second wave of bittersweet sadness washed over her. No, she would never forget Venice. Never forget her time with Danny there.

But Beth wasn't going to live in the past any more – she

lived in the present. And she had to get on with her life. No matter what that entailed.

'Come on. Follow me,' she urged Jodi, willing herself to put the melancholy out of her mind. It seemed as if fate was playing a cruel trick on her just then. Placing a clue from this treasure hunt deep within a display of fantastic Venetian artefacts and history.

Jodi and Beth walked deeper into the maze of galleries to find the painting. Finally, the doorway to gallery 955 stood in front of them, and Beth paused one final time.

She wasn't one hundred per cent sure what lay beyond the door (except for Monet's painting, of course) but she did know that this was the final step, the end of the treasure hunt. The big finale.

'You want me to go first?' Jodi asked quietly. For a moment Beth thought that she might take her up on the offer, but she decided that wasn't right.

Since the very beginning, and every step along the way, Beth had doggedly pursued this quest herself. It was only right that she take the first step in the last clue. This was her puzzle to solve – this was *her* story. She shook her head. 'No, I need to go first.'

Taking small steps forward, she entered the gallery with Jodi behind her. The duo made their way delicately through the throng of people around them. Beth took in everything – every face, every piece of artwork, every display – until she was finally staring at the back wall of the gallery towards her prize.

Monet's painting.

Right away she knew that the replica that she had been given of *San Giorgio Maggiore* didn't compare to the real thing. And she knew that if the two were held up next to each other it would be a no-brainer as to which was the original.

Real versus fake. Imposter versus ideal.

But then Beth saw something else – something just as arresting as Monet's painting.

She gasped, her breath catching in her throat as the man who was standing in front of the painting admiring it turned around. Immediately, his eyes locked with Beth's and the two stood staring at each other, as if the gallery was suddenly empty of everyone except them.

'Oh my . . .' Beth heard Jodi say from beside her.

She'd been right all along.

It was Ryan Buchanan.

Chapter 34

'It *is* you,' Beth said simply, feeling at that moment as if she and Ryan were the only two people in the world. Her heart swelled with ... something – but she couldn't quite identify the emotion.

This entire thing, she thought. It was *exactly* like something out of a movie. This was usually the part where the background music rose in a crescendo and happily ever after would be realized. The would-be lovers would know that now that they'd admitted their true feelings for one another, there was nothing else holding them back.

Ryan smiled *that* smile at her – that one that had made her weak in the knees the first time they met, that made her forget everything – but for some reason it wasn't having quite the same effect just then.

She walked slowly towards him, gradually closing the distance between them.

'Beth, what are you doing here?' he said, looking genuinely delighted to see her.

'Hey . . .' she murmured quietly. 'It *was* you all along. I thought it might be. Especially after this morning . . .'

Ryan's face lit up with adoration. 'Beth, I think you and I both know we've been on the same wavelength right from the beginning,' he whispered, reaching for her. 'You're right. This morning, I knew that we were meant to be together, too; and now seeing you here . . . Did you end it with Danny then? I must admit I didn't expect that you'd do it so soon . . . But I'm delighted you did.'

Dealing with the last question initially, Beth shook her head, but for the first time she didn't feel guilty – just completely sure of what she had to do. 'Not yet, but I will now – now that I know it's really you.'

He chuckled, looking a little uncertain. 'Of course it's me. Who else would it be?'

'You know, you really had me guessing for a while,' she continued. 'I felt so confused at times, to be honest. But in the end, I got it right. I put all the pieces together and they led me here. Just like you said this morning, there are no coincidences.'

Ryan reached for her and pulled her into his arms. 'I think I fell in love with you the moment I met you,' he said. 'That day at the store. And I just knew we would end up together. I knew that you would be mine. And I was determined, no matter what, to make that happen.'

Though Beth had imagined many times what it might

feel like to have Ryan's arms around her, now that was happening she felt ... strange.

'Well, I admire your tenacity,' she said, wanting to keep talking for some reason. 'You certainly made a hell of an effort putting this whole thing together in such a short space of time.'

A brief look of confusion crossed his features, but then he chuckled. 'I did, didn't I?'

Beth looked at his face, unable to believe that this was really the end of the trail, and that she'd been right all along. Yet why did it all feel so ... *wrong*?

'Especially this morning,' she babbled on. 'You have no idea just how confused I felt last night. I was so sure that I had figured it out but yet something wasn't adding up. And then, of course, when the painting arrived while we had so conveniently gone to brunch, by the same bike messenger who has been popping up through this whole thing – well, I just knew for sure. You were trying to tell me I *had* figured it out, weren't you? That I shouldn't discount the last clue. And of course the painting led me here. You certainly did your homework. How incredible that the Monet was part of this exhibition, and that the boat exhibition was taking place at the weekend. What I don't get, though, is how you managed to rope in Tiffany's and the Waldorf ...'

Beth's voice trailed off, immediately sensing that some-thing was wrong. Ryan was silent and certainly wasn't acting like she'd expected, laughing and confessing everything about the entire set-up. Her gaze met his and just as she was about to ask him what was wrong, he spoke first.

'What are you talking about, Beth?' he asked. 'What painting?'

She furrowed her brow and tilted her head, pointing at the wall where the Monet hung. 'Well, that one, of course – or really, the copy the artist I met in the park last night had painted. You know, it's a very good copy, but seeing the real thing now – well, there's no comparison, is there?' She smiled. 'And of course, when it was delivered and I saw what it was, I knew that I was right about *The Thomas Crown Affair* being the movie in the clue.'

Ryan laughed nervously and bit his lip. 'I'm sorry; I don't mean to ruin the moment, Beth, but what clue? And what's all this about Tiffany's and the Waldorf? I'm sorry but I really have no idea what you're talking about.'

'Of course you do,' she argued, laughing, but her voice lacked conviction. 'Stop playing coy.'

But Ryan just continued to stare at her as if she was speaking a foreign language.

Trying to make sense of what was happening, as well as Ryan's obvious confusion, Beth's mind suddenly shot through a range of emotions – bewilderment, doubt and finally, understanding.

She took a hesitant step back, her heart thumping with adrenalin. 'You're not joking, are you? You really don't know what this is about.'

Seemingly taken aback by her sudden change in mood, Ryan appeared unsure what to do with his hands. He reached out for Beth momentarily, but identifying a very clear transformation in her demeanour, decided instead to stuff his hands in his pockets.

'I – I am actually not sure what I'm supposed to be joking about,' he said, looking deflated. 'What were you saying ... about movies and clues and stuff? And *The Thomas Crown Affair*? What the hell is that?'

Beth shook her head as if trying to convince him that he *must* know what she was talking about and was simply suffering from a temporary bout of amnesia, or determined to continue playing dumb. But if this was the case she couldn't determine why. Another movie re-enactment of some sort maybe? If so she certainly didn't think she'd seen it.

'Yes, *The Thomas Crown Affair*. The movie with Rene Russo and Pierce Brosnan. That painting was in it. *San Giorgio Maggiore at Dusk*.' She pointed again to the wall where the Monet was hanging.

Ryan turned to see what she was indicating, as if he hadn't been aware of what he had been looking at moments previously, and turned back to her. 'Really? Well, that's cool.'

But Beth was having none of this sudden ambiguity. 'Of course you had to know that, because how else would you have put the clue together?' She swallowed hard, feeling a chill creep up her spine.

But Ryan merely smiled and shrugged. 'Sorry, never saw that movie. And I had no idea about the painting.'

She stood open-mouthed, looking at him, trying to make sense of his words. 'You never saw ... wait. So, you just did a bit of research, then? Of course you did,' she continued, now sounding as if she was trying to convince the both of them. 'Hold on. So what about ...?' She thought back through each clue that she had been given. Surely there was some sort of mistake?

'What about *Romancing the Stone*? Have you seen that?'

He pondered for a second. 'Years ago, I think. But what does it matter if—'

'*Breakfast at Tiffany's*?'

Again, appearing to summon his memory, he nodded vaguely. 'Yeah, certain parts, here and there.'

'So when we were talking about movies all those times – my favourite New York movies,' Beth asked, everything gradually starting to become clearer, 'it was just simple chit-chat?' She swallowed as realisation finally hit home – and sunk in.

Again, Ryan looked baffled. 'Beth, I'm really not sure what you—'

'What about *The Seven Year Itch*?' she continued glumly, already knowing the answer.

To this, he smiled broadly. 'The Marilyn Monroe flick? Well, sure, I mean I know of it, but I'm not sure if I've ever watched the whole thing ... I mean, who doesn't remember that shot of her in that dress?'

Beth couldn't even be persuaded to smile at this point. 'Did you know that that scene was originally filmed right here in New York?'

'Seriously? Where?'

She raised her hands to her face and rubbed her temples, unable to believe what was happening. 'Oh, God. I got this all wrong.'

'Got what wrong?' Ryan asked, his handsome features falling once again into confusion. 'Hey, Beth, I know you love movies and everything, but is it really that big a deal if I haven't seen those ones? I mean, we have plenty of time to see them together.'

Beth turned her attention back to Ryan and realized that in just a few moments everything had changed. He didn't even *look* the same to her any more – she had miscast him. She had put him in a role he wasn't suited for. Everything was suddenly crystal clear, and she couldn't believe that she had got it so wrong.

She turned back to Jodi, who up until this point had been quietly observing the exchange from a distance. But it was clear that she had also figured out what was going on. She too understood Beth's mistake, and duly stepped forward to help out her friend.

'Sorry, Ryan, I think Beth's made a mistake,' Jodi said without looking at him. She was focused on Beth, who was looking unsteadily all around her, as if she was about to crumple to the ground. 'You OK, honey?'

She shook her head. 'No, not at all. It's not him, Jodi. I got it wrong and I thought I—'

'It's OK, an easy mistake.' Jodi cut her off when she realized that Ryan was still very much invested in this conversation. She turned to him and smiled the way a person might at a child. 'Ryan, sweetie, Beth's going to have to call you later. There's been a misunderstanding and I think that she needs some space.'

Her point was perfectly plain, but Beth was so embarrassed she found that she couldn't even bring herself to look at Ryan for his reaction. She wondered now if she had led him on throughout all of this, made him think there was a chance she would change her mind about being with him. Especially this morning.

The thrill of the treasure hunt and her suspicion that he was behind it had evidently modified her behaviour towards him accordingly. She was mortified. Was this all her fault? She had cast him in a leading role, and now knew that he wasn't her knight in shining armour, never really could have been. She had imagined Ryan to be someone that he was not; had imbued him with the most romantic and attractive characteristics of her favourite romantic heroes. Had she ever really seen him for who he was, or was she so completely taken by what she wanted him to be?

And something else was apparent to her.

There is *such a thing as coincidence.* Ryan's presence here alone was the biggest coincidence of them all. Granted, it was his day off too, this new exhibition was being promoted all over the city, and it wasn't unreasonable for someone new to New York to want to visit one of its famed museums, but still . . .

If Ryan wasn't the one who'd set up the treasure hunt, then his being here at the museum was immaterial.

And perhaps more importantly, Beth concluded then, it meant that the search was not yet over.

Her mind spinning with questions, Beth allowed Jodi to deal with Ryan, and slumped down on the bench directly in front of the Monet. She looked up at the painting and considered it. Real versus fake.

Feeling lost in a sea of confusion, she was summoned back into reality when Jodi sat down heavily on the bench next to her.

'I got rid of him. I don't mind doing your dirty work, honey, but I think you will probably still need to call him later. He's really confused and, to be frank, completely love sick over you,' her friend said.

Beth put her head in her hands and groaned. 'I can't believe I got this *so* wrong.'

Jodi stayed silent and Beth was glad that for once she'd decided not to offer her opinion. She already felt like enough of an idiot as it was – she didn't need Jodi hammering it home.

'Well, you know what this means then, don't you?' her friend said, nudging her, clearly wanting Beth to snap out of it.

She groaned again. 'Of course I know what it means.' She looked up at Jodi and forced a smile. 'There's must be another clue. This thing isn't over yet.'

Chapter 35

Beth continued to sit on the bench in confused silence while Jodi worked through the possible options. Indeed, at that moment it was her friend who was more engaged in the treasure hunt because Beth was struggling to figure out how she felt, let alone what she should do next.

If Ryan hadn't set this up, then who had? And why? Billy? If so, then wouldn't he be here? As far as Beth knew he was still at his post in Gold Street, and would be all day.

Which left only one realistic possibility.

Danny's name automatically popped into her brain, but she couldn't fathom how – or why – he would do such a thing, given his recent preoccupations. Or was there a chance she'd got all that wrong too?

'Hey, Beth, come on now, snap out of it,' Jodi chided. 'Let's get on with this. You said it yourself time and time again. You need to finish this.'

She shook her head. 'I don't know. I mean, what's the point? And *who* the hell is behind this? If it's not Ryan – and it really couldn't be Danny – then why should I press on with it? You said it yourself; who else would do it? Who would go to this much effort?'

Jodi shrugged. 'I don't know, honey, but I am betting it's someone who knows you and cares about you. There's no other way to explain it. Obviously Ryan didn't know enough to do this for you. He cares about you, but he doesn't *know* you. But someone else sure does.'

Beth shook her head. Needless to say she had absolutely no interest in Billy, and would be mortified if this had anything to do with him. She was prepared to admit to herself now that part of the reason she'd pursued this so doggedly was because she'd suspected Ryan from the very start, and for as long as she was enjoying their flirtation, was only too happy to go along with it.

'This is nuts. I can't keep up with it.' She turned to Jodi and for the first time in the entire quest, realized she felt angry. 'You said it yourself. This isn't a romantic Christmas movie – some merry romp across New York City – and no matter what I might have believed, things don't always work out for the best. You were right all along.'

'Stop it, Beth. That's not you. You don't believe that. And I know what I said before, but I don't want *you* to be that way. I don't want you to turn out like me, all bitter and angry. Don't be like me,' Jodi repeated quietly, the last words catching in her throat.

Undeterred by her friend's pleading, Beth carried on. 'No, I've decided. That's it. I walked into this museum believing that something incredible was going to happen, that it would be ... transformative somehow, and do you know something? Regardless of what has happened in this room – and what has happened up until this point – I'm going to stay true to that. I *am* going to leave this museum a new woman. I'm going to start afresh. No more fairy tales and make-believe for me. I am going to see everything through a lens of clarity. I am going to be firmly based in reality and live my life knowing that movies are just pure fabrication. Nothing that happens on the silver screen happens in real life – at least not to most people.'

Jodi reached out and touched her friend's arm. 'OK, that makes sense, but what about the rest of the hunt? I'll still help you, you know. We can find the next clue, see this thing out and—'

'And then what?' Beth questioned, cutting her friend off, her voice growing louder, angrier and more heated. 'What's next? Another clue, and another and another? No thanks, I'm finished. No more – you're probably right too, Jodi. This could be the work of a stalker and I am not going to be some victim ...'

Beth *was* finished. She was angry, confused and she was also *incredibly* frustrated. She banged both hands against the bench in irritation.

'Whoa, Beth, calm down,' Jodi gasped, just as a loud

thud came from under the seat, as if it had been cracked in two.

Shocked because she hadn't intended to break the bench, Beth looked around to see if anyone had noticed what she had just done. Indeed, the noise had attracted a few stares from other people in the gallery. She looked down at the bench, her face heated with mortification. 'Shit, did I break something?' But the seat seemed intact.

Jodi chuckled. 'This is pretty solid wood, Wonder Woman. I don't think so. But seriously, no more going all Avengers-like on me – we're going to get kicked out of this place. And quit the stroppy toddler act too.'

This elicited a laugh from Beth and she finally began to feel her spirits lift. 'All right, point taken. Come on. I need to get out of here. Preferably before they throw us out.'

'But what about the clue?' Jodi reminded her, her attention back on the painting.

Beth waved a hand. She felt exhausted by it all. 'I meant what I said. I'm finished. No more clues. I'm going home.' She stood up and, waiting for Jodi to follow her lead, she placed her hands on her hips and arched her back, stretching. 'I'm seriously tired. I think I need to go home and sleep – or take Brinkley out for a walk – or something.' She closed her eyes and moved her head around on her shoulders, releasing tension in her neck. When she opened her eyes again, Jodi was still stubbornly sitting on bench, staring at her. 'Come on, I'm ready to go. Let's get out of—'

But as Beth looked down at Jodi, she noticed there was something *under* the bench, something that had not been there before. Of that, she was sure.

'Hey, what's this?' She squatted down to retrieve the object and realized that this must have been the cause of the thud that they had heard just a minute ago. Something had fallen off the bench; perhaps a bolt or something that held it together ...

Reaching out and picking it up, all at once Beth realized what it was.

A key.

'Where did that come from?' Jodi asked, bending down to look.

But Beth didn't answer. What was a key doing under the bench? She peered beneath the seat, looking at the bottom, and realized that it seemed to have fallen from the underside of the wood. An errant piece of duct tape had been holding it in place, along with a piece of paper.

A note.

Suddenly, and despite herself, Beth felt herself being pulled straight back into the search. Without a doubt, she knew the key was the next clue. This is why she had been brought to the Met, to this exhibit, this gallery and this painting.

In the film *The Thomas Crown Affair*, she recalled that by hiding a briefcase under a bench just like this in the movie, Pierce Brosnan had been able to carry off the heist at the Met. This clue was channelling that scene.

Beth reached under the bench for the piece of paper, releasing it from the duct tape. It was folded over like a note. She sat back down next to her friend and, key still in hand, she unfolded the paper.

And as Beth read the words written on it, her breath caught in her throat.

You are too romantic about Manhattan, as you are about everything else.

Chapter 36

The answer to everything hit her at once.

Suddenly she knew exactly who was behind it all, the coffee cup that had sent her to Tiffany's, the boat exhibition, the Waldorf Hotel, the Bethesda Fountain ... the painting of Venice.

Hell, when she was struggling with the *Seven Year Itch* clue, he'd even handed it to her on a plate!

Danny.

And now, Beth realized – her mind racing as all the pieces suddenly began falling into place – thinking of the Waldorf in particular ... now she understood why the name Yussopov had seemed so familiar to her. It was the surname of Angelina from the boat. She must have been the woman in the suite. But who were these people? Clients of Danny's, perhaps? She knew that his firm did some advertising work for Tiffany's, and maybe the hotel too, but ... Beth's mind raced. How her boyfriend had managed it all, she didn't know. But one thing was for sure, he was the one behind this treasure hunt.

Her heart soared. How could she have not seen that?

'It's Danny,' Beth said to Jodi, tears in her eyes. 'He's been behind it all along. How could I have not known that? I'm such an idiot ...' She thought again about the clues from the beginning. Yes, there were some unanswered questions, but one thing was for sure: each and every clue had been orchestrated by the man she had been so certain she was losing.

Of course there was still one major unanswered question. Why? Why would Danny do all of this – go to these incredible lengths – if he was having an affair and about to leave her for another woman? Beth frowned. Was it some roundabout way of telling her?

No, no way. Danny wouldn't dream of doing something so hurtful, especially at this time of year, with only days to go to Christmas. But still the puzzle remained, what was the point of it all?

Jodi seemed to read Beth's thoughts. 'Why would Danny do all of this, honey? OK, maybe he wanted to put some spice or romance back into your relationship, I can understand that. But what about that woman you saw him with yesterday?'

Beth shook her head, confused too by the same thought. 'I have no idea. But I have a feeling I'm going to find out pretty soon. I need to go to him. Now.'

Beth hustled across the gallery floor towards the exit.

Danny was waiting for her now, and she was almost positive as to where. The slightly altered quote on the note had made sure of that. Another movie quote, but one Beth understood (and Danny knew she would) very well.

Jodi, struggling to catch up with her friend, peppered her with questions as the two made their way to the front lobby of the Met. 'How do you know where he is now? What did the note say? Where are we going?'

Beth stopped and turned to face her friend as they exited onto Fifth Avenue.

'Not we, Jodi. I'm sorry. I have to do this next part on my own,' she said softly. 'And you want to know how I know where he is?' She reflected on one major movie-worthy memory from their shared past, and realized just how unbelievably blind she had been. She couldn't deny it, but now love – real love – bloomed in her heart. This was reality. Danny knew Beth to her core, and she couldn't believe that she had taken that for granted.

'He was too romantic about Manhattan, as he was about everything else' was a quote from a favourite movie, and though the line was uttered by the main character, Isaac Davis, Danny had always teased Beth that it summed her up perfectly.

'Jodi, I need to take back something I said to you before,' she smiled, giving her a quick hug. 'I was wrong about something.'

'Makes a change ...' her friend said wryly. 'No seriously, what do you mean?'

'Sometimes movie moments do happen. I shouldn't have ever said that they didn't.' Beth turned on her heel and ran down the steps to hail a conveniently empty passing cab.

She opened the back door and jumped inside, leaving Jodi standing bewildered outside the Met.

'Where to, sweetheart?' asked the driver.

Beth sat back in the seat and smiled, not needing even to think about it. This time, she knew exactly where to go. 'The East River at the foot of 58th Street.'

Travelling in the cab, waiting to reach her destination, Beth mulled through everything in her mind. And while some things seemed to add up, she kept coming back to the same question over and over. Why would Danny do all of this for her if he was in love with someone else? Why would he arrange this treasure trail for her – orchestrate so much, down to the very finest and minute details – if he was having an affair?

She tried to consider why she, in turn, had believed that someone like Ryan – who really didn't know her at all – would go to such great lengths to woo her.

Staring out the window of the car, she felt that familiar wave of melancholy wash over her. She knew that she had been fickle in her affections for Ryan, and she felt terrible about that now. But she couldn't change the past – she could just get on with the future.

'Any spot in particular you want to be dropped off?' called the cab driver from the front seat. He looked up at

the sky. 'Hope you've got an umbrella; looks like it's starting to snow.'

'Just the foot of 58th, thanks. I'm meeting someone
there.'

The cab driver gave her a thumbs up. 'You got it, sweetheart.' He slowed, pulled to the kerb, parked and turned
around to face her. 'It'll be ten even,' he said. 'Hey, I don't
know if you're a movie fan at all, but bit of trivia for ya . . .'
he continued, and Beth smiled, already anticipating his next
words. As she handed him the money along with a tip, the
guy continued, 'Yeah, so Woody Allen and Diane Keaton
filmed a pretty famous scene here for *Manhattan*. You ever
seen that movie?'

Beth nodded and smiled as she opened the car door.
'Once or twice.'

She knew without a doubt that Danny would be here waiting for her. As she walked from the street and neared the
bench where they'd sat so many years ago – where they had
in effect fallen in love – she had a brief moment of fear.

What if he had put her through all of this and brought
her here today, just to break up with her. To say goodbye?
She stopped walking as the thought crossed her mind,
but then shook her head, trying to clear the thought.
No, Danny wasn't cruel. He knew how much she loved
Christmas. He would never do something like that at this
time of year. That can't be it, she thought.

But then what about the affair? Wasn't cheating cruel?

Beth didn't know the answer to that, and she let the question hang in her imagination, as the bench – *their* bench – came into view.

It had a sole occupant, and even from this distance, Beth knew that it was Danny. She would know him anywhere. Taking a deep breath and trying to prepare herself for what was to come next, she walked slowly forward until she was standing ten feet behind him.

In front of her, the East River flowed and she could hear the traffic on the Queensboro Bridge. It was different from that first time they were here together. Not as silent – not as peaceful. But it was still a special spot. And just then, as the cab driver had predicted, it started to snow. Which merely added to the magic and romance of the final step.

It was perfect.

Smiling, Beth took a deep breath and opened her mouth to speak. 'I'm here,' she said, loud enough for Danny to hear. 'I figured it out, all of it.'

She waited with bated breath for the man who she had loved for so many years to turn round, take her in his arms and tell her that he loved her, that he'd done all this to surprise her. For reasons yet unknown.

Finally, Danny did say something. But he didn't turn round.

'Come sit down, Beth,' he said in a strange voice.

There was something about his tone that immediately scared her, and that earlier fear – that he was about to break up with her, reveal the truth that he didn't love her any more – once again surged forth in her soul. But she did what he asked just the same.

Sitting down on the bench next to him, Beth faced him, even as he continued to stare out over the river. She studied his face. The face that she had kissed and expressed her love to so many times. Suddenly, it was as if she was seeing him with different eyes.

This wasn't a joyful scene, she realized, it was a heart-breaking one.

Danny's face was drawn, pale, *thinner* than she remembered it. When was the last time I truly looked at you? she wondered. She didn't know the answer, but now she felt frightened by what she was seeing.

'Danny?' she continued softly. 'I found the clue. I found all of them.' She placed the key on the bench between them. 'This one too.'

He nodded and sighed. 'I know you did. I knew you would and I'm glad.' He turned to face her and she couldn't escape the feeling that he was studying her somehow. Like he was trying to memorise the way that she looked because he would never see her again after this moment. Finally, he spoke again. 'I have something I need to tell you. Something I didn't know before I set all of this up.'

Oh God ... Beth saw the pain in his eyes and knew that this was it. He was about to confess. She suddenly realized that one of two things could occur. He would tell her that he was leaving her because he was in love with another woman. Or he would confess all and ask for her forgiveness.

She looked down at the bench and studied the key just sitting there. If he asked for forgiveness would she be able to give it? She looked back up at him and saw that he was struggling with the words – whatever he wanted to tell her was just not coming out. So she decided help him. Take the edge off and get it over with. 'It's about her, isn't it? That woman I saw you with.'

Danny's expression immediately changed, and he looked confused as he tried to determine what she meant. 'What woman?' he asked simply.

She bit her lip out of frustration. Here she was, giving him an opening to confess, and he was going to deny it?

'Danny, please, I saw you with her. Yesterday, going up Park Avenue on my way to the Waldorf. I was in a cab.' Beth paused and then realized that if he had set all this up, he surely must have been aware of where she was headed. 'I saw you on the street. With the dark-haired woman. You looked ... close.' Beth's voice cracked and she turned away from Danny.

'Adele,' he said simply.

She turned back, the name slicing through her heart. But at the same time Beth was thankful at least that he wasn't going to try to deny it, pretend it wasn't him; that she hadn't seen what she thought she had seen. 'Is that her name?'

'Yes, that's her name. That's who you saw.'

Tears prickled at the corner of her eyes and she felt her heart begin to break little by little. So it was true. He wasn't going to deny it. She couldn't believe it. At Christmastime, with the snow falling all around them in this picture-perfect scene, he was going to break her heart.

'Oh. So I see. OK, then,' she said breathlessly – and then, unable to hold back her emotions any longer, she decided to get it all out in the open. 'So all of this ... dragging me here ... it was just to tell me that we're finished. That it's over? Well, I hope that the two of you are very happy together, though I have no idea why you put me through all this – sending me all over the place like a rat in a maze – just to tell me it's over,' she cried, her words bitter. 'Why would you do something like this? And at Christmas ... ?' But she choked on the rest. She couldn't say anything more. She had to get out of there.

She stood up and headed off, away from their *Manhattan* bench, away from Danny. She wanted nothing more than to escape from this entire situation. She needed to get some-where on her own and try to get to grips with this in peace. Get to grips with the end of her relationship, her seven-year love affair with a man she'd been so sure was her soul mate. Why had he toyed with her like that? It was beyond cruel.

But Danny, apparently, was not finished, and as Beth tried to move away he caught up, grabbing her arm and spinning her round to face him.

'Wait a minute, Beth, please. Let me explain. You don't understand.'

'*I* don't understand?' she shot back, tears flowing openly now, as snowflakes fluttered across her vision. 'I understand perfectly. You're in love with someone else. Adele. How *exotic*. But why did you have to put me through all of this, Danny? Why couldn't you just come out and tell me that you didn't love me any more – and just break up with me? Why create this elaborate charade, this treasure hunt, only to lead me here to end it. *Why?*'

Danny ran his hands through his hair and looked at the ground. He took a deep breath and finally raised his gaze to meet hers.

'Like I said, that whole thing was set up long before … just … before. And yes, I admit I've been seeing Adele lately,' he confirmed quietly. 'But, Beth, she's not my lover. She's my oncologist.'

Chapter 37

Adele was his ...? Beth thought but couldn't even repeat the word in her mind, let alone out loud. Because she understood the significance. Danny wasn't having an affair, he was—

'Please. Sit back down. Give me a chance to explain,' Danny pleaded, taking Beth's hand and leading her back to the bench. Still reeling at what he had just said, she sat while he put his head in his hands. 'There's so much I haven't told you, and I just want to say in advance that I am sorry for that. It was wrong of me to keep it from you, but I really didn't know how to—'

'What's wrong?' she asked, swallowing the huge lump in her throat. 'Are you sick?' It was a stupid question, of course; why else would he need an oncologist, a cancer specialist?

Cancer ... All thoughts of an affair – of Danny having fallen out of love with her – had completely left her mind. In their place was concern – and pure and utter terror.

After what seemed like an eternity, Danny finally spoke.

'Yes, I'm sick, Beth. I'm very sick. I found out about a month ago – not long before Thanksgiving and way after I'd set this thing up. I should have cancelled, but to be honest I'd kind of forgotten about it, until everything was already in motion . . .'

Very sick. Oxygen seemed to disappear from the air all of a sudden, and Beth couldn't catch her breath. She felt as if a cold, icy hand was gripping her throat.

His voice broke. 'It's pretty bad, honey . . .'

Beth was desperate, yet at the same time reluctant, to know more.

'Adele – Dr Rovere – she's become a confidante of sorts over the last few weeks since I was first referred.' He took both of her hands in his and turned to face her, his voice soft. 'I have leukaemia, Beth. A rare form.' His voice cracked again, and for the first time since she arrived, Beth reached out to make contact with him. She pulled him close and was shocked when she realized he was crying.

Oh God . . . 'Danny, it's OK, let me help you. We'll get through this; I know we will. Tell me how I can—'

But he was shaking his head as she held him. 'No, Beth, you don't understand. You can't help me. I don't think anyone can. Yesterday, when you saw me on the street, Adele followed me out because I'd left my phone behind. She had just given me an update on my prognosis – and I was so overwhelmed and disorientated . . . She's been trying to help me, not just with the treatment but in how

I should be dealing with things emotionally. She tried to persuade me over and over that I needed to tell you, that having a support system would help, but I wasn't hearing her. What with Thanksgiving and now Christmas, I couldn't do it.'

Beth felt the spectre of dread settle over them. 'What was the update?' She knew that she had to ask the question, but she was terrified of the answer.

'It wasn't good news,' Danny said, pulling away from her. 'It's accelerating, Beth.'

Her mind frantically worked to process all this new information. Her Danny, the love of her life, was ill – seriously ill – for weeks and hadn't told her about it. Why hadn't he told her?

'Why didn't you tell me?' Beth pleaded. She was quickly understanding the gravity of the situation, but the fact that Danny had knowingly and purposely excluded her from being a part of this devastating news cut her to the core.

'I'm sorry,' he whispered. 'I'm so sorry. It was wrong. But I did have my reasons.' She waited for him to continue, and after a quiet moment he did. 'You've always been light and life to me, Beth. Everything about you is sunny, happy, serene. And you see the good in every situation – I love that about you. And I suppose I knew that if I told you what was going on, that all of that would change. It would blight your soul, make you unhappy, anxious, worried. Of course it would change you and everything about our life, and I didn't want you to change. I just wanted you to stay you.'

Beth understood and now more than ever she also realized that what she'd been thinking at the museum and what Jodi had said before was true – she lived in a fairy-tale world – avoided reality. And because of that, it had encouraged Danny to think her fragile, weak ... unable to deal with real life. That was why he had kept her in the dark.

'You thought I couldn't handle it ... the reality.' Beth looked down at the ground, ashamed to her core. She felt like a complete idiot.

Danny reached out and raised her face to his. 'No, it was me who couldn't handle that,' he said. 'When I heard, my first reaction was to deny it all, pretend it wasn't happening and the longer it went on without telling anyone, the longer I could convince myself that it wasn't real. Telling you would only make it real. So no, you're not the weak one Beth – I am.'

'What about your folks? Do they know?' She wondered now if this was the reason he hadn't asked her to come with him to Queens. But chances were Mae and Rick couldn't possibly know about it either, or Beth would have surely found out. His mother would be devastated and there was no way she would countenance keeping secret something of this importance.

He shook his head. 'Like I said, I just haven't been able to talk about it, especially with the holidays coming up ...'

She reached for him then, and the two of them held one another for a long time, saying nothing, still trying to understand why – *how* – he had suffered through so much mental anguish alone. Yes, he might have been protecting himself, but knowing Danny as she did, Beth guessed there was some measure of trying to shield her from the reality too.

Then, as Beth tried to get to grips with that notion, her thoughts focused on the even more distressing prospect that her future could be devoid of the man she had loved for so long.

She swallowed hard and held Danny tighter. She understood now that he was, and always would be, the love of her life. Eventually she pulled away. 'But people fight these things all the time, don't they? You're strong and still young and otherwise healthy, so surely there must be some hope, some chance ... ?'

But Danny was pulling away. 'No, Beth. There's no silver lining in this scenario. Adele says there's something like a one in ten chance of beating it – and that's only with a lot of expensive medication. We can't afford that ...' He put his head in his hands again and Beth was anguished as she recalled how he'd suggested cancelling their medical insurance last year to save money when his hours were being cut. 'It's just ... I don't really know what to say ... there's been so much to think about.'

She sat forward, grasping on to the fact that there was some hope, however small. 'Danny, we'll do whatever we

361

have to. Don't give up just yet. I know you and you're not a quitter. Neither am I – I found my way here, didn't I?' she teased, trying to lighten things a little.

But the very notion about how she *had* ended up here raised afresh the question that Danny hadn't answered yet.

'The hunt. This elaborate treasure trail. All over New York ... the marina, Tiffany's, the Met. The Waldorf. What was it all about Danny – *why* did you do it? Especially in the middle of all this?'

He sniffed and sat forward. 'There was actually a different reason behind that to begin with, but then I realized ...' He seemed to be about to say something but then stopped and picked up the key. 'Like I said, it was set up a long time ago, and I'd kind of forgotten about it until the people involved let me know everything was in motion. But this, the last clue in particular, was a last-minute inclusion.' He indicated the key. 'You remember when we locked our love on that bridge in Venice that time?' Beth nodded. Of course she did. 'Look, please understand that I only want you to be happy. That's all I ever hope for you. That you are happy. With or without me. And ultimately, even though you now know the truth – *especially* as you now know the truth – I just want to give you that option.' He turned the key around in his fingers, and looked away into the distance. 'I know about Ryan, Beth.'

At once it felt as if all of the air had been sucked out of the atmosphere. 'Ryan from work? What about him?' she replied, baffled by this turn in the conversation. With everything else that was going on, at this point Ryan was almost a distant memory, and she couldn't believe she ever thought he might ever have meant anything. It was a stupid dalliance, a boost to her ego. She was an idiot. But how could Danny possibly know anything about how she'd been feeling ... ?

'Look ... I don't blame you for anything that might have happened with him—'

'Danny,' she said, immediately on the defensive. 'Nothing happened, I promise you, I would *never* cheat on you—'

But he put up a hand, silencing her. He wasn't angry, just resigned. 'I believe you. And I know you wouldn't cheat. But what I'm saying is that I know about Ryan. I met him, sort of. At the store. I saw you two together and well, I saw that you looked happy, too. Like you used to look all the time with me. Hell, I know that I haven't been the best boyfriend, partner, lover, anything lately, and that's why I understand if your head was turned. I've taken you for granted in a lot of ways, but I also love you enough to let you go if that's what you want.'

He handed Beth the key, which she took limply and right then it dawned on her what it all represented. It was the key to the padlock from Venice, the spare. At the time neither of them had been sure what to do with it, and not wanting to ruin the romance of the moment, she remembered Danny had eventually just put it in his pocket and Beth had never thought about it again. 'If you want to leave – especially after what you know now, I won't stop you. I want you to be happy, Beth, even if it is with someone else. I won't tie you to that promise.'

Her mouth fell open as she figured out what Danny was trying to tell her: that he was giving her the option of leaving him – of ending their relationship – if she didn't want to deal with this new reality. No strings attached. He was giving her the option to unlock their vow.

But there was no *way* she was going to use the key – metaphorically or otherwise. She only wanted Danny. For a lifetime, just like they'd promised. Even if – she realized, her heart twisting – that lifetime might be short.

Still holding the key, Beth put her face in her hands and allowed herself to cry freely. She felt Danny pull her close, wrap his arms around her and breathe into her hair.

'No, of course I don't want anyone else. I don't want anyone but you. No matter what. No matter if it's years, months, weeks even – I want to be there for you. It's you and me for a lifetime – we promised each other that years ago, on that bridge in Venice – and I still want that. You know me, inside and out. No one has ever known me the way that you do, but you are wrong about something.' She grasped his hand, willing him to listen. 'I can handle this and so can you. I've realized some things about myself lately, and I understand that life doesn't always play out the way it's supposed to. But I also know that we can always do the best with what we have. You have to trust me, though. You have to let me in.'

Turning her face to his, she felt all the barriers that had

been put up between them over the past few weeks come crashing down. And she knew that Danny had accepted her words, was thankful for them even, when he took her face in his hands and kissed her with abandon.

He kissed her the way he used to when they first met – when he and Beth had nothing but time available to them. Beth vowed to herself that no matter what, they would make the most of what little they had left.

'No more wasting time, Danny,' she whispered. 'It's us – in this together. We're a team. And I'll be with you every step of the way.'

Danny put his forehead against hers and closed his eyes. 'Are you sure?'

She encircled his neck with her arms and covered his face with kisses.

'I've never been surer of anything,' Beth said. 'I'm not giving up on you just yet; I'm not giving up on us.'

Satisfied, Danny kissed her again and finally raised a smile. Beth was pleased to see some of his former self in his eyes and she breathed a sigh of relief. It was true that she was a perpetual optimist, and she *wouldn't* give that up. Nor would she give up hope. It was too precious – and powerful.

Feeling her relax a little in his arms, Danny broke their embrace.

'OK, well, in that case I guess I should tell you there's one more clue. The one I had in mind all along to give you when I started this thing. Before I got sick.'

'What do you mean, you had something in mind all along?' Beth said, confused and a little taken aback by this unexpected turn in the conversation. 'I thought the whole point of the trail was the key?'

Danny was smiling. 'Nope. Actually it was something entirely different. I just had to change direction a little when Ryan came into the picture, just in case . . .'

He reached under the bench and presented her with the final clue. 'But I have a feeling you'll solve this one easiest of all.'

Epilogue

Beth sat quietly, in a private space called the 'Reflection Room'. It was located in a wing of the church not far from the nave. Out front, so many people were gathered, waiting for the ceremony to begin.

She wasn't quite ready to face them all yet. She needed just a bit more time to herself. And reflect she did. It had been a whole year since that day by the East River, but it felt like an eternity. So much had happened.

Much of it was still very raw to Beth, and now, as she stood up – thinking quietly about Danny's last few weeks in the hospital – she realised that despite everything they had been through, all of the worry and suffering, there still was something to be thankful for.

And she still had hope. Beth had promised Danny that day on the bench that she would always have hope and she intended to continue to live by that promise.

She crossed to the lone window in the room and peered

out. From this vantage point she was able to see the snowy parking lot of the church where people were still arriving.

This whole affair was a lot bigger than expected, but then again, everyone loved Danny.

Beth had chosen the church that Danny had attended while growing up in Queens. While she wasn't overly religious, she knew it was important to Mae and Rick for the ceremony to be held in their church, and she didn't argue.

Suddenly, she saw some familiar faces filing in, all bundled up against the winter cold with hats and fur coats. Yuri Yussopov, and his wife, Lin, who it turned out was a good client of Danny's. The Madison Avenue firm had been involved in the marketing and advertising of the Manhattan Sailing Exhibition, and explaining his intentions for the treasure trail, Danny had in advance enlisted Lin and her husband's help with the boat and the hotel.

She watched the Russian couple in their mink coats and hats hurry inside. Danny and Beth had much to thank them for over the last year – not only for playing a pivotal role in bringing them together, but also for sending a lot of additional business to Danny's firm – saving his job, his income – and being so incredibly over-the-top kind while he was in the hospital. Beth felt her eyes mist up thinking about Yuri and Lin's overwhelming generosity. She promised herself not to cry, however – not yet.

Turning her attention elsewhere, she then saw Courtney, their teenage dog walker and neighbour, with her boyfriend, Steve, another participant in setting up the hunt, who worked as a part-time bellboy from the Waldorf for the holidays. The Tiffany's salesperson was another one of Danny's business contacts and, like all the other players, had promised in the early days – before he'd got sick – to help him out with the hunt once he'd explained the reason behind it.

Then there was Adele, Danny's doctor and a woman whom Beth had also become very dependent on over the last twelve months. She was kind, but formidable, as if helping Danny through his illness was some kind of personal mission for her. Yet there was no doubt she'd been a tremendous support through it all.

As had Billy. Beth smiled when she saw the doorman approach, hand in hand with his girlfriend, Claire. Far from a potential suitor for Beth, the Scotsman had been wooing a different woman entirely, but hadn't wanted to reveal anything about his new relationship while it was still in the early stages. It seemed Beth had interrupted him wrapping a gift for Claire when he'd been flustered in the lobby that time.

Another thing she'd got all wrong.

Her thoughts moving automatically to Ryan then, and Beth wondered how he was getting on back in LA. Apparently he'd decided that New York wasn't the place for him and had quit his job in Carlisle's in the New Year, and moved back to the West Coast. Beth guessed she had more reason than he to be embarrassed about what had happened, but of course, she had other things on her mind by then.

How nice of them all to come, she thought. So many people, going out of their way to be here for us.

At that moment, a quiet knock came from somewhere behind her and Beth turned towards the sound. 'Come in.'

Jodi poked her head in and Beth immediately caught a whiff of all of the flowers – their gorgeous scent wafting from the church all the way to this room. She had briefly glanced in earlier – she had never seen so many flowers in her life.

'They're ready to start,' her friend announced quietly.

Beth took a deep breath. She needed to steel her nerves. She had known this day was coming for a while now and she had agreed to keep her side of the bargain. She'd promised Danny a long time ago to love him for ever, and she was determined to honour that promise.

After all this was over, it might be fitting to return to Venice for a while; to reflect, revisit some happy memories, regain some equilibrium – something that Beth knew would be very much needed after all this.

'Are you ready, sweetie?' Jodi asked her.

Pausing to take a deep breath, Beth grabbed Jodi's arm. 'Hold on, just a second. I just need a moment.'

Her friend nodded, understanding. 'Of course, take all the time you need. They can't start without you.'

Turning back to Jodi, Beth nodded. 'OK, I'm ready.' Straightening her shoulders, she swallowed, and offered a small smile.

Jodi stepped forward and took her arm, providing her

support as they left the room. 'The place is packed to the rafters. You have so many people who care about you and Danny,' her friend commented. 'Trevor can't believe it. He says he's never felt so much love in a room.'

Much of it coming from the woman beside him, Beth thought smiling. She and Trevor had been going strong for a year now, and she was delighted that her friend had found her happy ending at last.

Happy endings . . .

Beth once again felt tears in her eyes. 'I'm glad that we're doing it all like this. It feels right.'

'It *is* right,' said Jodi, squeezing her arm. 'Everything is just how it is supposed to be.'

The pair walked down the hallway towards the church porch. The interior doors were closed and Beth knew that once they opened, all eyes would be on her. The significance of the occasion once again rested on her shoulders, and while her nerves were definitely going haywire in her stomach, she owed it to Danny to handle it right.

OK, here goes . . . Exhaling deeply, she looked down at her feet.

Bridie's vintage ostrich feather and jewel-encrusted heels – the final piece of Danny's treasure trail – sparkled in the late afternoon sunlight, as if winking at her.

She had made him a promise last year by the river when he'd presented her with the final clue – one that she was indeed able to solve instantly. Though it had nothing to do with a movie, its significance was unmistakable.

371

Beth looked up at her dad, who stood to the side of the entrance smiling, waiting to take her arm and lead her up the aisle.

It was Christmas Eve. And today was the greatest gift that anyone could ever give her. The gift of a lifetime – with Danny.

So today, wearing her grandmother's vintage shoes to marry the love of her life in her beloved city of happy endings, Beth was placing her bets on the 'for better' part of that promise.

It made for a much better finale.

Acknowledgements

Lots of love and thanks to Kevin, to my lovely Carrie, and our family and friends for their continued support.

Special thanks as always to Katie, Becky, Alice and all at Curtis Brown, especially the wonderful Sheila Crowley – I'm incredibly lucky to have not only a terrific agent, but a great friend.

Huge thanks to the lovely team at Simon & Schuster UK for their enthusiasm, kindness and Trojan efforts on my behalf, in particular my brilliant editor Jo, who is a joy to work with and whose suggestions improved this story no end. And the inimitable Sara-Jade Virtue; such a terrific champion of women's fiction, always tireless and passionate in her efforts and support of authors, to whom this book is dedicated.

To the fantastic Jennifer Weis and the lovely people at St Martin's who do such a great job with my books in the US and give me a wonderful excuse to visit NYC (as if one was ever needed).

Also big thanks to Helen, Simon, Declan and the team in Dublin, who look after me so well, and heartfelt thanks to all the booksellers in Ireland, the UK and beyond who give my books such terrific support, and who are always so lovely and welcoming when I visit.

Last but certainly not least, massive thanks to readers from all over who buy and read my books. I'm so very grateful and love keeping in touch through Facebook, Twitter and my website www.melissahill.info. I really appreciate your support and very much hope you enjoy *The Love of a Lifetime*.

Win a two-night Champagne heritage break with

Hand PICKED
—— HOTELS ——

Arrive at the hotel of your choice and unpack in your Executive bedroom for two nights of indulgence. You will be spoilt with welcome Champagne and canapes followed by a three-course table d'hôte dinner for an evening at leisure.

Wake up to a traditional breakfast, before exploring the grounds of the country house hotel and then retreat to the spa for a sumptuous 25 minute treatment of your choosing. While the afternoon away with a traditional Champagne Afternoon Tea in a classic lounge before retiring to your room for a restful sleep.

Included in the prize:

- Two nights in an Executive bedroom
- Pre-dinner Champagne and canapés on the first night
- Three course table d'hôte dinner on the first night
- Champagne afternoon tea on the second day
- 1 x 25 minute spa treatment each to be taken during the stay (if a spa hotel is selected)
- Full traditional breakfast both mornings
- Valid for redemption until 31st January 2017, from Sunday to Thursday
- Subject to availability
- Based on two people sharing
- Check in from 3pm, check out by 11am

Hand Picked Hotels is the leading collection of architecturally splendid country house hotels – built for pleasure and continuing a centuries-old tradition of offering guests an indulgent country house visit. The 20 award-winning hotels are renowned for exquisite food, fine wines and bespoke service in stylish, relaxing surroundings across the UK and Channel Islands, including 10 spa hotels, with locations ranging from the New Forest and Jersey to the Cotswolds and Edinburgh. For more information visit www.handpickedhotels.co.uk

Melissa Hill

A Diamond from Tiffany's and Other Stories

It's been two years since Ethan Greene and Gary Knowles collided one fateful evening outside Tiffany & Co on Fifth Avenue. A mix-up with their shopping bags sent each man's life on an unexpected trajectory, and while Gary and his fiancée Rachel are heading for the altar, Ethan's love life is not so settled.

Rachel's dreams are within her grasp; her restaurant is going from strength to strength and she and Gary are set to be married amongst family and friends at an idyllic New York location. But when they arrive in the city only days before the ceremony, Gary seems distracted and restless. Could he be having second thoughts?

Ethan is anxious to see Terri again at the wedding; he truly felt they had something special, and plans to use the time in New York to prove to her that their relationship deserves another chance.

Will the romance of New York and Tiffany's work its magic on the couples once more?

Melissa Hill

The Hotel on Mulberry Bay

Mulberry Hotel, perched on a clifftop above a
sweeping bay, was once the heart and soul of pretty
seaside town Mulberry Bay. Run by the Harte family
for years, the place itself is almost as beloved
as cheery landlady Anna.

The hotel was also once home to thirty-something
sisters Eleanor and Penny, and while youngest sister
Penny still lives close by, it's been some time since Elle
has visited. But following a family tragedy, Elle
is forced to return from her busy London
life and reassess her past.

When it becomes apparent that the hotel is in
dire straits, Elle and Penny are unprepared for the
reaction of their father, Ned. He steadfastly refuses to
give up the family legacy, revealing that he's given up
something equally precious once before. Startled by
their father's surprising revelation, the sisters unite,
with the local community behind them, in their
efforts to save the hotel – and, in the process,
heal the fractures in the Harte family.